He was familiar with the stove and small space, reminding her again that he'd grown up in this establishment as much as he had the grocery store across the street —maybe more than Paul, who had been groomed to take over his father's place as co-CEO of the C&O chain.

He added Gruyère to the bun, the melty cheese making her mouth water. He put prepped sliced mushrooms into the pan, whisking them with butter and some herbs before carefully cracking an egg in another pan.

He sandwiched the mushrooms between the cheesy bread, and then poured the béchamel sauce he'd been preparing on the stove on top. The sunny-side egg crowned the meal. Absently, he wiped the edge of the already-clean plate, and then placed it in front of her with an economy of motion, along with silverware, then leaned against the counter.

Whatever self-consciousness she felt about him watching her as she ate vanished when she put the first bite in her mouth.

It was a glorified grilled cheese sandwich, and she was about to pass out with pleasure.

By Alisha Rai

The Forbidden Hearts Series
HATE TO WANT YOU
WRONG TO NEED YOU

Coming Soon
HURTS TO LOVE YOU

The Pleasure Series
GLUTTON FOR PLEASURE
SERVING PLEASURE

The Campbell Siblings Series
A GENTLEMAN IN THE STREET
THE RIGHT MAN FOR THE JOB

The Bedroom Games Series
PLAY WITH ME
RISK & REWARD
BET ON ME

The Karimi Siblings

FALLING FOR HIM
WAITING FOR HER

The Fantasy Series

BE MY FANTASY
STAY MY FANTASY

Single Titles

HOT AS HADES
CABIN FEVER
NIGHT WHISPERS
NEVER HAVE I EVER

Wrong TO NEED You

Forbidden Hearts

Alisha Rai

AVONBOOKS

An Imprint of HarperCollinsPublishers

WRONG TO NEED YOU. Copyright © 2017 by Alisha Rai. All rights reserved. Printed in the United States of America. No part of this book may be used or reproduced in any manner whatsoever without written permission except in the case of brief quotations embodied in critical articles and reviews. For information, address HarperCollins Publishers, 195 Broadway, New York, NY 10007.

First Avon Books mass market printing: December 2017

Print Edition ISBN: 978-0-06-256675-1
Digital Edition ISBN: 978-0-06-256674-4

Cover design by Nadine Badalaty
Cover photograph by Michael Frost
Cover image © bioraven/Shutterstock (tattoo)

FIRST EDITION

17 18 19 20 21   QGM   10 9 8 7 6 5 4 3 2 1

For Tai, Ash and Pinky.

Chapter 1

SOME WOMEN were seduced by a voice or a touch or a look. For Sadia Ahmed, it was hands.

Or, at least . . . *His* hands.

They were big, the perfect size to grasp her ass and grip her tight. Or to wrap around her neck while his thumbs settled into the hollow at the base of her throat. Or to cup her breast and lift it to his mouth.

Sadia picked up a glass and started drying it, her actions precise and unhurried. She was certain her face didn't give away the fact she was fantasizing about sex with a patron sitting in the dive bar. Her libido might be hot, but her facade was stone-cold. She was a mother, a widow. To a lot of people, she'd discovered, those two titles took precedence over being a woman.

She didn't mind letting people keep their illusions. It made her life easier and she wasn't a disruptive person by nature. Someone else could shock the world, so long as she could dream about what she pleased.

Out of the corner of her eye, she contemplated

what she could see of the anonymous man's hands. He wore a baseball cap pulled low, and the bar was dark, so his body was all she had to moon over. His body was enough.

His fingers were long and elegant. They were big enough to fill her up with one, but she'd demand two. Hidden under the soft cotton of her shirt, her stomach clenched. He could play her like a violin, which was appropriate. He had the hands of an artist. Attached to a body that belonged to a fighter.

Her gaze drifted over what she could see of the rest of him. Wide chest, broad shoulders, thighs like tree trunks, biceps like whoa.

Unf.

Sadia carefully replaced the dry glass and picked up another one. Over the past week, she'd gotten really good at surreptitiously peeking at her mystery man during each of her shifts. On Monday she'd noticed him for the first time, sitting in a darkened booth in a far corner. On Wednesday he'd chosen a seat which was better lit, enough for her to grow obsessed with thoughts of his fingers on her and in her.

Though it had been busy earlier tonight, she'd consciously kept an eye out for him. Once the Thursday crowd had thinned out, her gaze had been drawn to him like a magnet to metal. Another dark booth, another dark cap pulled low to hide his face. Alone, nursing the ginger ale he'd ordered. His quiet stillness set him apart from the rowdy people who usually filled this bar.

"Hey, Sadia."

Sadia started. She regrouped quickly and gave her boss a cheerful grin which hopefully masked the filthy thoughts in her head. "Hey, what's up?" Michael had owned O'Killian's for at least as long as she'd been working here, off and on since her twenty-first birthday.

"I wanted to thank you again for picking up so many shifts this week."

She tossed her towel over her shoulder. "No problem. You know I'll take the hours." The tips were good. With a young son, she could always use extra money. She wanted to keep her bartending skills sharp.

Those were all the reasons she gave people when they asked her why she was still tending bar when she had her hands full with the café she'd inherited from her husband. They weren't false.

They weren't completely true either, but the whole truth would cause more than a few raised eyebrows.

My husband had debts he didn't tell me about. The tips give me grocery money.

I'm terrified the café will go bankrupt on my watch. I need a fallback career.

And there was one other good reason, but she really couldn't share that one with anyone. That reason was her secret.

"I know, you're so great about being flexible." Michael ran his hand over his bald head. He was an older, short, squat man, kind and soft-spoken. It was nice to take a break from being the boss at the café and work for someone else, especially when that someone was a decent person. "Listen, I have something to ask you."

She nodded, hoping he wasn't planning on changing next week's schedule. Between child care and staffing the café, she needed her shifts set in stone as early as humanly possible. Last minute changes were a nightmare for her to manage.

His eyes darted around, and he inched closer. "Well, my wife's been bugging me to ask you, and I know it's a little unprofessional but . . . is it true Nicholas Chandler hired a skywriter and a marching band to try to win Livvy Kane back?"

Sadia puffed out her cheeks, relief and amusement and annoyance mingling.

All week. This had been going on all freaking week. The Kane/Chandler drama-llama was a staple of this town, so of course everyone was curious.

She and Livvy were going to have some words when the woman got back from wherever she'd run off to with her old flame. The problem with being the best friend and former sister-in-law to half of the town's most infamous couple was that everyone assumed she knew what the hell had happened to take Livvy and Nicholas from sworn blood enemies back to the lovebirds they'd been in their youth. Sadia kept having to disappoint them. "I'm pretty sure there wasn't any skywriting or a marching band involved."

Michael looked disappointed. "He did whisk her off to France, though? My wife heard that from her hair stylist."

Sadia shrugged. For all she knew, her best friend

was in France. She'd received a text from Livvy which said she and Nicholas were going somewhere private to work through their issues. Sadia had been worried, until she'd spoken to Livvy's aunt Maile. Livvy had called Maile, citing terrible reception, but saying she'd be in contact as much as possible.

So long as Livvy was letting someone know she was alive, Sadia supposed she could wait for a full explanation. Sadia had texted back that she was happy if Livvy was happy and she was available to talk if her friend needed her.

And she was trying really hard to keep that attitude up. It was just difficult to not feel a little slighted she'd found out about their romance with the rest of the town, when Nicholas had publicly declared his love for the woman.

Livvy was her best friend, damn it, even if they hadn't been in close proximity to each other for the past decade. Sadia should have known what was going on in her life.

There are things you never confided to Livvy about your marriage.

Because she'd been married to the woman's older brother, with whom Livvy'd had an already rocky relationship. Sadia hadn't been about to add to it. "I really don't know where she or Nicholas are. Or whether they're even together," she tacked on.

"Oh, I get it. Don't want to gossip. Admirable."

Sadia nodded, ready to accept this excuse, since it was the, what, fifteenth time she'd had this conversation?

Livvy, you owe me a couple nights of child care for leaving me behind without even a public statement to spread.

Michael patted a handkerchief over his forehead. "Anyway, again, hate to even ask you, the missus was curious."

Yeah. The missus.

"You can take off, if you like."

"Are you sure?" She was already whipping the towel off her shoulder.

"Yup. Closing time soon and it's quiet. Go get some rest. Your son will probably be up early." Her boss smiled, and it was only through sheer force of will Sadia didn't physically cringe at the trace of pity she saw there.

Her late husband had told her more than once not to lecture him about how much pride he had. He'd tap her spine. *This right here, made with pure steel.*

Fine, she was proud, and accepting pity wasn't something she was good at. Unfortunately, since Paul had died over a year ago, she'd had to get used to the sad looks and understanding pats and special treatment. They came from such a well-meaning place, so she appreciated them as much as she could when they made her so wildly uncomfortable. "Yes, Kareem's an early riser. Will do."

Michael moseyed away to talk to the other bartender, Jason. Probably to see if Sadia had shared any juicy gossip with him.

As she was finishing signing out on the computer, the hairs on the back of her neck stood up.

Someone was watching her.

Casually, hoping against hope it was who she thought it was, she glanced over her shoulder at Mr. Perfect Hands. Who whipped his head away to stare at the wall.

Her palms grew damp. It could mean nothing, of course, but this was the first sign of interest she'd gotten from him.

Sadia glanced at her watch. It wasn't quite two. She could steal some time for herself.

Her body flushed hot, getting ready for the chase. Her chases were short by necessity, but she liked the excitement of the pursuit almost as much as sex itself.

She glanced around. The few patrons left in the place were all busy with their own conquests or thoughts, the staff occupied with getting ready for closing.

She moved quickly, pouring whiskey, fresh lemon juice, and maple syrup in a shaker with ice and then straining it into a glass. She garnished the cocktail with a lemon peel.

With each step toward Mr. Perfect Hands and away from the bar, her brain calmed, her walk becoming more confident.

This. This was the secret reason she kept this job, the one her family, her in-laws, the employees at the café, and the PTA moms at her son's school could never know.

I can find adults I don't know who can take care of my physical needs with little to no emotional demands.

Sure, lots of locals came here, but she'd lived in

Rockville all her life, and she knew how to avoid them. There were more than enough strangers for her to flirt with. Have sex with.

She hadn't realized how hungry she'd been for human touch until a few months ago. She and Paul hadn't slept together for almost a year before his death, and she'd been starving. The visiting nurse who had broken her dry spell had seemed startled by Sadia's enthusiasm, but she'd quickly gotten on board.

After her, Sadia had found more men and women, the ones she felt safe and comfortable with—she was a good judge of character and no assholes were allowed to apply for bed privileges. She never took them back to her home, no. It was usually their place, which tended to be hotel rooms.

The encounters were quick and hurried, long enough for them both to get off, and then Sadia booked it. This was a necessary physical itch she needed to scratch, and she scratched it as quietly as she could, at a time when she wouldn't feel guilty about not being with her son. Kareem was asleep when she was working at the bar, tucked safely into his bed with one of her sisters sleeping over in the same house.

No one could know about this. This was for her, and her alone, the one thing she took for herself.

As she drew closer to the man in the booth, he shifted, his arms bunching and releasing. On another guy, she might suspect that he'd bought his red Henley a size too small. On him, she wondered if he could even find a size that fit him. Getting dressed was probably a daily battle of him versus fabric.

That was a battle she would pay to see.

He kept his head down even when she came to stand next to the booth. She cleared her throat slightly, and placed the drink on the table in front of him, next to the now-watered-down glass of ginger ale. "Hi there," she said, and made sure her voice was as low and husky as she could make it. Though that dumb baseball cap was pulled so low it obscured most of his face, what she could see of his profile was perfect: full lips, sharp jaw, blade-like nose.

She wanted him to look up so she could check out the rest of him, but he didn't. He didn't acknowledge her at all.

"I made this for you. I hope you like it," she tried again, and nudged the glass closer to his pinky. Up close, she could spot tiny scars on his flesh, little white marks marring the toasty light brown of his skin, like he'd been nicked a number of times. They didn't detract at all from the beauty of that goddamn hand.

She shifted, disappointment coursing through her when he didn't so much as move. She was about to walk away when he spoke. "I didn't order anything."

A shiver ran down her spine. Oh damn, that voice. It was a voice made of fine sandpaper wrapped in velvet, raspy and low, like he didn't use it much.

She could have an orgasm with that voice whispering filthy things in her ear alone, not even touching her. In fact, she might make him do that, if he was game. Flustered, she fiddled with the ends of her ponytail. "On the house."

Banter. Flirt. Dance. She took another step closer. Getting married to her high school sweetheart meant she'd never really had much of a chance to hone her flirting skills, but at the ripe age of almost thirty, she was getting pretty good at this whole dance. "It's called a revolving door," she said, making sure her voice was as intimate as his. She could have given him the exact year of origin of the drink— 1929—but she was never sure who would appreciate her drink-based nerdery.

If she wanted to sleep with the guy, she didn't need him to adore all of her. She just needed him to physically want her as much as she wanted him.

"I don't drink."

That stymied her. Who came to a bar and nursed soft drinks? "You hang out in strange places then."

No answer. No eye contact. Ah, balls. Well, she'd shot her shot, and if he wasn't receptive, there was nothing she could do about that.

Her lips twisted and she picked up the glass. "Well, have a good night."

She froze when his hand wrapped around hers. Her stomach dropped at the callouses on his palm. Ah god. They would feel so good on her body.

She licked her lips. "Is there a problem, sir?" She made that sir as seductive as she could, trying to promise untold delights and sexual pleasure.

Well, as much delight and pleasure as could be

packed into forty-five minutes or so, of course. It was late, and she did have an early morning tomorrow.

His hand tightened on hers. "Sadia."

She jolted, staring down at his cap. She should be uneasy he knew her name, except she was more concerned with how he said it.

Like he'd said it a million times, in a million different ways. Like he knew her.

A suspicion niggled awake at the back of her brain, and she rejected it with a single shake of her head. No, it couldn't be. This man was so much bigger than the boy she'd known and loved. He'd been tall then, yes, but lanky, long hair hiding features that were a little unfinished.

That boy had left town following a string of tragedy and never looked back. Not even for her. Not even when she'd begged him to.

Livvy said he'd been in town, that he'd be back.

But Livvy wasn't here now, right?

She catalogued his beautiful, perfect hand. The nicks were new, and so were the callouses. But those fingers, now that she was really looking at them . . .

His wrist twisted. There was a scar there. She'd been there when he'd gotten it, the first time they'd met on the playground in third grade. He'd taken down a bully for her, and the kid had shoved him against a fence. A nail had sliced into skin.

His head raised, and suddenly she was peering into a pair of dark eyes she knew better than her own.

They were remarkably similar to Paul's eyes.

Which made sense, because this man, the man she'd been lusting after, whom she'd mentally undressed and fucked over the past week, was her late husband's brother.

"Jackson?" she whispered.

Chapter 2

JACKSON KANE hadn't planned this.

If these last few weeks were chapters in his life story, that was probably what they could be titled: I Didn't Plan This.

He hadn't planned on staying so long in this town. He definitely hadn't planned on remaining here when his sister, the reason he'd come home, wasn't even here. And he certainly hadn't planned on engaging in some light stalking of his sister-in-law.

Ex-sister-in-law? Former sister-in-law? What did you call your brother's widow?

Off-limits.

"Jackson?" she repeated.

Since his cover was blown anyway, he took advantage of Sadia's shock to drink her in. The glances and peeks he'd limited himself to hadn't been nearly satisfying enough.

She looked softer, like someone had taken the picture he'd had in his head of nineteen-year-old Sadia Ahmed and blurred the edges. Her hair had once been so long she could sit on the straight dark strands, but it was shorter now. The straight brown mass was pulled into a high ponytail, the end curling over her shoulder. Everyone who worked at the bar wore black pants or jeans and a tight-fitting black shirt. Her pants were some stretchy material that molded to every curve. Her top slipped down over her shoulders, baring golden-brown skin a couple of shades darker than his.

Other employees showed more flesh but it was hard to register other women when Sadia was in his vicinity. It always had been. That hadn't changed.

Every moment he'd spent spying on her, he'd told himself he was only curious, that this was no different from looking up people from your past on social media, but that was a lie. Because a long time ago, in a galaxy far, far away, he'd loved Sadia with all his soul.

She'd loved him, too. As a brother. As a best friend.

Not anymore, though. He hadn't loved anyone in so long, he barely knew how. His relationship with his sister was proof of that. And judging by Sadia's face, she wasn't exactly brimming over with love for him.

She moved her head from side-to-side, and he frowned, realizing she was shaking. "Sadia." Without being fully conscious of it, he changed his grip on her hand, stroking her fingers. Her skin was so soft.

She was one of the few people he'd ever been okay with touching and being touched by. He slept with women, yes, but they didn't hug. They fucked, rough and without emotional engagement, and then they walked away, neither of them glancing backward.

"Hey." He ran his thumb over hers, but her shaking only intensified.

Her eyes glinted, and his hand fell away. If he was unused to talking and hugs, he was massively unaccustomed to women crying on him.

But nothing startled him as much as the low growl that erupted from her throat. "Hey? Is that all you can say to me? Hey?"

He glanced around, but the place was loud enough and dark enough that no one was paying attention to them. "Calm down."

Her eyes opened so wide he could see the whites all around her pupils. "You. Did. Not. Just tell me to calm down."

He eyed her. He had told her that, but she seemed to be getting angrier. The opposite of calm.

"You want me to calm down." She nodded. "Why don't I do that, Jackson? Why don't I calm down? Because what's there to be upset by? You only disappeared from the face of the earth for ten years. Ignored every single email I sent you. Ignored your nephew's birth, your sister and mother's pain, your own brother's funeral."

He flinched. There had been something ironic about being in a jail cell when his brother had died a little over a year ago, but processing that irony had been far beyond his capabilities.

She wasn't saying anything but the truth. Only a monster would have ignored every word she'd written to him over the past decade. Only the most uncaring of people wouldn't have at least called her when her husband—his brother—had died.

That's what he was, what he'd aspired to be. Alive, but unfeeling. His heart beat, his blood pounded, his organs functioned. That was it. That was enough.

Or he'd thought it was enough.

"But I should calm down. No need to be upset." The tears trembled on her lower lashes. "Fuck you, you selfish—"

"Useless, assholic dick," he finished, softly quoting her last email to him.

The tears spilled over. "And fuck you for never responding to me. Not even when I begged you."

Oh.

His frozen heart hadn't been tested by Sadia's tears. Every single one that slipped down her face flicked against his defenses like acid. "Sadia. Stop crying."

Her eyes grew even bigger. Ah, shit, he'd said the wrong thing again. "Don't you ever tell me what to do." And then she grabbed the drink she'd made him, and with a flick of her wrist, dashed it in his face.

She whirled away and stomped off, jerking at the knot of the apron strings tied right above her ass. Her round, cuppable, squeezable . . .

He jerked his gaze away. God, no. He couldn't think of her ass. Or her thighs, jiggling with every step.

He licked his upper lip. The alcohol was dripping

down his neck, into his collar. He wasn't much of a drinker anymore, but whatever she'd given him was smoky and sweet. Like her.

God, if he'd ever wondered what a flirtatious all grown-up Sadia would be like . . . no, he had to scrub that from his memory like he'd scrubbed so many other things.

Jackson mopped up his face as best he could, tugged his hat lower and came to his feet.

His bike was hidden at the far corner of the parking lot, far out of the spill of light cast by the bar's broken neon sign. He leaned against the metal and chrome, and waited. After about fifteen minutes, a car engine sounded from behind the café, and then a tidy crossover drove out of the parking lot.

He was imagining the wetness on Sadia's cheeks as she drove away, right?

He sagged against his bike and burrowed his head in his hands, scrubbing his eyes. There were no tears there. He hadn't cried in . . . well, since he'd been a kid, in this very town.

Slowly, he put on his jacket and his helmet, got on his bike and headed in the opposite direction. He wanted to follow her, but his motorcycle would be too obvious in her tidy residential neighborhood. And he knew that because he'd already cruised by her place a few times.

It's a wonder no one's called the cops on you yet.

He was playing it pretty fast and loose with surveillance in a place where local law enforcement didn't exactly have a great opinion of him.

Jackson revved his engine and took a sharp

left turn, his headlamp slicing through the post-midnight gloom. The streetlights were spaced few and far apart, but he didn't need them. He could maneuver the roads in this town with his eyes closed. A decade of self-imposed exile couldn't change that kind of muscle memory.

He'd been born in Rockville, the second son of local royalty, the grandson of a man who had helped carve civilization out of a patch of frozen land in upstate New York. Growing up here had been idyllic. Until the last couple weeks he'd lived here. A jail cell was never pleasant, especially for a kid who had grown up privileged.

He hung a right, barely glancing at the library where he'd whiled away most of his after-school hours or the high-end florist where he'd bought a corsage for Sadia when he'd taken her to the junior prom.

For the first time since he'd come back, he inhaled deeply. The air smelled like wood chips and apples, firing up some long dormant part of his brain. It smelled like home. The last place he wanted to be, and the one place in the world that didn't want him.

Jackson slowed as he approached the town's main square. He looked left, then right.

A single car zoomed through the intersection, and he knew he was imagining the driver surveying him, but he hunched his shoulders anyway, trying to make himself smaller. The last thing he wanted was to be recognized by some longtime resident.

Jan, you'll never believe it. I think I saw Jackson Kane on the road. No, Paul's younger brother. Remember? He burned down the C&O. Well, he was never tried, but everyone knew he did it. He left town right after and guilty men don't run.

He could leave again, now.

If he went right, he'd hit the on-ramp for the highway. It would take him about seven hours, give or take, to get to New York City. He had a gig scheduled there in less than a month. His duffel and all his shit was still back in his seedy hotel room, but he had no attachment to any of the stuff he carried. Abandoning them here wouldn't matter.

A car drove up behind him and he waved the vehicle around him. Jackson held his breath. The car cruised by and took a left.

He looked after the red taillights. Left was not an option for him. Going left meant he'd head deeper into town. In three minutes, he'd reach the supermarket his family had once owned. The café Sadia now owned.

Jackson shivered. The wind was cutting through his leather jacket, and dry leaves whirled in the street. He wasn't cold, though. On the contrary, sweat was gathering on his upper lip.

He turned his right turn signal on. Looked around the empty intersection, like someone else would come rolling up to tell him what to do.

The tick of his turn signal echoed the pounding of blood in his veins. He eased off the brake. Skated forward a foot. Then another.

Then he hung a left.

Two and a half minutes later, he maneuvered between the two legacies of his parents. On one side of the road was a huge building. The last time he'd seen it, at least half of it had been burned out.

A Molotov cocktail could do a hell of a lot of damage when that cocktail hit a gas line. They'd rebuilt it bigger, and the name on the front was different now.

Chandler's.

It used to say C&O. His mother's father, Sam Oka, had laid the first brick of that store, alongside his best friend John Chandler. The Chandlers and the Oka-Kanes had been intertwined in business and family for two generations, until one icy night ten years ago, when Jackson's father had driven headfirst into a tree. Maria Chandler, Nicholas's mother, had been in the passenger seat. Robert and Maria had both died.

Instead of playing the grieving widower, Brendan Chandler had taken the opportunity to swindle a depressed Tani Oka-Kane out of her half of the C&O empire.

And, as gossip would tell it, in revenge, Jackson had burned down the flagship C&O.

He turned his bike away, into the café's empty parking lot. Kane's Café was spelled out in red backlit channel letters, the neon colors spilling onto the pavement.

He killed the engine of his bike and took off his helmet, swiping his hand over his hair, unused to the short strands. Unlike the new building that had taken the place of C&O, this small, squat building was homey instead of grandiose. His father's parents had been popular, gregarious individuals who had moved here from Hawaii when Robert Kane had been a baby. The townspeople had been delighted when the Kanes' only son had fallen in love with the reigning princess of the C&O empire.

Jackson got off his bike and walked toward the building. With a quick glance around, he circled the place and went to the back door. The black magnetic key holder under the drain pipe was still there, all these years later. His grandfather had been forgetful as hell.

He opened the back door and stepped inside, holding his breath for an alarm, but all was quiet.

He walked to the front, careful to keep the beam of his phone's flashlight away from the windows. It looked exactly as he remembered it: the red booths, the white counter, the cheerful, ever-changing local art on the wall.

He ran his fingers over the gold lettering of the café name on a menu stacked next to the register. Jackson bet Paul had gotten a kick about keeping their family name on a small part of this town, directly opposite Chandler's. No one had been angrier about losing their stake in C&O than Paul. Until the night their mother had signed their shares away, Paul had been the golden heir-apparent, the future co-CEO of the grocery store empire.

The sharp prick of pain took Jackson by surprise. He'd gotten too good at avoiding the ghosts of his past. Not much happiness, yes, but no pain either.

He rested his hand against the lettering of the name, against that apostrophe in Kane's that denoted it a possessive. Even though he was dead, this was Paul's, Jackson reminded himself, perversely eliciting that painful kick. The business, this town. The woman he'd been spying on like a fool.

I miss you.
I think about you all the time.
I love you.
Come back.

Without conscious thought, he rubbed his finger over the screen of his cell. Every single email his former best friend had sent him over the past decade was housed in that phone, and he knew them by heart. They were the reason he had any electronics at all, so he could carry that inbox with him wherever he went. The modern-day equivalent of wrapping a stack of letters with a ribbon.

They'd started shortly after he'd run. Sometimes she'd sent multiple notes in a week; sometimes there would be a long stretch between them. They'd finally stopped over a year ago, with a few words. **Jackson. Paul's dead.**

And then, a couple weeks ago, he'd woken up in Hong Kong, grabbed his phone, and nearly rolled off the bed when he'd noticed Sadia's name in his inbox. **So, motherfucker, I want you to know your sister is back home and dealing with all sorts of shit on her own: your mom, Nicholas, his dumb family. If you care about her at all, maybe you could check in with her. Though I know that's a long shot, because you're a selfish, useless, assholic dick who doesn't care about anyone but yourself.**

If you care about her at all . . .

When he'd exiled himself from this town and everyone he'd once loved, he'd thought he excised every soft part of him he possibly could. It had been a necessary protection. Feelings could be manipulated. Stone could not.

But that had been an illusion. He'd learned exactly how much he still cared when he discovered Livvy was going to be in arm's reach of Nicholas. His fear for his twin had been palpable. The man had once devastated her so badly, she'd wanted to die.

He'd thought he'd played his part well, that she wouldn't go back to Nicholas, that she'd be fine, and they could all go their separate ways, but he'd been wrong. He didn't have to play his voicemail to recall the message his twin had left him a week ago. "Hey, it's me . . . Livvy? I, um, wanted to tell you that Nicholas and I are going away for a bit. Maybe a couple of weeks. I know this seems like a sudden about-face, but he, um . . . anyway, we're talking, is all. I'll call you when I'm able. Don't worry about me." Her voice softened. "I don't expect you to stick around for me. I know you may even already be gone, and that's okay. I love you, Jackson."

He stared out the front window. *I don't expect you to stick around for me.*

And why should she? He might have held Livvy all those years ago when she screamed she wanted to die, but he'd been scarce since then. She'd had another depressive episode after Paul had died, she'd told him last week. He hadn't even known.

Isn't that what you wanted? You can leave now. There's no one for you here. No one who expects you to stay. No one who needs you.

His gaze drifted over the window, to the Help Wanted sign there. He could easily read the mirror image text reflected in the glass.

CHEF NEEDED

He narrowed his eyes and switched to the web browser on his phone. It took about five seconds to discover a chatty reviewer—Sally R. from Rockville— sadly lamenting that the longtime chef had left Kane's and the owner's cooking left a lot to be desired. Jackson checked the date. Two weeks prior.

Rick had left? The man had taught Jackson how to cook.

Jackson scrolled through a few other reviews, his frown growing as he noted the complaints about burned baked goods and subpar lunches. Unless things had changed drastically, Sadia wasn't a chef.

But he was.

He'd wondered why was she working at the bar. The café would never have the income potential of the C&O, especially without upgrades, but it had pulled a comfortable income for his grandparents, and he assumed, for Paul and Sadia. Did she need the extra money?

He could picture Livvy with her arms crossed over her petite frame. *She always stood by you. You owe her, Jackson. She needs you.*

Oh fuck.

A couple of things were blindingly obvious: Sadia needed a chef.

He was a chef.

She hated him, quite rightly, because he had wronged her. Which meant . . . he did owe her, in ways Livvy didn't even know.

It was practical and logical for him to stay and lend a hand here, in his family's old café, while he waited for Livvy to come home. He was probably the last person alive who knew this place as well as his grandparents.

And, goddamn it. He *wanted* to stick around.

He stuck his phone in his pocket and rolled his neck. It was a good thing he didn't require much sleep. A scout of the kitchens, a shower, a shave, and he'd be back, ready to do battle with Sadia to win the privilege of helping her.

He licked his upper lip, tasting the whiskey she'd thrown in his face. He had no doubt it would be quite the fight.

Chapter 3

Sadia gasped, her eyes flying open. Before she could even fully see, she had her phone in her hand, rescued from the pillow no one slept on. She squinted at the time, bringing the phone close to her face so she could make it out.

She let out a breath, some of her panic subsiding. She'd once luxuriated in waking slowly and carefully, making her way through each layer of sleep. Since Paul had died, that had changed. Now she woke up every day in a jolt, fearful of oversleeping.

There were only so many hours in a day, and so many things she needed to accomplish. Wasting time on sleep could be disastrous.

She turned off the alarm that wasn't scheduled to go off for another twenty minutes and stared at the ceiling, the predawn light from outside creeping through her curtains. Her eyes were gritty and tired. It had been a while since she'd had a sleepless night. She was so exhausted lately, sleep was almost always guaranteed. Especially on nights she pulled the late shift at the bar.

But then, last night had been a bit of an anomaly.

Don't dwell on it.

She'd tossed and turned for a long time, her anxiety ratcheting up every time she'd noted the time and her brain had automatically calculated how much sleep she would get. Three hours, then two, then one. Finally she'd dozed, her eyelids overpowering her mind.

She'd hoped she could wake up and pretend Jackson had been a dream, but that wasn't possible. Two minutes. She'd allow herself two more minutes of dwelling, and then she'd get up. She could spare two minutes in her schedule.

Sadia stretched, the muscles in her shoulders aching from days of hunching over a stove and a desk. She'd been operating in fight-or-flight mode since Paul had died, and it had only grown more intense any time she had a tiny setback. Seeing Jackson was a setback.

She'd tried to be understanding when Jackson had fled town after he was released from jail, but he'd been a part of her life for so long, she hadn't been able to stop herself from talking to him. After she'd received no response after the first year or so, she'd assumed she was emailing into a void. Those letters had become an outlet for her, a place to store some of the thoughts she didn't or couldn't say out loud. She'd only stopped when Paul had died because she couldn't justify the time she'd spent on writing frivolous notes no one read.

But then she'd discovered he was responding to Livvy's emails to that same address. Which meant he must have gotten hers, too.

Ignored every single email I sent you. Ignored your nephew's birth, your sister and mother's pain, your own brother's funeral.

She hadn't confessed what had really caused her the most pain, though. He'd ignored *her.*

Rage and hurt swirled inside her. She'd loved him so, and she thought he'd loved her. But in the end, she'd been easy to ignore and delete.

She hugged the anger close to her. It was good and honest, and quite frankly, she'd rather be mad than think about how many hours she'd spent imagining his hands on her body when he'd been some anonymous hot person in her bar.

Nope, nuh-uh. She slammed that door shut. She could only hope he hadn't realized she was flirting with him. That would be mortifying.

She glanced at her phone again. Her two minutes were over. There was nothing she wanted more than to pull the covers over her head like she had when she was a child dreading school, but she was an adult now, and had to be an adult.

It was the worst.

Reluctantly, she rolled out of bed and stripped her leggings and T-shirt off, dropping them into the laundry basket on her way to the bathroom. Crack of dawn wasn't her specialty—especially after a sleepless night—but until she found someone as trustworthy and reliable as Chef Rick, who had been employed at Kane's since its opening, she'd be making this early morning trek.

Her shower was brief and barely long enough

to wash the sleepiness or her disquiet away. Paul had always intended to install a larger water heater in this home, but they'd always been short on time and energy, and she balked on spending the money on it now. There was enough hot water to fill Kareem's bath at night. Good enough.

Her hands slowed as she ran the soap over her breasts. She looked critically at her body. Jackson had gotten *jacked* over the years. Like, muscles on top of muscles and then another layer of muscles. His arms might have their own zip code. She'd never been completely svelte, but having a child had only made her softer. She poked at her squishy belly and frowned.

What are you doing?

She shook her head and finished soaping up. That's right. She'd already used her two minutes to think about Jackson, and this snap of insecurity was not like her. Her body was healthy and capable, and, as she'd discovered time and again, capable of giving and receiving pleasure. She was happy to have it, squish and all.

She barely paid attention to what clothes she put on. Her wardrobe had slowly evolved to clothes she could wash and wear and could be easily mixed and matched. It was more efficient, and she had tried to become as efficient as humanly possible. She wielded lists and journals and pens the way other people might wield swords.

If she had to organize her life down to the last minute, she'd do it. It was one of the many tools she used in her never-ending quest to prove to herself and the world that she was Sadia Ahmed, Official Non-Failure of a Person.

Once she was dressed, she opened the small box she kept on her vanity. This time, too, was scheduled in her morning routine. Inside the top lid was a picture of her and Paul from their senior prom. Paul was handsome and looked smug in that carelessly arrogant way he'd had. She was beaming in a silver sparkly dress. Kareem loved this picture, and she did too. They were madly in love and secure in their places in the world: her, the middle child of successful, doting physicians; him, the heir to a fortune and the future co-CEO of a national corporation.

Three years after this, they'd eloped. Still madly in love but their roles in the world turned upside down.

She caressed the only other object in the box: his and her wedding rings. She and Paul might not have had the picture-perfect marriage, but his death had left a hole in her life. She'd been told more than once by well-meaning people that she needed to grieve, and she smiled and nodded. They didn't understand. She didn't have uninterrupted time to grieve. Just minutes here or there. "I miss you. I'm doing my best," she whispered. After a beat, she put the box down, snapping the lid shut.

She was putting on her socks when she heard a door open down the hall. She quickly grabbed the backpack that held her stuff for the day and her clothes for the night. If she was very lucky, she'd have time to run home after school so she could help Kareem with his homework and feed him a snack. In case she couldn't, she needed to be able to transition into her bartending uniform, like Wonder Woman spinning into her crime-fighting outfit. Only the tired, single mom version of the superhero.

She jogged downstairs and raised an eyebrow to find Ayesha reading at the breakfast table and Jia popping a pod into her coffee maker. When she worked at the bar at night one of her younger sisters stayed at her house. Lately, since she'd been heading out to the café before Kareem even woke up, they'd also been coming by or staying in the morning, until he got on the bus.

They were lifesavers. "Hey," she whispered. "Jia, when did you come over?" When she'd left last night, Ayesha had been the one ensconced on her couch, quietly studying and eating chips. Jia and Ayesha's medical school wasn't far from Sadia's house, so they were the ones who usually slept over.

Ayesha closed her textbook, rolled her eyes and answered in a similarly quiet tone. "This one"— she pointed a finger at her twin sister—"killed her car battery. She just got here. Took a cab so I wouldn't have to go get her."

"I don't understand why the trunk has a light inside it. It's so easy to forget to close it." Jia glanced up from the coffee maker. Her kohl-lined eyes widened. "Whoa, rough night?"

Sadia's eyes narrowed on the twenty-four-year-old's guileless, smooth face.

Ayesha blew out her breath. "You can't say that. That's rude."

Jia blinked at them both. "But she normally doesn't look like that. So it's kind of a compliment, I thought."

"Nope," Sadia said. "Definitely rude."

"It's mostly the bags under your eyes," Jia added helpfully.

Ayesha rose. "Jia, stop talking."

Sadia rubbed her finger under her eye. "Had a bit of insomnia."

"I can help you with that. I got my makeup kit with me."

Sadia hesitated. Normally she'd demur, but then she thought about her flash of insecurity in the shower. A tiny boost in confidence might be in order. She glanced at her phone. "Can you do it in three minutes?"

Jia scoffed. Most med students probably didn't look like fashion plates at five in the morning, but her little sister could have stepped off a magazine cover in her pretty, long blue-and-white dress and black faux-leather jacket. Her hijab matched her dress, two scarves wrapped to create a zigzag pattern over her scalp. "I can do a full face in two and a half."

Sadia didn't doubt that claim. In college Jia had started a blog with makeup and fashion tips, and it had grown into videos and podcasts. She dropped into a chair at the counter while Jia rummaged through her designer backpack.

Ayesha went to the fridge and pulled out a carton

of milk, then grabbed the Raisin Bran Sadia kept in stock for her younger sisters. "So, listen," Ayesha started. "We need the dirt on the Chandlers. Everyone at school has been asking us about it."

Jia approached with a small makeup pouch. "And we have to say we didn't know, even though our sister is related to them." She dabbed a hefty amount of concealer under each of Sadia's eyes, then carefully smoothed it into her skin.

"I'm not related to the Chandlers." She closed her eyes when Jia pulled out her black eyeliner.

"You're related to Livvy, and Livvy is apparently with Nicholas again, so it's basically the same." Ayesha clinked two bowls on the island.

"Don said—"

"Ugh, I hate that guy. He can't even tell us apart yet." Sadia didn't have to open her eyes to feel Jia's sneer. Though the twins were identical, they were perpetually baffled anyone could ever mistake them for each other. Ayesha was quiet and contained where Jia was brash and loud, Ayesha cautious where Jia was impulsive. Jia favored brightly colored clothes and vivid makeup while Ayesha tended to choose more neutral garments and rarely wore makeup or jewelry. Today, Ayesha wore a beige sweater and dark jeans, a simple black scarf covering her hair.

"Anyway, Don said Nicholas closed the Chandler's out on Main, put up a huge banner announcing he was in love with Livvy, and asked her to marry him with a Super Bowl ring he won in a poker game."

Jia stepped away and Sadia blinked her eyes open, the eyeliner foreign on her usually naked lids. "Why a poker game? He's a CEO, not a poker player."

"Because all rich manly men play poker?" Jia guessed.

"And happen to possess Super Bowl rings?"

Jia shrugged. "I'm just passing the rumors on, I'm not saying they make sense."

Sadia relented. "I can confirm the first of those two things is true."

"But they did fly to a private island in the Caribbean, right?" Jia whisked a brush in powder.

"They're off somewhere. I don't know where."

"Are they together then?" Ayesha asked.

"Guys, I don't know. Tell Don and all your other friends you're clueless. We're not gossips, and we're certainly not talking about Livvy behind her back."

"Sadia—" Jia began in a cajoling tone.

Sadia shook her head firmly, forestalling her. "Nope. You're right, Livvy's my family. And your family, by extension."

As she'd expected, that quieted both of her sisters. Family was everything.

Sadia softened her tone. "Are you done yet?" she asked Jia, hoping to distract her sister. "I don't want anything heavy."

Jia pursed her bright red lips at her. "I wouldn't give you heavy makeup. You need something light, which won't wear off during the day. A touch of eyeliner and some of my super long-wearing lipstick . . ." She rummaged through her backpack and pulled out a tube of mauve liquid lipstick. "Hold still." She carefully lined and filled in Sadia's lips, then stepped back. "Et voila."

Sadia ducked her head and glanced at her reflection in the toaster. "Oh. Not bad."

Ayesha grinned. "You're the prettiest of all of us, MashAllah."

It had been so long since she'd put any makeup on, Sadia wanted to steal another second to admire her face, but she was already over the three minutes Jia had promised her. "Pshaw. It's Jia's skills."

Jia winked. "My skills are good, huh? But this time I had solid source material."

"You are a pro."

"I know. I should do this full-time."

Sadia gave a distracted smile. "Ha, yeah. Okay, I have to go." She came to her feet. "Kareem ate all his vegetables last night, so he gets a bag of chips in his lunch today."

Ayesha's lips twitched. "Seems like a good balance."

Sadia checked her phone and shoved it in her pocket, mentally calculating this delay into her schedule. "Thanks, both of you. I swear, I'm going to hire someone any day now." Mentally, she crossed her fingers. She had to find a chef soon. She simply couldn't afford a nanny or daycare. Since Paul had died, between her four sisters, her parents, Aunt Maile, and Paul's mother, Tani, she'd somehow managed to cover most every gap when she couldn't be with her son, but this early morning business was a bit of a challenge.

"No problem. We're up. I gotta do some reading anyway." Jia replaced her makeup pouch in her bag and pulled out a textbook. All four of her sisters were conscientious to a fault when it came to homework. Not Sadia, for whom school had been a constant form of torture.

"Thanks. I'll see you both tomorrow night?" Her family tried to get together once a week or so for dinner. With the five sisters and her parents' own busy life, it wasn't always easy.

Ayesha shoved one bowl toward her twin and dug into her cereal. "Yup. See you then."

The road was empty for her drive to the café. She turned on public radio, her favorite. Kareem always whined when she put it on, so she took advantage of the times he wasn't in the car.

She relaxed, listening to the segment on baseball players. She'd never cared much for sports, but she liked looking at baseball players. And their butts.

Her fingers twitched on the wheel, and she overcorrected, swerving back to the road. Maybe she should just not think about sex or butts or hands for the indefinite future. Her libido was clearly a problem lately.

She parked in her spot behind the café, then pulled her journal out of her bag. She liked to make a quick outline of her day, carrying over the tasks from the day before she hadn't had a chance to get to.

She surveyed the list, then added one more item. *Only think about Jackson for a cumulative one hour today. Do not email him or read your past emails to him.*

This was the first time Jackson had ever made her official to-do list. He'd traditionally been reserved for times she'd been playing hooky from her actual responsibilities.

At the very bottom, she wrote the words she wrote on every day's to-do list. *You can do this, and if you can't do it today, you'll do it tomorrow. You are not a failure.*

She made sure no one in her family ever saw her journal. They wouldn't be cruel about her affirmations, but self-care wasn't a concept her parents were hugely familiar with.

Sadia was so focused on running through her mental to-do list it took her a moment after she entered the café to realize that the lights were on in the kitchen. Had she not shut them off the night before? That was weird, for her. She didn't like to waste a dime more on electricity than she had to.

A pot clanged against metal and her eyes widened. The scent of cinnamon and carbs teased her nostrils. She readjusted her keys in her hands so the metal poked through her knuckles. She doubted many attackers crept into a closed café and cooked, but she'd watched enough television to know serial killers came in all shapes. She pushed open the door of the kitchen, ready to attack.

Then she stopped. Oh damn. This was arguably worse than a serial killer. A serial killer would just try to kill her. Jackson, she might kill.

Jackson had swapped out his long-sleeved shirt for a white T-shirt, which left his deliciously muscular forearms bare. A black tattoo peeked out from under his sleeve, thick, swirling geometric lines following the dips and curves of his biceps.

She tore her gaze away from that perfect golden flesh to stare at the stained apron wrapped around his narrow waist. "What the hell?" She wasn't sure if her words were directed at her or him.

He cast her a quick, sidelong look out of those beautiful black eyes. "Hi, Sadia." He went back to kneading a large lump of dough, like they'd said everything they needed to say to each other.

Not even. "Uh, what are you doing here?"

"Baking." He nodded at the cooling racks, which held trays of croissants and muffins, golden and luscious, the scent making her mouth water. They were all things that had been on the Kane's menu from before she'd been tapped to run the place, but they somehow looked better than anything that had ever graced their display cases.

You just think that because you didn't have to make them.

"I can see that." She put her keys away and stepped into the room fully, letting the door swing shut behind her. "The question is, why are you here, baking?" She was kind of proud of how rational and calm that question sounded, given that she'd thrown a cocktail in this man's face a few hours ago.

Because she was calm and rational. She rarely lost her temper.

"You need help."

She waited, but he just kept working the dough. She gritted her teeth, having forgotten this aspect of Jackson's personality, his brevity with words. He'd never understood everyone couldn't see into his brain. "No. I don't."

"You do."

"I can assure you, I'm doing fine."

He pounded his fist into the dough. "You've gotten bad reviews since Rick left. You're coming in here at the crack of dawn and working shifts at a bar to supplement your income." Another glance, and she straightened her shoulders defensively. "You're clearly exhausted."

Her eyes narrowed. Well thank God Jia had dabbed some concealer on her, or he might have been really moved to pity at her haggard appearance. "I'm not exhausted." Yes she was. "Wait, we have bad reviews?"

Paul wouldn't have gotten bad reviews.

The richest people in this town had sided with the Chandlers following Robert Kane and Maria Chandler's deaths and the C&O's subsequent explosion, but Kane's had catered to the average folk, and they'd been sympathetic—if curious—about the Kanes' fall. Paul had been charming and magnetic. The café had never been a big moneymaker, but it had done okay. If Paul hadn't passed away, the loans wouldn't have been such a big deal.

She didn't have Paul's proprietor personality, and she definitely wasn't a chef. No wonder their reviews sucked now.

Jackson turned the dough over. "A few. People can tell Rick is gone."

"Oh."

"Don't look so discouraged."

She automatically squared her shoulders. "I'm not discouraged."

"I can help."

"Are you a baker now?" Her question was serious, not sarcastic. She'd googled Jackson more than once over the years, but the top hits remained the C&O fire and his subsequent arrest. Jackson *had* been in culinary school when everything had gone down and his family was torn apart.

"I'm a chef. I can bake adequately."

"Wait, really?"

He grunted.

That wasn't any kind of answer. "Do you work at a restaurant somewhere?"

"I work in a lot of places."

"Like a personal chef?"

He dipped his head. "I have gigs. Got one in about a month. I can help you until then."

She took a deep breath, feeling the situation spinning out of control. Spinning out of control was not on today's to-do list. She opened her mouth to firmly make it clear that she didn't need him right now, but he had to go and distract her by bending and peering into the oven, his shirt riding up enough to reveal the base of his spine. She almost swallowed her tongue at the twin dimples there.

Whoa, had those always been there?

She ripped her gaze away from his butt. His rather nice butt.

She was sure he'd always had one of those, but she hadn't really considered it nice before now.

Focus. No butts, no hands. Sex is reserved for the bar at night with anonymous consenting humans. This is not the place, and he is not the human. "What the hell is this, Jackson?"

"What do you mean?"

"You. What's your game? Loitering at the bar, coming here?"

"There's no game."

"There must be a game. You disappeared forever, and now you're back and you honestly think you can walk in here and take—" She took a deep breath, inhaling and exhaling. No, she was not going to lose control like she had last night.

"There's no game," he repeated. "You need help. I can help you."

"Since when do you want to help me?" She couldn't hide the bitterness, though she was proud of herself for not shouting.

"Since I knew you needed help. I have no ulterior movies. This is a practical arrangement."

Goddamn it, it was like he knew she'd love anything that made rational sense.

Because he knew her, or at least, had known her from the time she was a tiny human. Sadia had been a pretty easy target for teasing at their prestigious prep school—though she had two older sisters, her parents hadn't really been up to speed on what was considered cool amongst American kids. Sadia had had to be on constant guard for people making fun of her hair and her lunch and her clothes.

Until Jackson had gotten involved.

Jackson had only had to lurk at her side, and

bullies had scrammed. For most of her childhood and young adulthood, not one day had passed that Sadia hadn't seen Jackson or Livvy or both of them.

But then he'd left, and he'd deliberately ignored every overture she'd made to him. Her spine stiffened, that anger poking at her again. "No, thanks. I'd rather not. I—" Her phone rang, startling her.

She glanced at the screen and frowned. "Hang on." She turned her back and answered. "What's wrong?"

"Nothing," Ayesha said in her soothing voice. The girl would have an excellent bedside manner when she graduated medical school. "But, um, Kareem just threw up."

Oh, no. "God—"

"He's fine! Promise. I called Noor and she said there's a stomach bug going around the school and it would probably go away in an hour or so. He's curled up in bed right now, asleep again."

Their oldest sister's son was in Kareem's grade, so Noor would know, but Sadia couldn't prevent the lurch of fear in her own stomach.

"Jia has class right now, but I can stay until noon or so? Do you think you can get someone to look after Kareem by then?"

A rush of love flooded through Sadia, so hard and fast she could barely speak. What on earth would she do without her sisters? "I'll, um . . . I'll figure out something for the afternoon. Let me call you back."

She hung up and tapped her phone against her

thigh for a second. Her older sisters and parents would all be at work, and Maile was usually occupied during the day. Tani was still recovering from her broken hip.

And she couldn't leave because . . .

Because they didn't have a chef. Only they did right now.

Son of a . . .

She gritted her teeth and faced the man who was driving her nuts. "My son is sick." *The boy you've never even met.*

Jackson wiped his fingers on his stained apron. "I'm sorry to hear that."

"He doesn't get sick much."

Nothing, not even a peep of curiosity.

She inhaled, trying to banish the hurt and anger in favor of rationality. "You can stay for the day. I'll show you around this morning—"

"Sadia, my name is on the door. You don't have to show me around." He touched the stove. "I learned to cook right here. I've cooked for you here before. Go home now and be with your son."

Her fingers twitched. Every instinct was screaming at her to run to Kareem, but she'd learned sometimes instincts couldn't win. She couldn't simply leave Jackson here, not without introducing him to the staff and making sure he really did remember the menu.

Kareem was safe and snug in his aunt's hands for a few hours. She'd take care of this portion of her responsibilities. "I'll stay until noon," she said firmly. The back door opened and she glanced at the kitchen door. "That's Darrell now. Let me introduce you to him."

"How much staff do you have?"

The question was sharp enough for her to frown. "Two or three people right now. I'm trying to hire more."

His face tightened as heavy footsteps sounded on the tile outside. "Hm." He turned to the stove.

Away from the door.

She stared at his back, and the way he'd folded his shoulders in. What was he doing?

Darrell walked through the swinging doors, looking far fresher than her, but he was barely nineteen, so that was acceptable. He was dressed in a pair of jeans and a casual button down, with bright orange sneakers. Sadia had cut out the uniform policy a few months ago, mostly because she hadn't been able to afford purchasing uniforms and she hadn't wanted the staff to have to do it. He smiled at her and pulled his earbuds out of his ears. He was currently taking a gap year between high school and college. Most importantly, he was sweet, dependable, and customers liked him. "Hey boss."

Oh, and he treated her like a boss, and not Paul's incompetent widow. Paul's employees had been loyal to him, and adjusting to her had taken some time. Some of them had quit. She knew she was in a high turnover industry and the employees coming and going weren't a reflection on her abilities, but she couldn't help but feel a little twinge.

Darrell raised an eyebrow at Jackson. Or his back, rather. "Uh. Who's this?"

"We got a chef. Just for the day," she hedged. "This is—"

"Jay," Jackson cut her off before she could say. He didn't turn around.

Darrell seemed unfazed. "Nice to meet you. I'm Darrell." He went to the cooling racks and grabbed two trays of baked goods. "I'll put these in the case. They look awesome."

Sadia sniffed. She knew that wasn't a dig at her cooking. Jackson's buns did look objectively awesome.

His *cinnamon* buns. Gawd.

Darrell paused at her side. "You can go do whatever you need to do, boss. I'm sure me and Jay can handle things for a while."

Sadia glanced between him and Jackson, who hadn't bothered to look Darrell in the face once. "I'll be in my office for a little bit, and then I'll have to leave before lunch, probably. Let me know if you have any problems." She'd cram in as much paperwork as she could in between checking up on Jackson. If he could manage the breakfast crowd, he would be able to manage lunch without her.

After Darrell left, she reminded Jackson, and herself. "It's only for today."

Jackson dug his hands into the dough, his long fingers manipulating the flour.

Gah. Wrong place. Wrong time. Wrong person.

He stretched the dough out between his strong, capable hands. "Whatever you'd like."

Chapter 4

ONLY FOR today? Not a chance.

Sadia needed him, maybe more than she knew.

Jackson twisted the knob to turn the right burner on and cursed. Still nothing. The kitchen only had two functioning burners. How was any chef supposed to work efficiently without the proper equipment?

Granted, the crowd wasn't as busy as he remembered it being for breakfast. He and the kid in the front had easily handled any food orders, the teen calling them out and Jackson pushing them through the pass-through. He'd slipped into his place in the kitchen as easily as a person slipped on a pair of jeans.

All of the Chandler and Kane kids had been expected to work when they were young, despite each family's wealth. Robert had assumed both his sons would take the lead in the C&O empire he'd married into, so he'd been more than a little disappointed when Jackson had chosen to work with Rick.

Jackson consciously unclenched his teeth. He

wished he could have had the kind of uncomplicated relationship with Robert that Livvy had had. Their father had been more than ready to indulge his only daughter. His sons were supposed to be strong, successful men, and Robert had really only had one idea of what strength and success looked like. Paul had fit that mold. Jackson had not.

He'd had his mother, however. They'd been similar, both quiet and reserved. Jackson swiped at the back of his forehead with his hand, shoving thoughts of his mother away.

It was hot in the little kitchen. He'd scoped out the A/C unit in the back during a break, a decrepit compressor that needed a new tune up. Had Paul changed anything in this place?

Don't second-guess me, little brother.

He froze, his brother's firm voice echoing in his head like he was standing in the room with him.

Only he wasn't there. He never would be again.

Jackson and Paul hadn't exactly been friends. In a lot of ways, Paul had been closer to Nicholas than him. But they had been brothers, separated in age by only three years. Jackson had no idea what their relationship would have been as grown adults, but as kids and young adults, Paul had seemed all-knowing and wise to Jackson.

Jackson's phone rang, and he fished it out of his pocket. So few people had his number, which was exactly how he liked things. His own list of contacts was laughably short.

He answered the phone, mainly because he knew

this particular caller wouldn't stop calling until he did. "Yeah."

"Jackson, my love. Not eaten by Bigfoot yet?"

Ariel Nelson was Jackson's partner, manager, ringleader . . . everything? After nine years of friendship and business partnership, Jackson wasn't sure yet what her title was, but she kept him and the rest of their team functioning. "Hello Ariel. Not yet." Ariel had been born and raised in London so anything that wasn't a major metropolitan city might as well be the Wild West as far as she was concerned.

"Good. I would be highly disappointed if my golden goose went and got himself eaten."

Jackson's lips edged up at the corner. Ariel had met him when he was a scared but talented twenty-one-year-old. She'd hired him as a sous-chef in her tiny restaurant in London.

When he'd left home, he'd lost his mother and his aunt, the two maternal forces he'd been closest to. Ariel had stepped right into that role so seamlessly he'd barely noticed that he'd tangled himself up in her until it was too late. She knew more about his past than anyone, save his family.

When he'd gotten too itchy in England, she'd been the one to propose a new business venture: a pop-up food establishment that could travel the world, on their schedule.

He'd only asked for anonymity as chef, and she'd agreed. In the beginning, they'd cooked together, but as he grew more skilled and developed his own style, she'd ceded the kitchen to him entirely. Without her organizational mind and business acumen, though, he'd be nothing.

"So what do you need? Are you ready to head to New York City? Done and done. You have a hotel room booked at—"

"No. I'm staying for a while."

Ariel was silent for a moment, and then came a gusty sigh. "Oh love, what are you doing?"

"I'm . . ." He looked around the kitchen, but it was quiet. Sadia was in the office, Darrell and his sister Kimmie taking care of any stray customers. "Helping out an old friend," he mumbled.

"I thought you were only going to be there long enough to check up on your sister."

"I'm still checking up on her." He hated that he sounded so childishly defensive, but something about Ariel made him regress. Maybe it was because she reminded him of his aunt. Same powerful, dynamic, but kind personality.

His lips twisted. Twice he'd driven past his aunt's home in the dark of night and been unable to knock on the door. He didn't know if he'd ever be able to.

"Uh-huh. Let me guess, the friend you're helping out . . . it's your brother's wife, yes?"

Of course she'd known. "Widow."

By Ariel's huff, he knew she'd caught the speed of the correction. "The one you're madly in love with."

Jackson straightened, his gaze shooting around

the room, as if someone could have actually heard that. "I was a kid then, Ariel."

"Feelings don't turn off." Her voice changed, and Jackson knew she was thinking of her late partner. "I know. Trust me."

"This is different," he insisted.

"The hell it is. That place is not a good place for you."

Hadn't he just told his sister the same thing a few weeks ago? Told her to hurry up and resolve whatever she needed to resolve and get the hell out of town?

He couldn't listen to his own advice. Probably because he didn't have the faintest clue as to what he was trying to resolve.

I don't expect you to stick around. "I'm lending a hand."

"Uh-huh," Ariel said, and she didn't sound at all convinced. "She has a child, does she not? What's your nephew like?"

"Sick at home." It had been hard not to demand answers to what kind of sickness Sadia's son had. Sadia had sent him so many pictures of the boy over the years, from the moment he was a tiny, squalling infant.

But pictures meant nothing. He didn't know the child, and the child didn't know him. "I haven't met him yet."

"You're going to, though." Ariel's tone softened. "Jackson . . ."

"It's fine. All I'm doing is working at my grand-parent's old café, is all." He pressed the phone tighter against his ear when she snorted. "She needs help, I have nothing else to do, and damn it . . . I owe her, Ariel." He wasn't here because he was still in love. No matter how beautiful she looked today in her relaxed sweater and skinny jeans, skin dewy and fresh, eyes somehow darker and more mysterious, bright red gloss slicked across her lips.

Don't think about her lips.

"I don't want you hurt, my love. You feel so deeply."

His fingers clenched around the phone. He had felt deeply once, but he'd learned his lesson. With deep feeling came deep pain. Selective memory and numbness had protected him for a decade. His heart was like a black-and-white television. It beat. It didn't feel.

I don't expect you to stick around for me.

Ariel was right to be worried. If he was thinking clearly, he'd be worried too.

Ariel made an unhappy noise. "Have you seen many townspeople? Is that angry mob treating you poorly?"

"No. I've barely had to see anyone. And no angry mob chased me out of town when I was a kid." More like quiet never-ending whispers, a trickle of awareness of people staring at him.

Jackson was so used to cooking behind a team of people who were dedicated to protecting his identity, he hadn't considered he'd have to interact with Sadia's staff if he worked here. He couldn't exactly swear them to secrecy. If Darrell had recognized him, he'd played it cool. Hopefully, that would continue.

It didn't take long for rumors to spread in this place, though. He'd have to think about that, once he got Sadia to agree to let him stay.

"You certainly made it sound like an angry mob. With pitchforks."

"No pitchforks." He turned around at the sound of the door opening, expecting to see Sadia, who had been checking up on him sporadically, if curtly. Instead, his gaze met the blue eyes of a woman he vaguely recalled from his youth.

Recognition crossed her face, and a shriek escaped her mouth, the tray of glasses she was holding crashing to the floor. "You?" she shouted, and pointed a finger at him. "What are you doing here?"

Jackson kept his gaze on her, wary, but not alarmed. Yet. "I'll call you back," he spoke into the phone.

"Who is that?" Ariel asked.

"Might be a mob representative."

JACKSON WAS a dream hire.

He knew exactly what he was doing, every dish was prepared better than anything she or even Rick had managed, he was efficient and capable. All morning, she'd been able to tackle her mountain of paperwork and trust he was handling the kitchen.

She was going to cry tomorrow.

Why do you have to let him go again? Keep him.

Because . . . because . . . because she didn't trust

him, because she didn't know him now. He might say he was going to stay for weeks and then bolt and she'd never hear from him again, no matter how many times she tried to—

She blinked at the computer screen and started typing again. She'd consider today a brief reprieve of at least some of her responsibilities and tackle tomorrow when tomorrow came.

She finished her email to their coffee bean supplier and hit send just as a crash and a high-pitched yelp came from the kitchen. Sadia shoved her seat back, worried over what she would find.

Which was Harriet, standing right inside the kitchen door, her hands over her chest. There was a tray of glasses shattered on the floor, Jackson crouched over, picking them up. Sadia tried not to think of what those glasses were going to cost her. She'd factored in a cushion for waste so she wouldn't obsess as much over tiny costs. "Is everything okay?" she demanded, and stepped inside, the door closing behind her.

Harriet whirled around to face her. The woman, like Rick, had been working at the café since the Kane grandparents had been alive. Her graying brown braid swung over her shoulder, her petite, almost fragile body vibrating. She stabbed a finger at Jackson. "What on earth is that criminal doing here?"

Sadia's mouth dropped open. Jackson kept his head lowered, face hidden. Out of the corner of her eye, though, she noted the almost imperceptible tensing of his shoulders.

Before Sadia could speak, Harriet pointed to the kneeling Jackson again. "Did you even know he was here? Did he break in?"

Sadia jolted to attention. Harriet's voice was loud enough to carry to Darrell and the customers, but more importantly, Jackson was right there.

She might be pissed as hell at him, but that didn't give anyone else the right to call him names. "Harriet," she snapped. "Watch it."

Harriet clamped her mouth shut and blinked. And why shouldn't she look surprised? Sadia wasn't sharp with the staff, even when she should be.

Sure enough, Harriet wasn't quelled for long. Her shoulders straightened, and she lifted her chin. "Darrell said we had a guest chef for the day. Tell me this man isn't actually working here."

Sadia smiled tightly, though inside she was seething. She'd never much liked Harriet—the other woman had had a proprietary attitude toward the café that occasionally annoyed Sadia. She was pretty certain the woman considered herself far more qualified to run the place than Sadia was.

And in the past, Sadia hadn't done much to correct her on that account. But she wasn't about to let her abuse Jackson. "We'll talk in my office. Not here."

Harriet set her lips but she complied, sweeping out of the room. Sadia cast Jackson a glance, but he still wasn't looking at her. She thought of his reticence with Darrell, and the truth dawned on her with the force of a sledgehammer.

She'd had a conversation with Maile about a week after Livvy and Jackson had skipped town. Livvy had kept in almost daily touch with her, but Jackson dropped off the face of the earth. Sadia had sat across from Maile at her kitchen table. *I don't understand why he had to leave.*

Sweetheart, you know Jackson. If there was anything that boy hated, it was attention. Can you imagine how he must have felt, walking out of that police station? Like a million eyes were on him.

Sadia frowned. And yet, he'd come here. To help her. Knowing it would mean at least a few people would see and recognize him. There was gossip about all the Kanes, but Jackson had been a special case. For him to be on the receiving end of that dreaded attention in a building that bore his name . . . oh, that was not going to be happening.

Damn it, damn it, damn it! She didn't want to feel grateful or happy or attracted or empathetic or anything else toward Jackson. She wanted that pure, uncomplicated mad.

While Sadia's anger grew with every step she took, it definitely wasn't directed at Jackson. She followed Harriet into her office and had barely closed the door before she whirled around. "You do not speak that way to him again," she said, and was proud of how controlled and calm her voice was. "Do you understand me?"

Harriet reared back, but she rallied quickly. "That man—"

"He has a name."

"He is a criminal."

Sadia crossed her arms over her chest. "Jackson is not a criminal. The charges were dropped."

"My cousin was the one who saw him burn down the C&O!"

Oh, fuck. Sadia had forgotten the connection. Harriet's cousin had been driving home on that Tuesday night over a decade ago when he'd claimed to have witnessed Jackson flinging something into the front glass of the C&O.

Based on the witness's testimony, the cops had descended on the Kane mansion, where the family was still in a state of shock over Robert's death and the loss of their half of the company.

Sadia hadn't been there, but Livvy had cried in her arms afterward over how the cops had turned the place upside down, finally discovering a gas can with Jackson's fingerprints in the garage. It had been flimsy evidence, but it had been enough to arrest him. Since the family was still wealthy, despite the recent loss of the company, the judge had denied bail.

"I forgot the witness was your cousin," she said, quieter. "But I didn't forget that he recanted." The recant had come after a couple of weeks, but it had come. Without anyone to place him at the scene, the prosecutor had decided to not press charges. Jackson had been released immediately.

He'd left town that night, before Sadia could even see him and reassure herself that her best friend was okay.

Harriet shook her head. "Someone got to him. Val wouldn't have just made up a story like that."

Sadia raised an eyebrow. "I'm sorry. Are you saying someone in my family paid off your cousin?"

"Or silenced him in some other way."

"And who did that, hmm? Who committed that felony? My elderly mother-in-law? My dead husband? My five-foot-tall sister-in-law?"

Harriet blanched, but invoking Paul, whom she'd actually liked, didn't stop her. "I'm . . . I'm not sure."

"But your cousin claimed he was intimidated into silence?"

The older woman pressed her lips tight. "No. He only said he couldn't be certain it was Jackson anymore. But I know my family, and he wouldn't have come forward at all if he wasn't sure."

"And I know mine." She didn't know Jackson now, or the Jackson who had been reading all her emails. But the Jackson she'd known all those years ago wouldn't have been able to stomach destroying a single thing. Especially not when there was a risk someone could be hurt. "Jackson is a Kane. He belongs in this establishment more than any of us."

Harriet drew herself up to her full height. "He may not have been tried, but I don't feel safe around such an unstable individual. As long as he's here, I won't be."

Sadia contemplated her options. She could assure Harriet Jackson would only be here for a day, or she could pacify her by kicking the man out immediately and take over the kitchen.

Or she could do none of those things, because she was pissed as hell, and not at Jackson this time. "If you'd like to take a small vacation, that's fine."

"Oh, it's not a vacation. I'll quit."

You are short-staffed. Calm her down.

Again, she thought of Jackson, silently picking up glass off the floor. She thought about the fact that Jackson had never once in all the years this woman had known him, treated her with anything but distant politeness and respect.

People had been so eager to believe Jackson was a criminal back then, and why? Because he was big and gruff and different? Everyone had learned not to say anything in Sadia's presence once she'd married Paul, but before that she'd had to defend Jackson more than once in the aftermath of the fire. "I'm sorry to hear that. You've been a good employee. Thank you for your years of service."

Harriet blanched. For a second, Sadia wondered if she'd walk back her threat, but then she stripped off her apron and threw it at her.

Snap.

There went her temper.

Sadia had a long fuse, and it took a while for someone to get on her bad side, but no one came into her establishment, badmouthed her family, and then *threw* things at her.

Good riddance. Harriet always had annoyed the hell out of her. Paul had complained, too, and he had at least had the ability to charm the woman.

As if she read her mind, Harriet turned at the

door. "Paul would not approve of this. Everyone knew he hated his brother."

Okay. That was quite enough. "I think I knew my husband better than you did," she said, her voice whisper soft. "And Paul would have never put an outsider above his own family." That had been one of the many things that had drawn her to Paul. They'd had similar values.

Her husband had sharply criticized Livvy for not staying home and been silent whenever it came to Jackson but there was no doubt in Sadia's mind he'd loved his younger siblings deeply. He just hadn't known how to show it to them, or prioritize his love over his pride.

But there was no way he would have stood for someone shit-talking a single member of his family, no matter how he felt about them.

"Are you sure about that?" Harriet had the nerve to ask.

"Yes."

"When people hear he's working here—"

Sadia clenched her hand around the apron and took two steps forward, using her height to her advantage. "Before you go, let me make something very clear. If I hear so much as one peep of gossip about Jackson or any other Kane, I swear, I will destroy you. Now, you may not believe me, because you think I'm so nice and harmless, but I assure you, when it comes to my family, I am neither of those things. Are we clear?"

Sadia wasn't sure what expression was on her

face, but it was enough to send the woman stumbling backwards a step. "Uh, yes. Yes."

Harriet left and Sadia took three deep, cleansing breaths. She couldn't freak out the way she wanted to, because she still had to go talk to Jackson. She checked her watch and groaned. And it would have to be a quick talk, because she needed to get to her son.

She met Darrell loitering outside the kitchen, eyes wide. "Did Harriet really quit?"

"Yes." Fudge, she'd have to explain. "Jackson is Paul's—"

"I know," Darrell interjected, then smiled at the confusion in her face. "I was alive when everything went down, you know. If you say he's cool, he's cool."

Her shoulders relaxed. "Thanks."

"My older sister's home. You want me to ask her to come in today?"

That solved one problem. Darrell's sister had worked at the café a few times when she was between jobs. "Yes, please. I would so appreciate it."

She waited for Darrell to leave and then faced the kitchen door, straightening her shoulders. What was her plan here? Sadia bit her lip. She was still pissed as hell, of course, but she could appreciate Jackson had actually made a kind of big sacrifice in offering to help her. It didn't make up for his abandonment, but . . .

She couldn't deploy the "Kanes belong in Kane's" argument at Harriet and not recognize it herself. Who was she to kick him out of a place that would have been his birthright if she and Paul hadn't married?

Damn it all.

Sadia pushed open the door slowly, thoughts churning. Jackson was at the stove, his face in profile to her, stirring something in a pot. The glass had all been cleaned up. She inhaled. "Jackson—"

"Have a seat." He nodded at the stool.

"I—"

"We can talk after you have a seat. You haven't eaten a bite today. Eat first."

"I'm not hungry." The smell of the food hit her and she recognized that as a lie. Her stomach was growling, and she did need to eat. She welcomed the few seconds to push back a talk where she wasn't even sure what to say, and trudged to the stool. "Fine—"

And then she shut up, because one didn't speak when watching art in motion.

His motions were precise and controlled, his hands a blur as he cut open a brioche bun and tossed it on the grill. He was right. She wasn't a chef, but she knew good cooking when she saw it. Their menu here was decidedly simple: baked goods, pastries, sandwiches, and soups. Their customer base came from their use of fresh ingredients and people who had grown up in town and needed an occasional dose of nostalgia in the form of an old-timey café.

The latter group wasn't going to stick around forever, though. People moved or passed away. That business would slow and then stop.

Don't think about that now. Right now, she simply wanted to watch Jackson move.

He was familiar with the stove and small space, reminding her again that he'd grown up in this establishment as much as he had the grocery store across the street—maybe more than Paul, who had been groomed to take over his father's place as co-CEO of the C&O chain.

He added Gruyère to the bun, the melty cheese making her mouth water. He put prepped sliced mushrooms into the pan, whisking them with butter and some herbs before carefully cracking an egg in another pan.

He sandwiched the mushrooms between the cheesy bread, and then poured the béchamel sauce he'd been preparing on the stove on top. The sunny-side egg crowned the meal. Absently, he wiped the edge of the already-clean plate, and then placed it in front of her with an economy of motion, along with silverware, then leaned against the counter.

He'd remembered how she took it—no ham, extra cheese. She used a knife to cut the egg. Rick had never crafted an egg this perfect, the silky yolk spilling over the sandwich. Whatever self-consciousness she felt about him watching her as she ate vanished when she put the first bite in her mouth.

Hell, it was a glorified grilled cheese sandwich, and she was about to pass out with pleasure.

She'd eaten probably hundreds, no, thousands, of these vegetarian croque monsieurs in this very kitchen over the past twenty years, and this was the most delicious one, the pinnacle of sandwich making. What was that? Thyme? Ugh, she didn't know. She didn't have a chef's palate.

"It's good?"

Perfect.

She glanced up at him when she realized she'd consumed half the meal without saying a word to him. There was an unreadable expression in his eyes as he watched her, his body still. "It's great," she admitted, and kept eating.

"Do you love it?"

She was imagining the intimate tone to his voice, but she shivered anyway. "I do."

He went silent, and too soon the sandwich was gone, the egg yolk and béchemel and a couple mushrooms the only remnants on her plate. If he hadn't been here, she might have licked the ceramic.

She patted her lips with the napkin and then took a deep breath. "Harriet—"

"Quit. She told me on her way out. I'm sorry."

"I'm not. You belong here. She has no say over that."

If he was surprised at her defense, his stoic expression didn't betray a trace of shock.

"Are you still willing to work for a few weeks?" she asked.

He nodded.

With him working here, she would actually have the time to find another chef. Juggling everything and headhunting had been beyond her capabilities. *Temporary.* He'd be temporary, of course. She couldn't forget that, could not grow to depend on him in any way. "You know you might have more unpleasant run-ins with other people?"

"I can handle them. I didn't expect Harriet. I'm good at not being seen unless I want to be."

Uh, how? He was so stinking big. Impossible to miss. "We're open until six most nights, but the kitchen closes at three, so you don't have to stick around after that. We close all day Mondays."

He nodded again.

"I'm going to pay you."

His rejection was immediate. "I don't want your money."

"You can't work here for free."

"I don't *need* your money."

"This is kind of nonnegotiable." She speared a mushroom that had fallen out of her sandwich and popped it in her mouth.

"If you try to pay me, I'll come in before you do and make all the food for the day."

"If you do that, I'll . . ." A spurt of amusement hit her. Had she ever negotiated with someone to force them to accept her money?

"You'll what?"

Yeah, what would she do? She couldn't threaten to call the cops on him, because she wasn't heartless.

Jackson, if you don't do what I say, I'll . . . I'll hug you!

It was a threat from their childhood, but they were hardly children anymore. She didn't know this man enough to banter with him. "I mean it. I will not accept you working for me for free."

"We're at a stalemate then." He lifted a shoulder. "It's okay. I can break in every day."

She paused. "Wait. You never told me how you got into the café this morning."

The enigmatic look he gave her told her she wasn't going to get an answer to that question . . . and that he'd follow through on his threat.

She scowled. "Okay. What if I . . . pay you some other way?" Oh damn. Had that sounded as sexual to him as it had to her? She hurried to clarify. "Like, in room and board? Where are you staying?"

He named a rather crappy hotel and she wrinkled her nose. "I have an apartment above my garage." A trickle of pain ran through her, but she ignored it. "You can use that in lieu of wages."

Jackson scratched his chin. "At your home?"

"Sure. Yes. You shouldn't be staying in some hotel room. You're family." The last two words were more for her than for him. A reminder.

This was family. Family by marriage. And before she'd married Paul, Jackson had been family by choice.

She might be furious at him, but family came first. No matter what. And it wouldn't be weird at all to have a man she was suddenly attracted to staying in close proximity to her. Because she was in control of herself.

She would keep repeating that to herself.

He wiped his hand on the apron. "I accept. Thank you."

A trickle of pleasure ran through her at his acquiescence. Far too much pleasure than she should feel. Damn it, damn it, damn it.

Her watch beeped, and she got to her feet. "I won't have time to ready the guest room today, since Kareem is ill."

"Tomorrow is fine. I heard Darrell tell someone you don't usually come in on Saturdays."

Saturdays with a child meant sports and music lessons and wholesale grocery store runs, but recently, her sisters had been chauffeuring Kareem to all of those. "I didn't always, but since Rick quit—"

"Don't come in tomorrow. I can handle everything."

A day off would be a huge weight off her shoulders. If Kareem continued to be sick tomorrow, she would have to arrange childcare for him, and she'd simply be here worrying all day. But still. "I don't think that's such a good idea."

"I'll call you if I need you."

"You don't even have my number."

He pulled his phone out. "So give it to me."

She hesitated, but rattled it off, something hurting as she watched him input it into his contacts. Her phone buzzed in her pocket, and she put her hand on it. His number. "I'll still come in—"

"Sadia. Your son is sick. Take care of him. If we need you tomorrow, we'll call you. I'm a Kane, remember? This place is as much mine as it is anyone else's. I can handle things here."

Had he heard her conversation with Harriet? She searched his face, but his expression was guileless. "Okay," she acquiesced. To not come in on a Saturday seemed wildly luxurious, but she couldn't look a gift horse in the mouth, especially since she'd be spending today taking care of Kareem. "You can come over tomorrow after lunch, and get settled into your room. I'll text you my address."

"See you then."

"Yes. See you then." Three words she'd used to say so easily to Jackson. Words she hadn't said to him in forever.

He moved away to the freezer, surprisingly soundless on his feet for such a big man. "Go on. I got this."

She couldn't doubt his competency. Not now. "I'm still mad at you," she felt compelled to say. She was mad. Mad and annoyed and still a little distrustful and attracted. And part of her did actually want to give him a hug.

But mostly she was mad.

He didn't turn around. "You can be mad at me so long as you let me help you. I'm okay with that."

Chapter 5

Jackson is a Kane.

Jackson turned off the main road, into the quiet residential streets of Sadia's neighborhood, only half his attention on where he was going. The rest of his mind was on the words that had been looping in his head for over twenty-four hours.

He probably shouldn't have gone and eavesdropped on Sadia and Harriet's conversation, but he hadn't exactly had to press himself up against the office door to hear it. Their raised voices had carried to the hallway, where he stood in bemusement, listening to this woman he had wronged defend him.

Paul would have never put an outsider above his own family.

He'd gone back to the kitchen at that point. No need to hear anything more about what Paul would or wouldn't have done when it came to him.

Jackson had never cared for Harriet, even when he was a kid, standing at Rick's side, cracking eggs under the crotchety old man's eagle eyes. She'd always had a vague disdain for him, though she'd been plenty nice to Paul.

That wasn't unusual. Lots of people had liked Paul and steered clear of him. He didn't know how to make his body and face harmless through smiles and jokes.

Criminal.

A child in a front yard stopped bouncing a ball and stared at him. He should have rented a nice, inconspicuous sedan instead of the motorcycle. He'd gotten used to driving bikes all over the world, but here the metal and chrome was too loud and obvious. A car would have given him a barrier between him and other people.

He deliberately lowered his shoulders. Harriet's cousin had been the witness who had claimed to see him the night of the fire. Not everyone would react like that to him. What he'd told Ariel had been true. It had been quiet whispers, not screams, not demands he leave, that had driven him from this place.

His mother had once told him when he was a toddler he'd break down sobbing when someone looked at him for too long. It had been a joke in their family, but his aversion to attention was no joke to Jackson.

Even interacting with that child, Darrell, and his equally young sister who had come in and worked yesterday and today had been difficult. They hadn't looked at him with anything but curiosity, but he knew that they knew.

Jackson slowed. At least Harriet's blowup had gotten him the one thing he'd wanted—Sadia had let him stay. Not only that, but she'd taken the whole day off from the café. He'd heard her calling

Darrell a few times, presumably to check in, but whatever the boy had told her must have calmed her down. She'd texted Jackson once, but it had only been her address, which he already knew, thanks to his light stalking.

He pulled up in front of a tidy brick home. It was a far cry from the old Kane estate or even the upper-class home Sadia had grown up in, but it was a pretty nice place. Tidy, well taken care of, probably a few bedrooms, not too far from his aunt's home.

It was, no doubt, a terrible idea to be here. He could practically hear Ariel in his ear, tsking over him. His brain had short-circuited when Sadia had made her offer to let him stay at her place, the neural pathway that fed pleasure and pain to his mind getting jumbled up.

You had no choice. It wasn't like you could take her money.

It hadn't been because he wanted to be close to her for as long as possible. No, not at all.

He pulled off his helmet and swung off the bike. The detached garage was set a little behind the house, out of view of the street. Good. The more privacy he had, the better.

A metal staircase led upstairs to a second story. The door there was wide open, some bluesy tune spilling out into the air, telling him Sadia was probably still readying the place for his arrival. She'd always been worried about guests, even when she was young. He'd never seen her house or her room in anything but perfect condition.

He slowed as he walked past Sadia's SUV. He glanced inside and stopped at the toys spread over the back seat.

He'd overheard Darrell telling his sister that Kareem had recovered from his illness today, which was good. But he'd tried not to think too hard about the fact he would meet the boy soon.

"Kareem," a young girl suddenly yelled over the fence from the neighbor's yard, making him flinch. "Catch the ball." A childish giggle floated over the fence.

He felt a little creepy as he, well, creeped to the fence and peered over it. He caught a glimpse of a small child with silky black hair and he jerked back, flattening his back against the wood like he'd been caught doing something illicit.

Dear Jackson, the baby's here! He is so beautiful. I'm attaching a picture. We named him Kareem, but his middle name is Robert. My mother and Maile almost got into a fight at the hospital arguing over who he looks like more. I think he looks like a turtle. Or a gnome.

Livvy came home for a day to see him. Can you come too? I want you to meet your nephew, Jackson.

Jackson's eye twitched. When he'd gotten that email six years ago, he'd been sitting in a crappy Internet café in Berlin. He'd stared at the flickering monitor, unable to decipher how he felt.

Sadia's happiness had been evident not only in the glowing smile in the attached picture, featuring a little swaddled blob laying on her chest, but also in her words, and what she hadn't said.

He'd been able to read between the lines of Sadia's every email, the same way he'd always been able to read between her words when they spoke.

Sadia and Paul had eloped about a month or so after he'd left town. From that moment until Kareem's birth four years later, she hadn't mentioned her family, not once.

Jackson leaned against the fence and shoved his hands in his pockets. Christ. This kid's birth had been one of the few times he'd actually been tempted to come home. See his brother, his mother.

See the child who had lit up Sadia's face and managed to bridge whatever differences and issues Sadia and her family had dealt with. If the baby could mend bridges in Sadia's family . . . maybe Kareem could have mended the wounds in Jackson's?

Except children weren't magical and nobody could guarantee that kind of outcome. So instead of booking a flight, he'd gotten up and left that crappy German café and gone back to his rented flat.

Jackson pressed his hand against the weathered fence, letting the rough wood press against his flesh. He was a big man, so physically intimidating people avoided him. But here he was, contemplating coming face-to-face with this child, and all he knew was fear.

Paul's son. His nephew. The kid might have heard

stories about him from his parents or in school. He'd maybe have an idea in his head already of who Jackson was.

This was uncharted territory, and there were no guarantees as to what would happen, how either of them would feel, what they would say. He inhaled, then exhaled, long and slow. In a minute, he'd go find Sadia, and soon, he'd probably meet this child. But first, he needed a second to himself.

SADIA RAN the vacuum cleaner back and forth over the rug, the mindless movement calming her exhausted brain. She'd been up most of the night with Kareem throwing up. Just when she'd thought she should call one of her older sisters, he'd calmed, and they'd fallen asleep around dawn curled up in his bed.

He'd woken up almost completely recovered a few hours later, which was fantastic, but also meant their Saturday could continue as originally planned. They'd skipped soccer, but Kareem had been well enough for his violin lesson. Midway through that, Tani had called and asked if Sadia could bring Kareem over. Since they hadn't seen him much lately, Tani had pointedly added.

Sadia battled back the vague feeling of guilt. It was funny Paul's mother and her mother weren't better friends. They were both able to make her feel guilty for no reason.

Tani saw Kareem a lot. Since Paul had died Sadia had been overly careful to make sure his mother and aunt didn't feel slighted or like they weren't a part of her child's life. Sadia thought she was doing a good job of it, but then Tani went and said something like that, and . . .

Sadia blew out a breath. It wasn't a big deal. The only reason she was obsessing over her former mother-in-law was because it distracted her from the unpleasant task she was currently engaged in.

She glanced around the room. A few weeks after Paul's funeral, she'd packed up most of his stuff from the master bedroom and the rest of the house in large boxes, save for small mementos and photos and whatever she'd felt comfortable giving away. Strangely enough, she'd found herself unable to throw away the sympathy cards she'd gotten after his death, so those had gotten packed too. She'd stacked the boxes neatly against the wall in this apartment. She didn't miss the significance of her putting his belongings in here.

She and Paul had furnished this room simply, with only a bed and a dresser and a nightstand. The attached bathroom was equally simple and barren. They'd used it as a guest room now and again, for her sisters and some friends who had visited from out of town.

If Paul had lived, though, he might be living in this apartment right now.

Their marriage had ended not with raised voices, but with silences and increasing distance. The night before he'd died, the eve marking their anniversary, they'd sat at the dining table they'd bought together and Paul had given her an ultimatum.

We can't live like this anymore, Sadia. We have to get a divorce.

She blinked hard, feeling as betrayed and blind-sided today as she had then. Oh, she'd known their marriage had been finished for a while. But no one else had known about that, not her family or his, or any of their friends. Paul had been in the kitchen every morning before Kareem woke up, there to hug his son and make him breakfast before kissing her on the cheek and heading to work. Only the two of them had known those kisses were air kisses.

Sometimes childhood sweethearts could get married young and develop together. And sometimes they didn't want to grow together anymore. Sadia hadn't been happy about that, but she'd come to terms with it.

A divorce would have made it public. Everyone would know their marriage was over. Everyone would know she'd failed.

Her fingers tightened on the handle of the vacuum and she pressed the thing down harder on the carpet, leaving streaks. Paul had tried to reassure her. *I'll stay above the garage for a while. Make it a smooth transition for Kareem.*

She hadn't been able to verbalize her issues, that Kareem was only one of her concerns. When she'd sat there silent, cradling a cooling cup of tea, he'd sighed, kissed her on the forehead and retreated to the office and the couch he'd slept on there. The next morning, she'd discovered he'd left before she woke up, to go hiking on the trail they'd hiked on their anniversaries. The same trail they'd hiked after they'd eloped and toasted being young and in love and together.

He'd never come home.

She ran the back of her hand over her nose. She pushed the vacuum over the corner where she'd stacked all of Paul's boxes that were now in the garage, making sure that the carpet held no trace of the boxes' imprints. She had to get Kareem ready for dinner at her family's and get Jackson settled in here. She had no time for thoughts of Paul. Sadia walked the vacuum backward and right into something solid.

Someone solid.

All the hairs on her arms stood up, a bolt of electricity running through her. She stumbled forward in her jump away, the cord of the vacuum catching on her feet. It tangled around her ankle and she had that split second of horror that came right before a person face planted.

She braced for mortifying impact, but it never came. An arm snaked around her waist, plucking her completely off the floor for a second like she was a child. But she didn't feel like a child when she was brought back against a strong body.

Wrong place, wrong time, wrong guy's strong body, her brain screamed.

Oh but he smelled so right, a combination of sugar and fruit and cinnamon and whatever else he'd baked today. Did all chefs smell delicious? Had she ever even noticed what Jackson smelled like when they were young?

She looked down at the smooth, strong arm wrapped around her middle. Her gaze traced it to the hand holding her steady, fingers pressing into her waist.

Oh god. That hand. "Uh, I'm not going to fall now," she squeaked.

His fingers released her one by one, and then his arm was gone, but her middle was hot, and it had nothing to do with the fact that it was an unseasonably warm day out. She flicked off the vacuum and turned, careful with where she stepped now. "You surprised me."

He gazed down at her. He looked as good as he smelled, in dark denim jeans and another long-sleeved t-shirt, blue this time, his battered leather jacket thrown over it. How did he look so bright-eyed when he'd been up since the break of dawn?

"I'm sorry. I knocked, but you didn't hear me, I guess."

She fiddled with her T-shirt collar. She'd barely had time to shower and throw on fresh clothes today, but without Jia here today she probably looked as haggard as she felt.

One touch and you're fretting over your looks? Calm yourself. Jackson of all people doesn't care what you look like.

"I was trying to tidy up around here."

"You didn't have to do that."

"I did. It was dusty and dirty. This place has been closed up for a while."

Jackson walked to the bed and dropped his duffel on it. She busied herself with winding up the cord to the vacuum. Her hormones were clearly on the fritz and didn't need a visual of him standing next to the bed.

He shrugged off his jacket and tossed that on the mattress as well. "This is cozy."

"I hope it's okay."

"Nicer than a lot of places I've stayed in." He walked to the bathroom and stuck his head inside. He braced himself on the door frame, his biceps bunching up.

What places have you stayed in?

Not her business, and not like he'd tell her. She blurted out the first words that popped into her mind to distract them both. "I saw your mom and Aunt Maile this morning."

His back tensed. "Did you tell them I was here?"

"No." She'd considered it, but despite being their in-law, Sadia had decided it wasn't her place. Maile had been cheerful and Tani her regular distant self, so Sadia assumed they either didn't know or didn't want to talk to her about it.

"Thanks."

"Don't thank me." She'd been too tired to handle the inevitable emotions and questions. They would probably find out, and then they'd be annoyed at her for not telling them, but she'd deal with that then. "You should tell them you're here."

He didn't respond to that, merely moved away from the bathroom, keeping his gaze averted.

Not her circus, not her monkeys. "Maile said Livvy is doing okay." She almost added *if you care,* but thought that might be a little too bitter. "She doesn't have great reception wherever she's at, but she's checking in with Maile and Tani."

He paced to the nightstand and ran his finger over the wooden surface. "And where is she exactly?"

Her eyes narrowed. Jackson's tone was a little too casual. "Not sure."

"Nearby?"

Ah, yeah. She recognized this enough times from Paul's pouting when Livvy had started dating Nicholas. Her husband had glared at Nicholas every time they'd had a double date.

Sadia had thought it cute then. Maybe it was because she had sisters, or because she was simply too old and tired, but now she found this male posturing absurd. "If she wanted you to know her coordinates, she'd tell you. Or me."

"I only want to make sure Nicholas is being good to her."

"What will you do if he's not?"

He straightened. "Take care of him."

"You can't beat up Nicholas."

He turned around. "I don't see why not. If ever a man deserved a beating, it's him."

Sadia couldn't count the number of times she'd threatened to stab Nicholas over the years for dumping Livvy, but she shook her head and made sure her frown was forbidding. "No. They're together and we'll be happy for Livvy." Until she heard differently, at least. She'd keep her stabbing knife handy.

His mouth settled into what looked suspiciously like a sulk, but he grunted. In agreement, she sup-

posed. She needed a grunting-to-English diction-
ary for Jackson.

"I parked my bike on the street. Is that okay?"

She rolled with the change of subject. "It's fine,
but I can make some room in the garage."

"No, don't worry."

Her phone beeped a reminder. "I have to head
out—"

A patter of feet on the staircase interrupted her,
and a small whirlwind burst through the door.
"Mom!"

Kareem came barreling through the front door
and launched himself at Sadia. She caught him
automatically, staggering back a step, into the
vacuum. He was getting so big. He'd be tall, like
his daddy.

She smoothed his silky black hair back from his
round face. "Hey, baby."

"There's a motorcycle outside, whose is it—" He
craned his head around her. "Hi."

Her heart quickened. She brought Kareem
around to face his uncle. "Kareem, this is your
daddy's brother, your uncle Jackson."

Jackson was utterly still, his face expressionless,
black eyes locked on his nephew.

She forced herself to smile. "Uncle Jackson, this
is Kareem."

Kareem surveyed the man in front of him. "Are
you Aunt Livvy's brother?"

Sadia had told Kareem stories about Livvy and
Jackson even when Paul had been silent on them,
but her son was still young and trying to figure out

how everyone was related to him and each other. She waited for Jackson to answer, but when he was silent, stepped in. "Yes. He, Aunt Livvy, and Daddy were all brothers and sister."

Kareem looked up at her. "Does he have a potty mouth too?"

Sadia winced. She might be annoyed with Livvy right now, but having her home was generally great. Except for the fact that Kareem had already learned at least two swears from her.

Kareem's teacher wasn't impressed with Aunt Livvy at all. "It doesn't matter. We don't use grown-up words even if grown-ups do."

Kareem shrugged and looked back at Jackson. "Hello." After another moment, Kareem pressed tighter against her side and picked at a scab on his arm.

Sadia dropped her hand on his shoulder, disappointment making her heart ache. Her son was intuitive, and he was picking up on Jackson's clear discomfort. Livvy hadn't seen her nephew more than a handful of times in his life, but when she'd come home, she'd been affectionate and eager to grow acquainted with Kareem.

She shouldn't have expected the same from Jackson. She didn't know why she had. *Because you used to fantasize about laying Kareem in his uncle's big arms and watching Jackson melt.*

Family was everything. She'd sacrificed so much to give Kareem the protection of a large extended clan, and it had always hurt that she hadn't been able to give him all of Paul's family too.

Plus, Jackson had never only been her husband's brother. He'd been her best friend too. He should have loved Kareem on two fronts.

She had to remember that this wasn't the same Jackson she'd grown up with. Sadia rubbed Kareem's shoulder, ready to end this awkward meeting, but Jackson stopped her. "Hello," he responded.

JACKSON CLEARED his throat. His single greeting had been raspy and too rough, but he didn't know how to be soft and sweet.

Baggage could be a tricky thing. It could be carried over, gifted, inherited. Jackson might have turned his heart off, but he'd never been able to completely bury the surge of emotions he felt when he thought about his brother. Especially the bitterness or the anger.

Jackson hadn't wanted to meet Kareem, because he feared what he might feel. What would happen, if at first sight, Jackson discovered he loathed the child? What kind of monster would that make him?

He tiptoed around his own soul, his breathing coming faster when he realized there wasn't a shred of malice lingering there.

Curiosity. Nostalgia. A spark of something that felt dangerously like . . . affection. Or maybe something stronger.

No cruelty, no desire to punish Paul's son. Jackson's hands shook in relief.

Jesus, this boy was beautiful. He took after Sadia, with her skin and eyes and the same chubby cheeks she'd had as a child, but there was something in the shape of his face, his smile, his chin that reminded Jackson of his brother. Of him.

He seemed tiny though. Were all children so small? How did they accomplish anything?

He took a knee in an instinctive effort to get on the same level as this mini-human. "You look bigger than when I saw you last."

"When did you see me?"

"I—" he faltered, and didn't look at Sadia. "I saw you in photos." So many photos. Whenever he would see the little paper clip icon on any of Sadia's emails he'd always rush to open the thing and scroll through to get to the attachments.

Kareem took a few steps toward him, so he was within reach. A lock of the boy's hair was sticking straight up, and Jackson was hit with an urge to smooth it down, but he controlled it. He didn't know the boy and didn't want to startle him by touching him.

Kareem searched his face. "I saw pictures of you. Mom showed me. But you were little in them."

Sadia had showed her son pictures of him? Ah. "I was little once."

"Are you gonna live here now?"

"No, Kareem," Sadia interjected. "Uncle Jackson is only visiting."

I don't expect you to stick around for me.

Kareem cocked his head, not taking his attention away from Jackson. He took another step closer. "Where do you live?"

"All over." Everywhere and nowhere. He had no

place to call his own. Hell, he couldn't even claim a country.

He cast about for something innocuous to talk to the child about. He was, oddly enough, loathe to let this conversation end.

Motorcycles. The child had been talking about his when he bust in. "Do you like motorcycles?"

"Yeah. Can I ride yours?"

"No," Sadia said firmly.

Kareem smiled at Jackson, revealing adorable baby teeth. "Maybe Uncle Jackson will say I can."

Children were smart. "That's probably not a good idea." He felt like an immediate ogre when the boy looked crestfallen. "You could sit on it," he offered, then glanced up at Sadia, wondering if he'd spoken out of turn. "If your mom is with you."

She was watching them closely, a frown wrinkling her brow. After a beat, she nodded. "That would be okay."

Kareem brightened. "And then we take a picture of me so I can show my friends."

"Yes, it'll make a great photo op," his mother said dryly. Her phone beeped a reminder and like a Pavlovian response, she glanced at her watch. Sadia had always worn a watch when they were young, but he'd never remembered her looking at it quite this much. Then again, she did have a lot more to juggle now. "Okay, Kareem, come on. We have to get you ready for dinner." She spoke to Jackson. "Family dinner at my parents' house."

Jackson swallowed all of his questions about Sadia and her parents, as well as the lurch in the stomach at the reminder of his own parent. He didn't want to think about Tani. Not now. He nodded.

"Nooooo. I don't wanna go."

"We have to." Sadia nudged her son and grabbed the vacuum. He almost offered to carry it, but something told him Sadia was used to juggling a number of things.

"I don't wannnnnnaaaaa."

Wow. Apparently, the kid was also good at stretching a two-syllable word into nineteen.

Sadia didn't seem impressed. "Your cousins want to see you."

She must have uttered some magic word in there, because Kareem brightened. "Oh, okay. See you later, Uncle Jackson." The boy pivoted and ran out.

Jackson rose slowly to his feet. Sadia cocked her hip and it took a feat of strength for Jackson to keep his gaze on her face and not think about what her waist had felt like. Her butt had nestled perfectly in the cradle of his thighs, and there had been a small handful of flesh rising over her jeans waistband that had fit the cradle of his hand.

Yeah, he wouldn't think about that.

"Is there anything you need before I leave?" she asked politely.

Perfect hostess. "No. I'm fine."

"I didn't think to have any food up here waiting for you, but if you want to use our kitchen, feel free."

Oh god no, he couldn't use her kitchen. If touching her waist and staying above her garage felt intimate, cooking at the stove in her house, for him, would be equivalent of seeing her naked.

He shook his head decisively. "I'll figure something out for dinner."

She hesitated, searching his face. "Text or call me if you have any questions on anything."

Jackson nodded. He wouldn't, but it probably made her feel better to say that.

She closed the door behind her and he sank onto the bed, linking his hands between his knees. He glanced around the tiny room. It was devoid of personality. He'd stayed in hundreds if not thousands of similar rooms over the years, some better, some worse. None of them had ever felt like home.

And neither does this. You're here temporarily, and only because Sadia wouldn't have been able to let you work for her for free.

He pulled his phone out of his pocket and pulled up his contacts. He scrolled through, pausing on Sadia's name, then going back up to Livvy's. His finger hovered over his sister's name and the message icon.

Getting in touch with someone wasn't as easy as pressing a button, though it should be.

He tossed the phone and rose to his feet. He would go back to the café and rearrange everything until it was exactly how he liked it in his kitchens, and then he'd play around with some recipes. He could hyperfocus and bury himself in the scent and touch and taste of food. Whenever he was in a new foreign place, the kitchen was his one constant, the place that universally accepted him and gave him a home. A place to help him deal with uncharted territory.

He rubbed his chest. Because while this town might be familiar, whatever he was feeling? That was definitely not.

Chapter 6

Sᴀᴅɪᴀ's ᴘᴀʀᴇɴᴛs had always been eager to give their five daughters every advantage they could beg, borrow, buy, or steal for them, which had resulted in five overscheduled daughters. With Farzana having her own successful OB-GYN practice and Mohammad a professor at a medical school, the elder Ahmeds had been overscheduled too. That was why they'd insisted the family come together at least once a week for a meal. The dinners were generally formal affairs in the big dining room, the grandkids eating on a sheet spread out in the living room. Since everyone save Sadia was in the medical field—her older sisters' husbands were both doctors as well—most of the talk was dominated by science stuff that went right over Sadia's head.

Sadia preferred the moments after the meal, when she and her sisters cleaned up while the four grandchildren played with their grandparents.

She plunged her hands into the soapy water at the sink, letting the feminine voices rise and fall around her. Inch by inch, she could feel the stress of her life melting away as she scrubbed the pots and pans. She could forget her business debts, the things she had to do for work tomorrow, her mixed emotions for her ex-brother-in-law/chef/former best friend. Not for long, but for now.

In the early years of her marriage, Sadia had missed these dinners. She'd been too stubborn to attend without her husband.

She'd known they wouldn't be thrilled when she and Paul had eloped, barely two months after Robert Kane had died, but she hadn't expected her parents to react as violently as they had. Her father had stood quietly, frowning in the corner of his massive study while her mother had sobbed on the couch. Sobbed until she started screaming at Sadia, swearing that she wasn't about to keep paying for her college education when she'd gone and done this foolish thing, throwing her life away for some boy.

Sadia had gone twenty years toeing the line with her parents, desperately trying to excel at the things that came so easily to her sisters, but she'd snapped in that moment. Secretly, she was relieved at the idea of no more school—she wasn't good at it anyway. She'd told her parents they could either accept her husband or not, and then stormed off.

For four years, she'd only had strained contact with her parents, though she'd still seen her sisters, at least. Jia and Ayesha had cooked up schemes to stage a reconciliation, while Noor shook her head and her second-oldest sister Zara offered to refer them all to family therapy. Nothing had worked until Kareem had been born.

Sadia had held him in her arms in the hospital, and called her mother and cried. Her stoic, stubborn mother had wept too, and Farzana and Mohammad had been at the hospital that day.

Her parents, for all their faults, adored their grandchildren, and Kareem was no exception. He was doted on as much as Noor and Zara's children.

Some people might call her parents snobs or elitists, and maybe Sadia would have done the same ten years ago, but with age came wisdom, and she could afford to be more charitable. Her parents simply had very definite ideas of what success looked like for their children and Sadia struggling to make ends meet wasn't in that picture.

Sadia had shown up to dinner with her newborn the week after his birth, and she'd considered herself blessed to be able to reconnect with her family. Paul had been happy she was happy, but he'd refused to come, and her parents had never demanded it. Sadia figured they were a little relieved he didn't come around to increase the tension and serve as a reminder of their estrangement. It had smarted, especially when her sister's husbands were welcomed so warmly, but she hadn't known how to force either of them to bridge their differences.

Kareem's giggle floated through to the kitchen, and Sadia smiled reflexively. It was the best sound.

"I'm thinking of opening a second practice," Zara announced, and accepted the plate Sadia handed her to dry. Sadia's second-oldest sister was a psychiatrist with an athlete's body, glowing skin and shiny hair. Her husband, Al, was similarly glamorous, tall and fit, an Ethiopian immigrant who had charmed everyone the second Zara had brought him home from medical school. He was on call at the hospital tonight, which was a shame. Everyone adored Al.

Noor tapped her fingernails on the counter and flipped through the magazine that someone had left on the island. At thirty-seven, Noor was the undisputed matriarch in training. She was firm and no-nonsense to the point of painful bluntness. Sadia could only aspire to be as practical as Noor was.

Her husband was an incredibly sweet pediatrician who didn't speak much. Rohan was probably sitting with their father in the living room, a faraway look in his eyes. He was often distracted by something happening in his too-brilliant brain. "Have you had an accountant look over your finances?" Noor asked. "You don't want to rush this."

"The practice is doing so well," Zara said. "I want to capture the rest of the territory before someone else comes in."

Noor nodded. "You could do a small second practice, and funnel the larger cases to your other practice."

"Yes, that was my plan."

Sadia continued scrubbing the pots. She often had nothing to contribute to discussions like these, but they seemed less exclusionary in the kitchen than they did in the dining room.

"Mama, look at my nails!"

Zara glanced over at where her only daughter sat at the breakfast table and beamed at the girl's tiny blue-green tipped fingernails. Jia was bent over the girl's other hand. "So pretty, Amal."

"They're mermaids," four-year-old Amal said seriously. She'd gotten her tight curls from her father, but otherwise, she looked just like any of the five sisters had at that age. As the only granddaughter, Amal was the recipient of much pampering.

"Mermaid tips," Jia corrected her. She winked at Zara. "I'm trying out a new breathable nail polish this company sent me. Amal was nice enough to volunteer."

"She'll volunteer all day." Zara turned back to drying the dishes. "Maybe I can bribe her to eat with nail polish," she murmured, her voice lowered.

"It's a phase. Don't worry so much." Sadia rinsed off a glass. "Kareem is so picky, but he breaks down when he's hungry. He whines, but he eats."

Noor looked up. She was bespectacled and plump like their mother, and with the recent gray hairs she'd acquired, was well on her way to looking like Farzana. "Noah and Jacob always eat everything, MashAllah."

Zara smiled sweetly at Noor, though there was an edge to the expression. "Well, you never have any problems with your children, do you?"

Noor fluttered her eyelashes at her younger sister. There was barely eighteen months separating them, so they'd often been in direct competition with each other in a way Sadia had not. "Not really, no."

Ayesha grabbed the stack of dried dishes to put away, conveniently getting in between the two eldest before a painfully polite fight broke out. "Hey, we should talk about the finishing touches for Mom and Dad's anniversary party, yeah?"

Sadia handed the last plate to Zara, drained the water in the sink, and dried her hands. "We should. We need to finalize everything." The party was in only a couple of weeks. Sadia had taken the lead in organizing everything, because well . . . organization was one of the few things she did excel at.

She grabbed her planner from her bag, sat on one of the stools at the bar, and ignored her sisters' groans. "Things go smoother when we write them down," she said firmly. "You know that."

"Are we talking about the party?" Farzana hustled into the kitchen and beamed at them. She was small and round, shorter than all her daughters.

"I thought this was supposed to be a surprise party." Jia didn't look up from where she was putting the final touches on Amal's nails.

Farzana waved that away. "The details will all be a surprise for us. But I did want you to add someone to the guest list."

Sadia waited, her pen poised on the paper.

"There's a new resident in the group. From Egypt. He's handsome. And single."

Uh-oh. "That's nice," Sadia said slowly.

"I think you should meet him," her mother finished gently. Gently and firmly.

Oh shit. She'd known this was going to happen soon. Her parents had started to hint about a month ago that she ought to go out and date, but she'd managed to brush it off so far. She put down her pen. "Why?"

"It's time for you to find a nice boy. Kareem could do with having a father figure in his life."

"He has many father figures. I'm not interested in meeting any men or women right now," she responded. Just as firmly.

Her mother ignored the part about women. Sadia had always been open about her sexuality, and her mom had been just as open about ignoring it. It might have bugged Sadia, except she was far too used to accepting the things she couldn't change. Especially when it came to her parents.

"You might change your mind once you meet him," Farzana exclaimed.

"I won't." Her family had no idea what her emotional state was right now. How could they? She could barely wrap her mind around it. "I'm too busy now anyway," she added, trying to find an excuse her family would accept.

Busyness, they all understood.

"Busy with the café?" Noor made a dismissive noise. "Sell that place, Sadia. One of us can find you something better to do."

A busy job in one of their practices, probably. She'd been a stay-at-home mom for years and had a small amount of experience running the restaurant. What else was she qualified to do?

Sadia swallowed, feeling her self-esteem deflate, as it always did when she measured herself against her sisters. Her list of career milestones and daily accomplishments paled next to theirs.

I got through another day.
I showered.
I got out of bed.
I combed my hair.

They weren't the kinds of accomplishments her family was used to.

But they were hers. And she didn't need to get entangled in a romantic relationship now, when she was still smarting from the failure of her last one. "The café is doing fine, thank you."

Her mother opened her mouth, about to launch another attack, but her husband crowded into the kitchen behind her. Noor's eleven-year-old and six-year-old sons hung off his neck and back, while Kareem clung to his legs.

Mohammad Ahmed was growing skinnier as he aged. With his ill-fitting clothes and wild hair, he looked the part of the absentminded professor that he was. He had wrinkles around his eyes and mouth, but they mostly came from smiling and squinting. The man could never remember where he put his glasses. "Are we talking about the party? I don't want it to be formal. No suits."

Matchmaking for her daughter forgotten, Farzana whirled on her husband while his grandsons dropped off of him and ran over to Amal, who was delicately blowing on her nails. Sadia tried to grab Kareem, who had chocolate smeared on his chin as he raced past. He was too fast for her, but not too fast for Zara, who caught her nephew by the collar, wiped his face with a napkin while he struggled, and released him, all in one smooth motion.

"I want to wear my new dress," Farzana said. "The dress code will be fancy."

"Daddy, you wear suits every day," Ayesha interjected, her tone as soothing as always. "What's the big deal?"

"The big deal is that I wear suits every day and I don't want to have to wear one at home."

Farzana folded her arms over her large chest and narrowed her eyes at her husband. Dressed in brown from her head to feet, she resembled a very tidy, plump sparrow. "You cannot dress up to show that you are happy to be married to me? What will people think?"

Sadia pursed her lips and noted that all her sisters had occupied themselves with other things: Noor staring intently at her magazine, Zara examining the crown moulding, Jia cleaning up her nail polishes, and Ayesha straight-up staring at the floor.

What will people think, loaded with that incredulous concern, was like their mother's trump card, carefully deployed and capable of shutting any of them up. The only time it hadn't worked on Sadia was when she'd made the decision to elope with Paul.

Sure enough, her father pressed his lips together and backed down. "Fine. We can dress however you want. Kids, come. We have ice cream in the freezer downstairs."

The kids whooped and ran toward their grandfather, Kareem launching himself into his grandfather's arms, little Amal scurrying to catch up. Farzana followed after the procession, scolding. "Be careful not to hurt your back."

"I am, I am."

Once they were out of earshot, Sadia breathed. "I'm glad they settled that themselves." She crossed out *Finalize dress code* on the list.

"Seriously. I knew that was going to be an argument." Jia joined them at the counter and leaned against it.

Zara patted Jia on the back absentmindedly. She'd been ten when the twins were born, and was almost as maternal with them as she was with her own daughter. "You did a good job on her nails."

"Oh thanks." Jia's laugh sounded forced. "It's like it should be my job, right?"

The words rang a bell in Sadia's head, and she glanced up, frowning. It was weird, Jia repeating that same phrase she'd said yesterday to her. And with that intonation.

Like she wasn't joking.

Noor snorted. "Yeah, right. Don't quit medical school while you chase being an Internet sensation is all."

"I mean . . . I'm not far from being that sensation, though, you know?" Jia licked her lips. "I could probably get there faster if I did do this full-time."

The sisters went silent, the only noise the kids' distant yelling from their parents' finished basement.

Sadia put her pen down. "Jia, are you saying you want to quit school to pursue this?"

"This hobby?" Noor asked in disbelief.

Jia stiffened, and Ayesha put her hand on her sister's back. She was the only one of them who did not look surprised. No shock there—the two of them rarely did anything without the other being aware of it. "It's not a hobby. It's a job. A good one, which pays really well." Each word was spoken carefully, like her sister had rehearsed them.

Noor raised an eyebrow. "As well as being a doctor?"

"Yeah, I mean, it could be better, even."

Zara cleared her throat. "Sweetheart, maybe we should all get together in my office some day this week and talk—"

"I don't need therapy," Jia said, cutting her off impatiently. "I need your support so I can tell Mom and Dad."

Sadia was the only one of them who had intimate knowledge of how her parents would react to one of their daughters dropping out of school. "They're going to be upset." Which was an understatement.

Jia nodded. Her eyes were shiny. "I know they're going to be unhappy. That's why I need your help."

Noor was shaking her head before Jia was even finished speaking. "I cannot support this, Jia. This is utter nonsense."

"Not nonsense, exactly," Zara soothed. "Jia, did something happen? Are you doing poorly in a class? Medical school was hard on all of us. It's not easy. But you can't quit simply because you didn't get a good grade."

"My grades are fine," Jia said. "I just don't enjoy it."

"You're not supposed to enjoy your job," Noor replied, with a touch of exasperation. "You're especially not supposed to enjoy school. You do it, and then you become the best at it, and then you have the money to do other things."

"My videos are earning lots of money right now. You don't even know."

Noor crossed her arms over her ample bosom. "You're right, we don't know. Are they earning more than anyone at this table earns?"

Jia glanced around the table. Sadia flinched when her sister's gaze lingered on her, telling her that yes, Jia probably did make more money than her.

"I think what everyone's trying to say, Jia, is that even if it is successful right now, banking on the Internet is a bit of an unreliable gamble," Sadia finally said.

"I know it's unreliable, and that doesn't bother me. I'm young and I can pivot if the bottom falls out of this, but it feels right to pursue it now."

Noor scowled. "This is a ridiculous discussion. You are staying in school."

Their little sister's shoulders squared. "No. I'm not."

Noor waved that declaration aside. "You are too young to make such a huge decision."

"I'm twenty-four! Mom was younger than me when you were born, Noor."

"That was a different time."

"Sadia was younger than this when she had Kareem!" Jia added triumphantly, and Sadia almost groaned. "And she never even finished college and she's doing fine."

Had her sister been sleeping all this time? She was the *bad* example, not the good one. Her parents never wanted her younger siblings to follow in the footsteps of the family screw-up.

Noor's nostril's flared. "Is she doing fine?"

Sadia inhaled hard, absorbing that hit like a wrestler absorbing a punch.

"Noor." Zara's tone was sharp, and she elbowed her elder sister. "Uncalled for."

Noor's lips tightened, but she shook her head. "Sorry, Sadia. I didn't mean for that to refer to Paul or anything."

Oh no. Sadia hadn't taken it as a comment on the ill-advisedness of her wedding. Her financial struggles were apparent and embarrassing enough. She was still the screw-up, even if they didn't know about her marriage.

This doesn't hurt you. Don't let this hurt.

"I can't support you in this," Noor said.

Zara frowned, furrows appearing on her smooth forehead. "I still think you should come by the office—"

"No." Jia looked at Sadia, entreating eyes on full blast. "Sadia. Come on. You understand, right?"

Sadia tried to avoid looking at her older sisters. Of course she understood. She understood perfectly. She'd hated school, had never excelled at it the way any of her sisters had.

But how could she rubber-stamp a decision that she knew would bring her baby sister a lot of criticism and heartache? Noor's reaction was nothing compared to what their parents would be. Plus, what advice could she give? She didn't regret her marriage, but Noor was right, she wasn't exactly the shining success story to come out of the School of Following Your Dreams.

Her parents weren't bad people; they just had a certain hierarchy of priorities. As far as they were concerned, Jia needed to stay in school and get her degree. When she was done with that, then she could find a nice boy to marry—one who was as well-educated and ambitious as the rest of the family was.

Ultimately, they cherished their daughters and wanted the best for them. They just didn't understand that each child's priorities might be different from theirs.

Sadia bit her lip, unsure of what to say.

At her silence, Jia's eyes teared up, and she whirled away to stomp out of the room. Ayesha gave them all a condemning glance, and followed after her.

Sadia was left with her older sisters. She looked down at the pad and doodled a picture while Noor and Zara spoke in hushed tones. Soon she'd collect her son and leave, go back to the world where she busted her ass to tread water and not drown.

Drowning was not an option.

Chapter 7

SADIA'S HOME was only twenty minutes from her parents', but Kareem fell asleep the second they got moving. Which was good, because she was in no mood to smile and mm-hmm at his animated chatter about his cousins. Her knuckles grew tighter around the wheel the farther they drove, her body trying in vain to reject the sense of failure hanging over her like a cloud.

At some point, Sadia would talk to her little sister and see what she could do to smooth things over, but not now. Not when she was angry and upset with the family she loved so much it hurt.

Is she doing fine?

She blinked away hot tears, the delayed reaction not unusual when it came to fights with her sisters.

Sadia pressed her hand over her heart, hating the swirl of emotions in there. She couldn't journal or plan those emotions away. She wanted so badly to be able to not hurt like this.

She pulled into her driveway and got out of her car, shoving her battered leather purse up her shoulder. When she was a teen, she'd used to sneak her mother's designer handbags out of her closet. Paul had loved seeing her all dressed up, and she'd loved how it made her feel.

After they'd been married a few years, they'd both grown a little too comfortable, and after Kareem had been born, forget it. She hadn't been unable to justify spending money on a purse or clothes for herself when the money could buy her son a new pair of shoes, or allow her to enroll him in some new activity that would enrich his life.

She unbuckled Kareem's belt and pulled him out of the seat. His heavy weight settled on her, making her grunt softly. One more growth spurt and she wouldn't be able to carry him at all. She pressed her face against his neck and inhaled, pulling in the scent of soap and little boy, trying to soothe herself.

"Do you need a hand?" The voice came out of the shadows of the garage, and she almost dropped Kareem.

A large shadow pulled away from the stairs, walking into the spill of the motion-activated lamp above the garage. Jackson. In all the night's excitement, she'd almost forgotten about him.

How, she wasn't sure. Forgetting that she had a very large, rather painful houseguest wasn't something she would normally do.

"I can carry my son," she said, surprise and lingering frustration making her tone sharper than she'd intended. Seeing the boy in his hands would be too much, would have her hoping for all sorts of nonsensical things she knew would end in disappointment.

The same way she'd always been disappointed when she'd sent an email and gotten no response. She needed to remember that disappointment where this man was concerned.

"Yes. I can carry your purse if you'd like," he offered quietly.

She shook her head. "I'm fine. Thank you."

With the practice of someone who had spent years juggling her son and other items, she made it inside her house.

She dropped her purse on the carpet and carried Kareem to his room, laying him on top of the unmade bed and stripping off his jeans. It was warm enough in the house that he'd be okay to sleep in just his shirt for the night.

He stirred when she tucked the comforter around him and opened his eyes. "Was that Uncle Jackson?" he asked drowsily.

Uncle Jackson. She'd tried to tell Kareem about his entire family, even the absent members. Paul had always grown quiet when she mentioned Aunt Livvy and Uncle Jackson, so she had tried not to do it in his presence, but he had never stopped her.

She sat on the edge of the bed, tenderness edging through the evening's distress. "Yes."

"Can I sit on his motorcycle tomorrow?"

That damn motorcycle. She didn't want her precious son anywhere near those dangerous machines, though she supposed there was no harm in him posing on the thing. "We'll see," she said finally.

A line furrowed his small brow. "That means no," he grumbled.

She pressed her hand over his head, smoothing down the lock of hair that always refused to stay down. "No, it means we'll see."

"How come you and the aunties were fighting in the kitchen?"

She faltered, and then she resumed the soothing motions. "No one was fighting. We were talking."

Kareem nodded, accepting this explanation easily. Paul had been bewildered by how loud her family was compared to his, but Kareem had been born into this. Raised voices weren't uncommon and didn't always denote anger.

She sat by Kareem's side until he fell back into a deep slumber, staring at his perfect, symmetrical, beautiful features. He'd taken the best parts of her and Paul, of that she had no doubt.

A sharp stab of pain worked its way into her heart. There was no one who knew and understood Paul's faults better than her, but Kareem should have been able to have his father longer. Paul had doted on his son from the second the boy had been placed in his arms. He was the reason her husband had kept up the charade of their marriage for as long as he had. Paul hadn't been able to stay away from his baby.

Sadia stood up from the bed and walked to the window, hesitating when she started to lower the blinds. The apartment's lights were out, but the moonlight gave her enough light to see Jackson walking around her car, closing her doors.

That was nice of him. Damn it.

Stay mad at him.

She was happy to, but her snippiness tonight was undeserved. He'd had nothing to do with the cause of her temper. That she could lay at the feet of her own sense of inadequacy.

She closed the blinds and trudged outside, nervously tugging at her blouse. It was one of her nicer shirts, but she'd lost some weight since she'd bought it so it hung baggy on her now. At some point, she'd have the money to have a changing wardrobe based on her body. Maybe.

Or maybe, if Jia did become a rich Internet superstar, Sadia could take a loan from her billionaire baby sister without guilt. A girl could dream.

The scent of cigarette smoke reached her before she could make out Jackson's features on the bottom stoop of the steps.

She'd been intending to be conciliatory, but she was so surprised she couldn't modulate her accusatory tone. "You smoke now?"

"Occasionally."

She inched forward. He scooted over, until he was pressed against the railing, and something compelled her to take the silent invitation and drop down next to him.

It was a wide step, and there was substantial distance between them, but she felt dwarfed and crowded. "It's not good for you."

"I'm aware." He paused. "You still have asthma?"

"Only when my allergies are aggravated."

He dropped the cigarette on the gravel and ground it out with the tip of his boot. "Sorry."

"You didn't have to do that."

"I've been in Europe for too long. I always take it up when I'm there. I know it's a bad habit."

She crossed her arms over her stomach. The tiny detail about his life away from here fed her curiosity and she followed the breadcrumb trail like a starving animal. "Where in Europe?"

"All over."

"Working?"

"Yeah." He hesitated, then continued. "I do pop-up restaurants."

"Oh. Like, temporary restaurants?"

"Yes. I have a small team. We scrounge around for empty restaurants all over the world, rig them up quickly, and then put together a business for a few weeks."

She inched closer, fascinated despite herself at this new glimpse she was getting of Jackson's past. "How often do you do this?"

"Almost every month, in the beginning. Now we go every few months. We're doing one in New York in a couple of weeks. It'll be our first one in the States."

"What's the name of your . . . of this venture?" She was so going to google this later.

"Kāne." He pronounced it differently, like KAH-neh. At her questioning look, he explained. "Same spelling. Kāne is the correct native pronunciation. When my grandparents came here, they got rid of the accent on our last name."

"No one ever told me that."

"I wouldn't have known either, if I hadn't spent so much time at the café when I was young. My grandfather told me." Jackson's face softened. "They were good people."

"I'm sure they were," she murmured. "I'm learning so much tonight."

He ducked his head. "I don't realize sometimes that I haven't told people stuff. I'm not being shady. You only have to ask."

Haha, what? Had she heard him correctly?

All thoughts of apologizing for her snippiness flew out of her head.

"I only have to ask?" She bit off each word. "Is that all I have to do?"

His silence only made her angrier, and she clenched her hands tight against her side. "Then tell me. Why didn't you ever respond to my emails, Jackson?"

His mouth opened, then closed. "I was ashamed."

She had to lean forward to hear him. "Ashamed of what?" She was the one who felt ashamed. She'd written as if he was reading every word she wrote, telling him the things she would have told him if he had been at her side. She'd treated those emails as her sounding board and confidante. He could have come and helped her and hugged her and responded to her at any time, but he hadn't.

"I was ashamed of not replying. And then, after

the first month went by . . . and then the first year went by . . . I thought it was too late."

"But why couldn't you respond in the first place?"

His face could have been carved from stone. "It was . . . painful."

"Painful to talk to *me*? Did I do something?"

"No. You never did anything."

Her nostrils flared at the non-answers. "You know what? Fine. You didn't say anything about me or when Kareem was born, and that's bad enough, but how could you not at least contact me when Paul died?"

Paul's dead. Please come home.

She'd sent that email five minutes after the police officer had left her house. Jackson had known before Tani, before Kareem. She'd had to write the words out, see them in black and white, in order to process them.

His body seized up, and she almost took it back. Almost. Almost got to her feet, apologized for making him uncomfortable, apologized for her earlier snappishness, which was all she had come out here to do, and walked back to the house.

No. Fuck it.

She didn't need to apologize. It was okay for her to be mad. This felt right.

She clenched her hands tighter. "Do you know what it was like for me? I don't even remember those days clearly. I could have used you." The guilt, the grief, the crushing sense of loneliness. She'd *needed* her best friend. Livvy had been there, but Livvy and Jackson had served different needs for her growing up.

"I couldn't come."

"Nuh-uh. I need a real explanation. That's not good enough."

He looked down at her. His black eyes were deep and unreadable. "I was in jail. In Paris. By the time I got out and got yours and Livvy's messages, the funeral had already passed. Weeks had passed."

She recoiled. "In jail? What the hell? What happened?"

His fingers drummed his knee. "I was involved in a protest. It turned ugly. I was the biggest man there and I got arrested. Took me a while to get it sorted out."

"What was the protest against?"

"Police brutality." The skin around his eyes tightened. "A young man was assaulted. It kicked off protests all across the country."

She vaguely recalled something about that in the news, but she'd been so splintered, she hadn't been able to really pay much attention to what was happening across the ocean. "Why were you involved in the protest?"

"Because it was wrong."

"That's not even your country, though."

His brow furrowed, like he didn't understand the words. "Principles don't have borders."

When Jackson had been arrested for arson years ago, she'd spent those weeks in a full-blown panic.

She'd known he was innocent, of course, but she'd also known the justice system didn't always work perfectly.

She'd gone to see him once while he was being held, but had spent most of their visit trying to be cheerful and not cry. After that day, he'd refused to see all visitors save for his sister and lawyer.

Her breathing came fast now, thinking of him sitting in other jail cells. She hadn't even known. "How many times have you been arrested since you left home?"

"Three."

"Why?"

He rolled his shoulders. At any other time, she might read his discomfort and back off, but not today. "Does it matter?"

"Yes. What were you arrested for? Were they all protests?"

"One other one was a protest. In London. For living wage."

She'd grown up hearing the Kanes and Chandlers recite the C&O motto. People. Quality. Fairness.

"What was the third?"

He looked away from her and didn't answer for a moment. "One of my staff was being harassed by his ex. I took care of the asshole. The cops came when we were fighting. They threw us both in jail, but the guy decided not to press charges."

She studied his stony face and ran this new information through her brain. From the moment she'd discovered Jackson had received her emails, she'd thought there would be no explanation for why he hadn't, at the very least, come running home for his brother's funeral.

Jail was a pretty good explanation.

And jail for these reasons? Perfectly in keeping with the Jackson she'd known, that every time he'd run afoul of the law, it had been in the pursuit of protecting and advocating for someone else. The only time he'd ever fought when he was young was when he was protecting her or Livvy.

People. Fairness.

"You could have called me when you got out." Her tone was plaintive. Yearning.

"I know. I didn't know what to do, so I did nothing. I'm sorry. I regret it. I regret all of it." The apology was plain, and without frills.

Just like him. Like he'd always been.

She may not have heard from him in ten years, and she still didn't understand him, but right now, right this moment . . .

She wanted to believe he was truly sorry. She wanted to believe he hadn't changed from the boy she'd adored, not deep down.

He was here, helping her. He didn't have to be. He could have kept on not doing anything, even after she'd sent him that last furious letter. Maybe, in his own clumsy way, he was trying to make amends.

It hurt to breathe. She looked down at his hand on his thigh. His fist was so tight, his knuckles had turned white.

This time, she couldn't bury her desire to comfort him. She placed her hand on top of his. A little tingle ran up her arm. His head jerked up. The whites of his eyes were too bright in the darkness.

His skin was hot and smooth below hers. It was familiar.

Jackson moved, and slowly, ever so slowly, his hand turned to cover hers. So weird, to feel the unfamiliar callouses on an otherwise familiar touch. The silence stretched around them, only the hooting of nocturnal animals keeping them company.

Part of her wanted to run inside. Or get in her car. Or go work on her journal for tomorrow.

All of those were rational, pragmatic ways to avoid Jackson and the tumult of feelings he'd knocked awake. With each stroke of his rough thumb, he tightened the crank of feelings inside her, giving her no outlet, except the one tiny acceptable one. "Can I hug you?"

He stilled. "Are you still mad at me?"

She reflected. "Yeah. Kind of. But I'm not embarrassed so much anymore."

"Why were you embarrassed?"

"I wrote to you like I was writing in my journal. Wouldn't you be embarrassed if someone you didn't know was reading your journal?" She ran her finger over his. "I know you, though."

"Oh."

"So can I hug you? It'll make me feel better. But I won't do it if you hate it," she tacked on.

The corner of his lips lifted, the most amusement she'd seen from him since he'd come home. He'd never been given to smiling much, but she was suddenly hungry for a proper grin. "You used to threaten to hug me, not ask."

"And you'd threaten to tickle me."

"You hated being tickled."

"Like you hated hugs."

"I never hated hugs. Not from you. I wasn't good at them, is all."

Ugh. She wasn't going to be mad at all soon if he kept this up. "It's very easy." She scooted closer and wrapped her arm around his back, her other arm going around his waist.

He went still. "This seems awkward." She swallowed the utterly inappropriate urge to laugh and craned her neck. Their heads were closer than she'd thought. She could count every individual lash on his eyes, the slight mark on his cheek from a scar he must have picked up at some point over the years.

"Loosen up."

He relaxed marginally, scowling when she couldn't stifle her laugh. "I told you I'm not good at this."

"Sorry, sorry." She released him to hoist his heavy arm up and snuck under it, pulling and pushing until she was snuggled up next to him. "See?" She put her arms back where they'd been and smiled up at him, feeling lighthearted and young for the first time in a while.

Oh it felt so good not to be enraged at him. She probably shouldn't have relented so easily, and maybe tomorrow she would change her mind, but right now, right here, she simply wanted to pull him close to her. For a brief moment in time, she didn't have anywhere to be, he was with her, and their friendship was perfect. "So easy."

He grunted. She thought he might have a smart retort, but his arms tightened around her and he pulled her even closer, until their upper bodies were plastered together. She laid her head on his shoulder and breathed deep, inhaling the scent of muffins.

He smelled like her friend.

"It would never have been too late," she murmured, and he stilled.

"No?"

"No."

JACKSON COULDN'T MOVE.

He didn't want to move, because if he did move, maybe he would discover that this was nothing more than a perfect, precious dream.

He felt too large and awkward, unsure of what to do with his hands. He finally settled on resting one on her waist and one against her head, her silky hair slipping through his fingers. It was awkward hugging someone sitting next to him, but again, he wasn't about to do anything to disrupt this.

This? This connection? This felt . . .

Like heaven. He closed his eyes. What if she stopped?

Sadia's fingers drifted over his side, rasping the cotton of his shirt over his too-sensitive skin. It couldn't even be called a stroke, but it settled him.

Her hair tickled his nose, carrying the scent of some sort of flowers. He wanted to bury his face in it, to absorb her so he'd never have to be without her. He wanted to coast his hands all over her, discovering every difference between the two of them. But that would be inappropriate. He'd always been acutely conscious of what was appropriate and inappropriate when it came to Sadia.

When had he fallen in love with her? When they were ten and he'd protected her from a bully? When they'd been thirteen and he'd made sure she wouldn't get in trouble for sneaking in late? When they'd been sixteen and he'd escorted her to their junior prom when her date had stood her up?

He'd spent an hour at the florist, picking out her corsage, a perfect red rose, because red had been her favorite color and the color of the dress she'd worn when they'd first met as kids, a detail she'd probably never picked up on. A bright crimson. He could still remember how her eyes had lit up when he'd slipped it on her hand. *You didn't have to do that*, she'd said shyly.

Because they were going as friends, but he'd memorized how she'd looked in her gold and red dress in a way no friend would. By the time their senior prom rolled around, he'd been determined to be her proper date.

Too late. His older brother had been the one escorting her to that.

That brutal reminder—Paul's, not his—splashed over him like cold water. *Your heart only needs to beat. Stay alive.*

He could care, and he could owe her, but he couldn't love her again. If he loved her, he'd hurt. Because this was and always had been a doomed love.

His arms tightened around her.

Finally she stirred and looked up at him, and he shifted at the same time, leaving their mouths within a hairsbreadth from each other. Her eyes were wet, her cheeks damp, and he realized with alarm that she'd been crying.

"Why are you crying?"

She bit her lip. "Because I missed you."

He lowered his head, and he wasn't sure what his intention was. To kiss her cheek, maybe, or to rest his forehead against hers. But their eyes met, and there was a question in hers. She lifted her face, bringing her lips closer to his. He accepted the unspoken request.

It was tentative, soft, the barest brushing of his mouth on hers. Jackson cradled her skull, taking his cues from her. When she pressed harder, he responded, flicking against her bottom lip. She opened up, letting him in. He swept his tongue inside, groaning when she shyly flirted with him. She tasted like mints. She'd brushed her teeth maybe, or ate one of the chocolate peppermints she used to keep in her purse. He'd tasted those mints plenty of times when she'd shared them with him, but never like this, on her lips.

He hoped he'd smoked so little of that cigarette that she didn't actually taste it.

He bit her lower lip, laving it when she whimpered and moved closer, pressing her back against the stairs, cushioning her head with his palm. He had a second to have the presence of mind to wonder if they were visible to anyone, but there were no lights here. They'd hear anyone coming from the road or the house long before the people saw them.

Her arms twined around his neck as he continued kissing her with deep, drugging kisses. He groaned into her mouth at her eagerness, insane with lust at how perfect and right she felt in his arms. His cock hardened, and it pulsed against his leg at this fantasy coming true.

He bit at her lips, pulled them deep. He felt like a kid jumping from couch cushion to couch cushion, unable to touch the floor. If he touched the floor, lava would get him. If he stopped kissing her, he'd start thinking. Or she'd start thinking. Either way, they'd both stop feeling.

He never wanted to stop feeling this, not in a million years. He'd waited so long for it. His whole life, or so it felt. He stroked his thumb over the arch of her throat.

She froze, and then her hands were shoving at him. His eyes sprang open and he leapt back so fast, he almost banged his head against the railing.

He knew what was coming. The lava.

She stayed half-reclined for a second, blinking up at him with wide eyes, and then she was on her feet, jerking at her wrinkled blouse, all the while a steady stream of "Oh my God, oh my God, oh my God," fell from her lips. She ran her hands through her disheveled hair. "Oh my God."

"Sadia," he began, but his voice was nothing more than a rough croak. He wasn't sure what to say.

Be smart.

Ariel had given him some great advice. Instead, he'd gone and complicated everything with a kiss so perfect he couldn't regret it.

The sheen of wetness in her eyes killed his lust. "Don't cry," he said quietly.

She swiped her hand over the back of her cheek like she was surprised to find tears there. "Oh God. What did I . . . what did we . . ."

"Nothing. We didn't do anything. I promise."

"I can't believe I kissed you," she whispered, and he stoically accepted the sting of disgust in her voice.

"I kissed you. And it was nothing," he repeated. That was right. He'd keep repeating that.

"No, it was something. You're . . . and I'm . . ."

"It was a momentary lapse. We're two healthy people, stress got to us, it's natural." He'd never tripped into a woman's mouth before, but he'd say whatever he had to say to get that stricken look out of her eyes.

He stretched his legs out in front of him, turning his body slightly away so she wouldn't see his erection. "Do you want me to leave?" *Please say no.* Because if she said yes, then he'd go.

"Leave? Leave what?"

"The house? Town?"

She blinked at him. He braced himself. It wouldn't take him long to pack, because he'd never unpacked.

He could call Ariel and be on a flight tonight. A flight to . . . somewhere.

He'd leave behind Sadia and the nephew he wanted to know and the family he couldn't talk to.

Please say no.

He didn't love her still. But he couldn't leave her.

"That's . . . No." She shook her head. "No, I just stopped being furious at you."

"You did?"

"I mean, not totally." She looked down at the ground and shoved her hands in her pockets. "You're not leaving. It's okay. You're right, this was nothing. We'll forget about it. Okay?"

"Yeah." No. He'd never forget it, not in a million years. But she didn't need to know that.

"Okay, good. I have to . . . um. I have to go. Good night." Before he could answer she whirled and paced away, her feet picking up until the gravel in the driveway flew.

He waited until she was inside her house before climbing the steps to his apartment. It took him a minute to strip all his clothes off and step inside the shower. Hot, not cold, because he knew there was only one thing that could relieve his erection.

He soaped himself up. Steam rose around him, fogging the glass, rendering him invisible, just the way he liked it. This was his secret shame. It always had been. He ran his hand down his belly and grasped his cock. He was thick with wanting the one woman he couldn't have.

He'd always tried to avoid giving his fantasy

woman a face, because he'd known exactly who his subconscious would sub in. He couldn't help it when Sadia crept in during his dreams, but he could when he was awake.

He braced his arm on the wall, the water beating down on his back and ass. His front wasn't cold. Not with his palm stroking his cock.

In his imagination, the door opened to an audience of one. She wouldn't watch. She'd slip inside and under his guard. Her nails would scrape over his clenching stomach, and she'd take over for him.

His fingers curled against the tile, but in his mind they were tunneling through her thick, dark hair. He'd drag her close and capture her lips and taste the chocolate mint on her tongue while she jacked him off.

Oh fuck. He squeezed his eyes tight. Chocolate mint.

His anonymous fantasy woman morphed, and her features became far too clear. He fucked his fist, the water starting to run cold, but he couldn't care. Not when a naked Sadia was standing in front of him.

In his dreams.

He'd tighten his grip on her hair and she'd respond, falling to her knees. He groaned, imagining the tongue that had been in his mouth rubbing against his cock, fingers that had been on his arms playing with his balls.

He widened his stance, his hips moving like he was fucking Sadia's warm, wet, willing mouth instead of his own rough hand. A few hard strokes and he came with a groan, the water washing away the evidence of his perversion. He rested his forehead against the tile and breathed deep.

It was nothing. They would forget about it. He didn't still love her.

His heart thundered in his ears.

Beat. Don't feel. Please don't feel.

Chapter 8

HE WAS in her head.

Half-asleep, Sadia rolled over onto her back, shoving aside the blanket, making it easier for him to touch her. He was crude and hurried, pushing her nightshirt up so he could get to her breasts. It was fine, she didn't need romance and hearts, not now.

She needed to be fucked. With fingers or a tongue or a cock or a dildo. She wasn't picky.

He sucked her nipples, teeth nipping her hard enough for a ripple of electricity to shoot through her body. The man's perfect hands slipped over the curve of her belly. He squeezed the roundness there, the result of pregnancy and genetics, a layer of padding unresponsive to crunches, before dipping lower.

She hadn't shaved or trimmed in a while, but he didn't seem to mind the hair, his fingers combing through it like she'd given him a treasure. His thumb dipped between her pussy lips, glancing over her hard clit, coming back to rub it when she gasped. He kept up that slow, circular motion that tightened the knot inside her belly while he moved down her body. Two fingers spread her lips wide and he licked her like she was a sweet treat. She squirmed, her entire body tightening.

He was so beautiful, big and muscular, muscles packed upon muscles. He sucked her clit in and his thick finger worked its way deeper inside her vagina, fucking her.

Oh fuck.

She sat up and fumbled to open her nightstand drawer, digging under various items she used for camouflage before finding her favorite vibrator.

She didn't need the frills today. She half-reclined on her pillows and spread her legs wide, rubbing the tip of the pink plastic against her wetness.

She turned the vibrator on, shuddering when she placed it on her clit and rotated it in a small, tight circle. This was enough. She didn't need to fuck herself with it to get off. In her head it was Jackson's cock, thick and engorged with blood.

She came silently, her teeth grinding into her lower lip as her body convulsed.

Her eyes popped open and she breathed deeply, resting the vibrator against her belly. She shut the thing off.

Holy shit. Bad enough to kiss her former brother-in-law. Now she was fantasizing about having orgasms with him?

She whimpered and screwed her eyes shut. What was wrong with her?

Should have stayed enraged at him. See where talking gets you?

It had been exactly one week since the two of

them had locked lips, and she was no closer to forgetting about it, though they'd spent the last seven days ignoring each other as much as humanly possible for two people who both lived and worked together. Sadia spent her days in the café locked up in the office or busying herself outside the kitchen. Jackson, for his part, left the house super early in the morning and returned late at night.

It didn't matter if she saw him or not, though. He was on her mind no matter what, even when she tried to schedule him out of it. The number of times she'd guiltily switched browsers away from work and typed the name of his pop-up into a search bar—well, she wasn't about to show him her search history, because it was absurd.

As was the fact that she had a world-renowned name cooking in a little café. There had been more than a few articles speculating about the anonymous chef's identity, but she was privileged enough to know that the man behind the restaurant specializing in comfort food from all over the world was her own Jackson. Foodies lined up for blocks when he came to their city.

She shook her head, wishing Jackson hadn't told her about his hugely prosperous, if secretive career. His success was intimidating as hell, and that was without factoring in their kiss.

That kiss. She'd tried every excuse and justification possible. A moment of temporary insanity, brought upon by the stress of the day and week and month and year? The struggle of holding it all together and pretending everything was fine? The seething resentment and frustration over her role in her family?

You were starved for sex, is all.

She wished she could grasp onto that last excuse, but she couldn't. Sex wasn't difficult for her to find when she went looking for it. In the right place, like the bar. Not in her home.

She grabbed her phone and checked the time, groaning when she realized she was five minutes past when she had to be up. It was Sunday, and Jackson had conveyed through Darrell that she didn't have to come in. That was good, because Kareem had an enrichment class, soccer, and a piano lesson today, which meant she was scheduled from minute to minute.

She rolled out of bed. No more. She honestly did not have space in her life to lust after Jackson of all people.

She got cleaned up, keeping herself focused on the task at hand. She paused once she was dressed and picked up the box with hers and Paul's rings in it. "I kissed your brother," she blurted out. Immediate relief ran through her at the confession.

She definitely didn't feel like she'd cheated Paul's memory, and Paul and Jackson being brothers wasn't some huge taboo, but all these intertwining relationships were contributing to how conflicted she felt. "I haven't felt weird about kissing anyone else since you died, but none of them . . ." None of them had made her feel anything.

She traced his face. "It wasn't because he reminded me of you, or anything like that. You guys were always so different. Maybe I just missed him a lot? I don't know. Anyway, in summation, I'm doing my best, but I also don't know what the hell I'm doing."

Sadia, babe. It was only a kiss. Everyone kisses. Relax a little.

Her lips wobbled into a smile, Paul's voice so clear in her imagination he might have been standing next to her.

That was right. It had only been a kiss. She would invite Jackson over for dinner tonight. He was her temporary employee and tentatively reunited friend. When she saw him, she was going to be cool and calm and pretend like nothing had happened.

Sadia prodded her son awake and made him a quick breakfast, then called the café. Kimmie, Darrell's sister, picked up the phone. "Kane's Café."

"Hey Kimmie, it's Sadia. How's everything going?"

"Great, no problems." Her voice was enthusiastic. Sadia could hear the crowd in the background.

"It sounds busy."

"Nothing we can't cope with. Jay's trying some new acai bowls and they're a hit."

She frowned. She hadn't known Jackson was introducing items off-menu. Not that it mattered, if they were making money.

As she said her goodbyes and hung up, Kareem looked up at her from the breakfast table. "Can I see if Uncle Jackson wants to play today?"

Sadia took a sip of coffee to hide her reaction. Kareem had asked the same question more than once over the past week. She understood it was the novelty about his mysterious relative that had Kareem so desperate to meet him, but she couldn't stop softening over how damn cute it was that he was so eager to get to know his uncle. She also didn't know how to tell him he couldn't see his uncle because mommy was freaking out that she'd kissed the man.

But no more. "Tonight, perhaps."

Kareem looked disappointed but then he brightened. "Can we go see the grandmas?"

The grandmas were what he called Tani and Maile. Sadia gave a strained smile. With Jackson working at the café, she'd managed to cut down on needing too much extra childcare this past week, which was a blessing. There was no doubt Kareem would happily tell her sisters or his grandparents about his newfound mysterious uncle.

She didn't want to deal with her sisters or parents pestering her with questions or her in-law's drama, and if that made her a jerk, so be it. She couldn't be a saint all the time. "Maybe tomorrow," she hedged. "Come on now, finish up your breakfast. We have a big day. I have to stop and get snacks for your team before the game."

"If you don't, Mrs. R will get mad. She's kind of a turd."

She closed her eyes and counted to ten. "Where did you hear that word, Kareem?"

"Is it a swear?"

"It's an impolite word."

"Aunt Liv—"

"New rule, okay? We don't repeat any words Aunt Livvy says or call anyone by those words."

Kareem pursed his rosebud lips. "None of 'em?"

"Not one."

"What if she says . . . butt?"

Sadia raised her eyebrow, struggling to keep a straight face when Kareem dissolved into giggles. Ah, yes. This was the only Kane she wanted to think about today.

"OH MY god, is it true Livvy and Nicholas eloped in Vegas and are in talks for their own reality show?"

Sadia stared blankly at the other soccer mom and then held out the box she carried. "I brought chips."

The well-dressed brunette accepted the chips without inspecting them, which was a sure sign that she was distracted by gossip. "You can tell me," she said. "I won't tell a soul."

"I have no idea where Livvy and Nicholas are," she responded, wishing she didn't sound so rehearsed. *More than free childcare. Livvy owes me like a million tattoos, if I ever get over my fear of needles.*

Rachel looked far from convinced, but she brightened. "Well, I also heard Livvy's brother is back in town. Is he as cute as he used to be?"

Dismay ran through Sadia. "I don't know." Damn it. Seemed threatening Harriet had only pushed off the inevitable gossip.

"Sure you do. He's working for you."

"I don't talk about family, Rachel."

Rachel looked taken aback for a minute, then annoyed. She glanced at the chips. "I see you got the regular chips. The kids like assorted, for future reference."

For future reference, you are kinda turd-like.

Sadia moved away and pulled out her phone. No one from the café had called her. She hesitated for a second, then opened her messages up.

How's everything going?

Jackson's reply was instantaneous, like he'd been waiting for her. **Fine. Don't worry.**

She chewed her lip. She should be more worried than she was. Jackson being at the café was more of a relief that she didn't have to be there than anything else. She paused for a second, then typed out her request.

Do you want to come over for dinner?

She hit Send, then glanced around, worried someone might know she was texting with the man she'd had a wet dream about, but no soccer mom was nearby to shame her, not even turd-like Rachel.

His response was just as fast as the last one. **Yes.**

Okay then. She nodded, trying to ignore the jump in her belly. She was excited to get back to their tentative truce after a week-long stalemate, was all.

She tapped her fingers on the back of her phone, then quickly wrote another message. **FYI, it seems like a few people know you're here, working for me. Maybe you should let your mom or Maile know before they hear about it from someone else?**

This was not her courting drama, but trying to

head it off. Eventually, Maile or Tani would find out, and then she'd have to hear about it.

Her phone buzzed. **Thanks for telling me.**

She waited, but that was it. Sadia suppressed her frown and looked up at her son's voice. Whatever. She had enough on her plate without Kane family dynamics.

She tried to concentrate on the game. It was itty-bitty soccer, so it wasn't exactly high stakes. Sadia was dedicated to making sure her son had as many opportunities as she'd had. Kareem should get the chance to discover what he loved and was good at.

Her mood lifted automatically as she watched the adorable five- and six-year-olds tumble around a grassy field. She cheered when Kareem managed to get a hold of the ball. "Good job, baby! No . . . Kareem, hug your friend when the game is over!"

She smiled when her son released his friend and gave her a thumbs-up. Her gaze drifted past the field, to the parking lot.

It took her a second to place the man sitting in a wheelchair at the edge of the lot, under the shade of a tree, but when she did, unease crept through her. Her smile faded.

Sadia didn't hate John Chandler the way her late husband had. Paul hadn't been able to stand the name or sight of anyone Chandler. While she appreciated that he'd lost way more than she could comprehend after Robert Kane and Maria Chandler had died, she'd also hated how it had shaped so much of Paul's life.

One of the reasons she hadn't taken her husband's name was because privately, she hadn't wanted to get swept up in the whole Kane/Chandler feud. Not that it had helped much. She'd felt like a traitor the first time she'd set foot in a Chandler's store after Paul had died, but she'd gotten over it, telling herself she wasn't about to feed her son anything but the best.

It was a punch to the gut to see John sitting in what she considered her domain, though, and by extension, Kane domain. Livvy and John had reconciled before her best friend had run off with the man's grandson, but why on earth was he here? Did he know another child in the itty-bitty soccer league? Because it wasn't like anyone would come be a spectator to a bunch of young children staring at the sky and bumping into one another and occasionally kicking a ball.

Unless . . . he was here to see Kareem?

Her maternal instincts bristled and she didn't even realize she was walking toward him until the distance between them dramatically shortened. When she was within a few feet, he took his attention off the children to calmly watch her approach, looking for all the world like he'd expected her. "Hello there, Sadia."

She stopped a foot away from him and linked her hands in front of her. "Mr. Chandler."

He was dressed casually, in jeans and a plaid shirt. John had never carried himself like the wealthy man he was. He smiled faintly. "You used to call me Grandpa John."

She had. The Kanes had treated the Chandler home as their own and this man as their grandfather, and she'd been part of the family from the time she was ten. "I haven't seen you in a long time."

"It has been a while." John looked out at the field. "Your son is growing fast."

Jackson had said something similar, but the difference between the two men was that Sadia had sent Jackson photos of Kareem. She hadn't sent John photos, and she was sure Paul hadn't. "Have you seen him before today?" The question was sharp, and she couldn't help it. She didn't like the thought of anyone viewing her son when she was unaware.

"I have," he said, surprising her with his honesty. "Not recently, though. I don't leave my home as much these days. I was curious."

"I don't really care if you were curious," Sadia returned politely. "If I see you lurking about my son again without my knowledge, I'll murder you."

He looked startled, and then he let out a sharp crack of laughter. "My god. No wonder Paul adored you so."

Her hands tightened around each other. She could still feel the imprint of Paul's lips on her forehead the night before he'd died, after he'd asked for a divorce. They may not have been *in* love, but Paul had definitely loved her, even at the end, just as she'd loved him.

John sobered, picking up on her mood. "I'm sorry about Paul. I want you to know that."

"Thank you."

"And I'm sorry I've been lurking, as you've said. I only wanted to learn as much about Paul's son as I could." He looked up at her, and she would have had to be a monster not to immediately soften at the sadness in his gaze. "He's the closest to a great-grandchild I'll probably ever know, Sadia. That was all."

She nodded slowly. Family. "I can understand that."

"I won't do it again. And frankly, I'm only here today because I wanted to speak to you."

"To me?"

"Have you heard anything from Nicholas and Livvy?"

She relaxed completely. Ah. This made perfect sense. "I have not. I understand they'll be back when they're ready to be back. Livvy's been check-ing in with her aunt and mother over the past couple of weeks, though."

John looked disappointed. "Nicholas is doing the same with his sister. I think he's trying to teach me and his father a lesson by not contacting us but . . . anyway, that's not important. I am thrilled the two of them are trying to work things out, of course."

She hummed an agreement. Yes, she was thrilled too. Still feeling a little abandoned, but happy. "If that's all you wanted to ask me . . . ?" She was poised to go back to her son and away from this vague feeling of betraying her family.

"Actually, there is one more thing. I heard a rumor."

Oh bollocks. She stayed, resigned.

"Jackson is back, I understand."

She bit her lip, not able to confirm or deny it, not even with this old man. The man's faded blue eyes filled with uncertainty. "Can you ask him to come see me?"

Ah God. "I don't know if I can, sir." For starters, she hadn't spoken to him in a week. Her peace offering of dinner hadn't even been cooked yet.

"Of course." John cleared his throat. "Don't mean to put you in a tough spot."

She hummed her reply.

John twisted around and removed a bag from his bag on his chair. "Can you, at the very least, give him this? Don't open it. It's for his eyes only."

She reluctantly accepted the cloth bag. It was heavy, like a book was inside. "I really don't want to get involved."

"Oh, I know. And I hate to ask you to do this, I really do." The wind shifted his shock of white hair. "But I need your help. That bag belongs to Jackson."

"John—"

"You get to a certain point in your life, Sadia, where you think about all of the mistakes you've made and the things that are missing. You think about all the people you'll never see again." He looked out toward the field and the kids there. A nostalgic smile played around his lips. "I loved Sam's grandchildren as my own, and that includes Jackson. I know he didn't set that fire. I don't want to hurt him. I miss him. I miss my family."

Her heart tumbled around and she clutched the

bag close to her chest. "Okay. I can't guarantee what Jackson's reaction will be, but I'll give him this."

"You don't look at it," he warned again.

"I won't," she agreed. She turned toward the field and cupped her hands around her mouth. "Kareem! Come here, please."

When she looked at John again, his eyes were wet. They grew wetter when Kareem came running toward them.

Sadia crouched next to John's chair and put her hand on his. It was soft and wrinkled.

Neutrality was as much of a stance as any action. John had, for all intents and purposes, been Paul's grandfather. And according to Livvy, he hadn't been behind the takeover of the C&O. He hadn't wronged her husband or her. She couldn't deny him or her son the right to at least be introduced to each other.

It was time to put this feud to rest once and for all. If Nicholas and Livvy did come back firmly in love, this wouldn't be the only time Kareem saw this man. If Sadia had to choose between neutrality and the bonds of family, she would always choose family.

Kareem glanced curiously between her and John. "Hi."

John cleared his throat. "Hello."

"Kareem, this is Daddy's grandpa. Your great-grandpa."

Kareem looked John over. "I didn't know Daddy had a grandpa."

John swayed toward her son. "He had a couple of grandpas actually. I was lucky enough to be one of them."

Kareem accepted that logic with ease. "Can your wheelchair go fast?"

"Kareem."

"No, it's fine." John's eyes lit up. "It can go pretty fast. I'll give you a ride sometime maybe."

"Cool." Kareem glanced up at Sadia. "I'm gonna go back to the game. Bye, Grandpa," he said casually to John, and ran away.

Sadia's heart clenched at the raw delight on John's face. "Listen, I'll bring Kareem by sometime, how's that?"

His throat worked. "You're a good woman, Sadia."

"Nah. Just selfish when it comes to family. I can't turn down people who want to love my son. But if you want to see him again, don't lurk. Call me. If you can track down my son's soccer games, you can use a phone."

"I will do exactly that." He caught her wrist as she moved away. "Sam would have been delighted his grandson married you."

She lifted a shoulder, uncomfortable with praise. "Thank you, sir."

He placed his hands back in his lap. "May I watch the rest of the game?"

"Sure. Do you want me to grab you a juice box from the snack table?"

"Cherry?"

"Fruit punch."

He deliberated for a moment, this multi-millionaire who had built an empire and a town out of nothing. "That would be nice."

Chapter 9

MAYBE YOU **should let your mom or Maile know before they hear about it from someone else?**

Jackson ran his thumb over the message. What a one-two punch, between a dinner invite and a reminder of his family. Sadia sure knew how to get his attention.

He knew Sadia had been avoiding him for a week, but he'd been happy to let her do so. He'd woken up every day with her taste on his lips and fallen asleep every night for a few fitful hours with the sound of her sighs in his ears. He spent the hours in between either working at the café, burying himself in food, or cruising around the surrounding areas looking for new suppliers.

Or cruising through his mom's neighborhood. Jackson looked up at the house he was standing in front of.

It was no wonder gossip had spread about him. He'd been so busy avoiding Sadia he hadn't been careful enough to avoid everyone else.

He slipped his phone into his pocket. He'd left the café as soon as the lunch shift was over and parked a few streets over from this suburban cul-de-sac, unsure of what he was doing, except the thought of Tani or Maile finding out that he was within a ten mile radius from someone else had left him vaguely ill.

On this late Sunday afternoon, the street was pretty quiet. This house had been a wedding gift from his mother's family to his father's, slightly nicer than Sadia's place but still nowhere near the grand estate he'd grown up in.

He'd known his mother had sold their childhood home and moved in with her sister-in-law, which was good. He might have complicated feelings for the woman, but he'd never wanted her to suffer. Living in the house she'd shared with her beloved husband would have been a death sentence for her.

Plus, he assumed she'd gotten a good amount of money for it. His mother had never worked outside the home, had been born after C&O was already turning a strong profit. He didn't know what she'd do for a living. Between the money she'd gotten for the company and the house, he assumed she and Maile were living comfortably.

He scratched the back of his neck as he walked up the winding sidewalk. The houses were close together, and if any of the neighbors looked outside, they'd surely be able to guess who he was. He looked too much like his father.

He went to the door and knocked lightly, not bothering to hesitate. If he hesitated, he'd leave.

There was no response. He knocked again.

Nothing.

He rested his hand against the doorknob. He could pick the lock—a trick he'd picked up from a particularly unsavory busboy he'd once known—but it was unnecessary here. The knob turned easily under his hand.

Unease slithered along his spine. His mother had had hip surgery not too long ago. Maile was no spring chicken. What if something had happened to his aunt and his mother had had an accident?

The door swung open and he stepped inside, closing it behind him. The house looked the same as it had all those years ago, when his grandparents and aunt had been the ones living here. Automatically, he took his shoes off.

It was dark and silent. He walked through the hallway on bare feet to the living room, peeking in there. There had been some changes here, but not many. New couch, new television. Same bowl of potpourri on the coffee table. Same framed family photo above the fireplace.

His heart clenched and he walked to the mantel. He remembered when it had been taken, the professional photographer called to the house. He'd been young then, maybe five or six, and he wore a somber suit that matched his brother's and father's. Livvy was held in their father's arms, looking disgruntled and cranky, her dress wrinkled and a bow lopsided in her hair. If he remembered properly, his sister had thrown a tantrum right before they'd taken the photo. Their mother had wanted her to wear a bright pink gown, but Livvy had been dead set on wearing her favorite dress, a white one with giant greenish-blue palm fronds printed on it. She'd won the battle of wills, because she wore the tropical dress in the photo, but she'd still been peevish. He touched a leaf. His sister had pretty much lived in that dress until it had fallen off her.

Paul had his arm around him. He was pressed right up against his big brother, his mother's hand on his shoulder. He brushed his thumb over Paul's face, then his mother's.

What the hell was he doing here?

A shuffle came from behind him, and he turned. His mother was leaning heavily against a cane in one hand, her other hand braced against the door frame.

They stood like that for a long minute. Her face was expressionless. He was sure he was also betraying nothing. That had been one thing they'd been good at, the two of them. Neither had ever been given to big displays of emotion.

They'd shared a special bond, the two quiet people in a household that could be chaotic. Or so he'd thought.

"What are you doing here?"

It was the first time he'd heard his mother's voice in a decade, and he couldn't stop himself from flinching. She didn't sound the same as he remembered. Her voice was higher. More thready. Though that could also have been the shock of seeing him.

He responded woodenly, trying to keep his tone as professional and crisp as hers. "I'm staying in town for a few days. I'm helping Sadia out at the café."

She wore the same light pink lipstick she'd always worn, but she had some wrinkles around her lips now and the color was bleeding into them. "I'm not asking why you're in town. Why are you here?"

He didn't know. Wait. No. He did. "I wanted you to know I was here. Before you heard from a stranger."

She snorted, an unladylike sound he'd never heard from her before. "I've known you were here for weeks. Since before Livvy foolishly ran off with that boy." She took two steps into the room. His body tensed, every instinct telling him to go help her, but unless something had drastically changed in her personality, she'd be annoyed if he did. She sat down on the couch and rested the cane against the arm of the sofa.

When he'd heard about his mother's accident, he'd asked Ariel to poke around. His partner had reported back that Tani was recovering fine. He hadn't worried further until he'd received Sadia's invective-laden email, and then he'd worried about Livvy.

Tani looked very small and fragile to his eyes now. Or maybe it was simply because he hadn't seen her in forever. Of course his mother would have aged in ten years, just as he had. "How is your hip?" he asked gruffly.

His mother stared straight ahead at the blank T.V. screen. "Fine."

"Where's Maile?"

"At the grocery store."

"Ah. Do you need—"

"No. I don't need anything from you. You can go now."

He flinched, the lick of pain vicious and not entirely unexpected. He'd almost made it to the door when she spoke. "I know you blame me."

He froze, his back to her, and she continued. "You blame me for not being there for you after your father died."

No. That wasn't right at all. He couldn't look at her, or he wouldn't speak, and he needed to tell her she was incorrect. "I don't blame you for that." He didn't know if Tani had depression like Livvy did or if her episode after their father died had been situational, but it didn't matter either way. He'd understood the depth of his mother's despair. How could he hold his sister while she wept and not have compassion for their mother?

If Tani would have allowed it, he would have comforted her then. But she'd retreated to her room alone, so all he'd been able to do was ensure the house didn't fall down around them.

His eye twitched. The hardest thing he'd ever done was scour his house for pills and sharp objects in fear of one of his family members doing something harmful, all while reeling from his own grief over their father.

"You do," she insisted.

"I don't. You were in pain. You loved Dad." His tone softened. "We all did." What he couldn't forgive was that she'd come out of that depression long enough to make a choice. One that had broken his heart.

"Then why?" Her voice didn't crack or betray a hint of emotion. "Why have you stayed away all this time?"

He risked stealing a glance at her. Her head was bowed, and the hair at the back of her scalp was thinning a little. "You told me to go with the police."

Her breath was sharp.

His hand curled into a fist. He didn't feel violent. He felt like a nineteen-year-old sitting in a prison cell, far from his admittedly pampered and wealthy upbringing. "You told me to go with the police, that nothing would happen, that I shouldn't talk to anyone. You said you'd fix it so I was out quickly." He'd looked into his mother's eyes, the woman he'd always been so close to, and trusted her.

"I—"

"Two weeks." He cut her off. He didn't like speaking, but now he was unable to stop. It was like something had flipped on the boiling pot of emotions he'd kept simmering for a decade. "You let me sit in a jail cell for two weeks while cops yelled in my face and my name was dragged through the news. Livvy and Maile were the ones who were trying to get me out. They were the ones who got me a lawyer, who visited me." And Sadia, too, though he'd refused to see her after the one time.

At first, he'd asked when their mother was coming. Livvy had finally told him Tani had retired to her room and was refusing to talk to any of them. About anything. Especially him.

It upset her too much, Livvy had told him apologetically, even though she'd still been in the grips of her own depressive episode.

"And all of that, I could forgive. I could say you were hurt and not in the right state to help me. But you knew, didn't you? You knew Paul lied to me. The minute you went along with that, you made your choice. You didn't abandon me before, but yes. You abandoned me then."

Her fragile fingers rubbed her temple, but she didn't respond. Didn't defend herself.

He shoved both hands in his pockets. "Can you tell me you didn't know?" And suddenly, he knew why he'd come here. "Tell me you didn't know Paul lied to get me to go with the police. Tell me that."

Lie to me now if you did.

But she didn't speak, and to be honest, he wasn't that surprised. He exhaled. "I'm glad you're okay. I'm okay too. If you ever need money, tell Livvy. She knows how to get a hold of me." With that, he walked out.

He was shaking as he strode to the front door. He opened and closed it quietly and then stopped on the porch for a second. The broad-shouldered, tall woman walking up the steps stopped as well. The reusable grocery bag in her hand dropped to the ground.

Aunt Maile had been his father's younger sister and a warmer, more nurturing woman didn't exist on the planet. He tended to shy away from boisterous, extroverted people—it was one reason he and his father hadn't been on the closest terms—but

Maile had understood and accepted his quiet personality without making him feel like something was wrong with him.

When he'd stood in front of her after being released from jail, she'd pulled him in tight and then given him a wad of cash. She'd known, without him saying a word, that he couldn't stand to be near his brother, in a town where it felt like everyone was looking at him with pity and alarm and fear.

She had streaks of gray in her dark hair now, and a few new lines around her eyes and mouth, but those could have easily come from smiles instead of age. Maile had always been a sharp dresser. Today she wore snug jeans and a purple top and cardigan, her long hair caught up in a jaunty ponytail.

He couldn't make her come to him. He walked toward her slowly and stooped down to pick up the bag she'd dropped. It was heavy.

A shaking hand caressed his cheek, and he allowed it. Maile was tall, taller than Sadia, and almost able to look him in the eye. "My God." Her eyes grew glassy. "You look like your father."

He shifted, uncertain, as always, with what to do at a woman's tears.

Luckily, she took the initiative, pulling him close. It took him a second, and he returned the hug. She squeezed him tight and he closed his eyes. He didn't know if he'd grown up or she'd grown weaker, but the squeeze wasn't as hard as he remembered.

When he was young and he'd grown overwhelmed and needed a time-out, she'd let him crawl into her big, soft lap and curl up there for quiet time.

He was too old to do that. He shouldn't even want it now.

She cleared her throat finally and pulled away. He was grateful to see she was smiling, beaming through her tears.

He was surprised, then, when her hand swatted across his chest. "Ow." He rubbed his pec.

"How could you come to town and not see me immediately?" she demanded. "Did it even occur to you?"

So Maile knew he'd been here for weeks too. A trace of shame crept through him at her outraged expression. "Yes. I didn't know how."

"You do exactly what you did. You walk up to me and you hug me," she lectured him. "That's all you need to do."

He ducked his head. "Yes ma'am."

"Well, you're here now." She breathed in deep. "You're home."

Home. He didn't have a home. Home had become wherever he could find a kitchen to cook in. "Temporarily."

"How long?"

"I don't know."

She couldn't seem to stop touching him, glancing pats on his shoulder and arms. Finally, she linked his hands with hers. "Livvy told me she's coming back in a couple of days."

He nodded, relief trickling through him. "She sounds good?"

"She's doing fine. Madly in love."

He had to swallow his cynical snort. "Okay."

"You don't think she's fine?"

"I think she's in love. Love makes you do all sorts of stupid shit."

Her eyes sharpened. "It does. It can also give you a secure base from which to do stupid shit."

He looked away. "I just don't trust Nicholas."

"Well, you don't have to. Trust your sister. She's an adult, and so is Nicholas. They'll either work this out or they won't."

He made an agreeable noise, simply so they wouldn't have to discuss this anymore.

"She'll be surprised you're still here. Frankly, I know I am. I've been waiting to hear you left."

"How did you find out I was here?"

She waved that aside. "I have eyes and ears all over this town. If I hadn't known you'd bolt, I'd have come running the second I heard you were at the café." Her lips held a nostalgic quiver. Like his father, Maile had grown up working in her parents' café. Also like his father, she'd had no culinary skills or interest in actually running the place. "I'm glad you're helping Sadia. She's a good girl. She could use a hand."

She might not have meant for the words to be harsh, but Jackson drew back physically. "I couldn't come before. I was—" Running. Avoiding any entanglements, keeping his few friends away from his weakest parts. "I didn't think I was needed."

"I didn't mean for that to be a scold, Jackson." A trembling hand smoothed over his cheek.

A great yearning opened inside him, and he had to beat back the urge to grab his aunt close. The tantalizing lure of being needed, of having someone to take care of.

He looked into her dark eyes. "I don't know what I'm doing here," he heard himself say.

Maile's brow wrinkled. "It seems fairly self-explanatory to me. You love Livvy and Sadia."

His rejection was immediate. "I don't love Sadia. I'm just helping her."

"Could you leave, if she hired help tomorrow?" Her smile was faint but victorious at his silence. "Love is like an addiction sometimes, isn't it? You get a taste, and you want more. Livvy, Sadia . . . they're good people to be addicted to."

He gave a jerky shake of his head. "Loving people means getting hurt."

"Sometimes. Loving people, reconnecting with the ones you've lost touch with, confronting your memories . . . that can all be painful. What's the alternative? To be alone?"

Yes.

He clenched his jaw tight.

She sighed when he didn't respond. "You could stay here while Livvy's gone. I could make up her bedroom for you."

"No." Staying with Sadia was difficult, especially after that kiss. Staying with his mother would be impossible. "I have a place."

She deflated, but then perked up again. "Will you come in for dinner?"

He was shaking his head before she could finish. "No. I'm okay."

"Have you seen—"

"Yes."

She pressed her lips together. As odd a pair as they made, Tani and Maile had always been dear friends. "She has so many regrets, your mother."

"I'd rather not talk about it." His words were gentle, but firm.

Firm enough that Maile nodded, though she looked displeased. "Do you want to sit here for a minute with me? We can talk some more?"

He wished he was the kind of person who could say yes, but his capacity to talk was rapidly dwindling. Once upon a time, Maile would have understood his silences, but maybe she wouldn't now. Maybe she would hurt him. Best not to find out. "I have to get going."

"I'll see you around, though? While you're here?" Her eyes were so beseeching, he felt like a jerk for making her beg.

"Yes. I'll come see you. At least before I leave."

Her lips wobbled upward in a smile. "Okay. I love you, Jackson."

"I—" No, he couldn't deny that he loved this woman. Not to her face. It would be cruel. "I love you, too, Aunt Maile." The words weren't as difficult to say as he'd thought, and he tasted the truth in them. The way her eyes lit up caused a little firework to go off in his chest. He placed his hand over his heart. It didn't feel gray or frozen. It felt . . . light. Scary.

Good.

Chapter 10

Sadia was already running twenty minutes behind schedule when her tire blew. The noise scared the stuffing out of her, and she swerved, coming to a stop at the side of the road, her rim making a scraping noise as it dragged along the road.

"What was that?" Kareem cried out.

She took a second to catch her breath and take stock of the situation. "A tire," she managed, trying to appear collected for her son. "We have a flat tire. No big deal. Sit tight while I change it."

"Can I watch?" He unsnapped the buckle that kept him in his booster seat.

"Sure." Her parents had started showing all their daughters how to do basic maintenance stuff when they weren't much older than Kareem.

Only ten minutes later, she had to throw the towel in. Whoever had tightened the lug nuts the last time she'd taken the car into the shop had done too good of a job. She'd pulled and pushed at the things, and they were absolutely not budging anytime soon.

She got back in the car and forced a smile for her

son, who was standing behind her seat. Her phone was ringing with an alarm reminder for Kareem's piano lesson and she shut it off, glancing at the watch. Half an hour behind schedule now. "No big deal. We might need a hand." She'd let their auto membership expire to cut down on the expense, but one of her sisters could probably come.

She sent a group text to her sisters, and one by one got three responses. Zara was almost two hours away, Ayesha wouldn't be able to leave her study group for another few hours, and Noor was on call. Jia didn't respond.

Her phone beeped another warning. If she didn't leave right now, there was no way Kareem would make his piano lesson.

She swiped a hand over her forehead, disheartened to realize she was sweating. Her breath was coming faster, too.

No, no, no. Don't let Kareem see this.

She'd only ever had a handful of panic attacks. One had been when Jackson had been arrested and it had looked like he might really go to trial. Paul had sat next to her then, stroking her hair and crooning to her. She'd felt so ashamed the next day, to make him worry about her when it was his brother sitting in a jail.

The others had all come after Paul had died, but usually late at night or early in the morning. She closed her eyes and breathed in deep, and exhaled. She did it again, in a desperate effort to stave off the attack.

"Mom?"

Without looking, she handed her phone over her shoulder. Maybe Rohan or Al were home and they could come help her. But she needed to focus on not having an attack, and not on using the device that might beep another reminder of how late she was getting. "Can you please call one of your uncles, sweetheart?"

JACKSON HAD just pulled into the driveway when Sadia called him. He picked it up as it was about to go to voicemail. "Hello?"

There was a beat, and then Kareem's childish voice. "Hi. We have a flat tire. Can you come help us?"

He frowned. "You have a flat tire? Where's your mom, Kareem?"

"She's here, she asked me to call you. I know how to use a phone."

"Seems like you do." And that was odd, that Sadia had asked Kareem to call. "Is she okay?"

Kareem's voice grew teeny. "Are you okay, Mom?" Then he was back. "She says yeah. She's just breathing like she's doing yoga."

What? Jackson's adrenaline spiked. "Listen, Kareem, there's a way you can send me your exact location. Can you open the app that has a map on it? There's a pin—" His phone buzzed.

"Did you get it?" Kareem asked.

Were all kids this technologically adept these days or was Kareem a genius? "Yeah, I did. Thanks." Luckily, they were only ten minutes away from him.

He made it to Sadia in half that time and immediately spotted her little crossover SUV on the side of the road. He got out and circled the car, coming up the passenger side.

When he opened the door, he knew something was up with Sadia. Kareem was standing behind her, his hand on her shoulder, his little face pinched. Her eyes were closed and she was almost white, she was so pale. Her breathing was shallow, and sweat had broken out on her brow. "Sadia." He placed his hand over hers.

Her fingers twitched and her eyes opened. He was floored to see the wetness there. "What are you doing here?" she gasped.

"I called him," the little boy piped up. "You told me to."

Her lips curled in, but she didn't dispute this.

"I think Mom's sick," Kareem whispered loudly to Jackson.

"Kareem, why don't you look through the photos on my phone?" Jackson handed the boy his phone. "There are pictures of places I've been."

The kid snatched it out of his hand. "Cool." He hopped back in his booster seat.

Hoping Kareem wouldn't hear too much, Jackson squeezed Sadia's fingers. "Sadia, I'm calling an ambulance."

"No," she whispered, and a tear fell down her cheek. "Please don't."

"Something's wrong with you."

"It's a panic attack. Please. No ambulance."

A panic attack. He searched her face, but he could only see the truth. "What do you need me to do?"

Her breath was low and shuddery. "Kareem can't see. Please, I need to go home. My bedroom."

He wiped the tear off her cheek. "I'll get you home, then."

Jackson changed the tire in record time, and then nudged her over so he could drive. Her breathing had grown more shallow, and her chest rose and fell, her hand covering her heart like she could slow its movements externally.

He knew Sadia was in rough shape when she didn't protest him helping her inside the home. Indeed, she leaned harder on him, giving him her weight.

Kareem still had Jackson's phone and trailed after them, swiping through all his pictures. Jackson glanced over his shoulder at the boy. "Why don't you find a movie for us to watch Kareem?"

"But I have a piano lesson."

Sadia went rigid in his arms, and Jackson tightened his grip. "We'll reschedule it." He wasn't sure if he was speaking to Sadia or Kareem.

She pointed him to her bedroom upstairs, and he sat her down on the bed and crouched in front of her. Her eyes were glassy, and her hair was coming out of her braid to stick to her neck. He didn't have much experience with panic attacks, but her symptoms seemed to be coming in waves, growing more severe instead of lessening. He grasped her hands. "Listen to me," he said quietly. "I need you to inhale and exhale deeply, in and out. Listen to my breath and match it, okay?"

She gave a tight shake of her head. "It's not working." She rubbed her hand over her heart. "Kareem is all alone out there and—"

"Kareem is fine in the living room."

Her tears spilled over her lashes. "I missed his piano lesson."

"That happens. Like I said, we'll reschedule it." He kept his tone as calm and steady as possible. "Do you have any meds for this, Sadia?"

For a second he didn't think she was going to answer, but then she nodded, lips tight. "I'm sensitive. They knock me out. I can't—" she gasped, her face scrunching up.

"You can. Where are they?"

She gestured to the bathroom, and he got up, moving quickly to the little room. Her medicine cabinet held the usual things and one prescription pill bottle. He read the label, shook out one little white tablet and came back to Sadia. "Do you need water?"

She stared at him miserably. "I can't fall asleep while Kareem . . ."

"I have him. I'll watch him while you sleep. Take it if it'll help you."

After a beat, she accepted the pill with a shaking hand, and popped it in her mouth. Her throat worked as she swallowed.

She didn't protest when he pulled back the covers and she crawled under them. He sat on the edge of the bed and held her hand while she closed her eyes, her face pinched while she breathed in and out. He wondered if she knew she was, actually, matching their breathing.

How long had she been having these attacks? She'd never had them when they were young. She'd never mentioned them in any of the emails she'd sent.

He wasn't sure how long he sat there, but eventually her breathing became more natural. Her eyelashes fluttered open, and her eyes were dazed now, but at least that panicked anxiety was gone. "Kareem."

He squeezed her fingers. "I'm going to go watch him now," he said quietly. "You rest. Wake up when you're ready."

She blinked up at him, then her gaze lowered to his hands. "You have the most beautiful hands."

She was asleep before he could react to that.

He finally allowed himself to breathe out in a rush.

Oh god. He hadn't felt fear like this in a long, long time. And later, when he had a minute, maybe he would analyze why he'd been so scared, but right now, there was a little boy in the living room who was probably taking Jackson's phone apart in boredom.

Jackson stared at her for a second longer, then rose. He closed her door only half way, so he could still hear her if she needed him.

He walked into the living room and stopped. Kareem was on the couch, feet up on the coffee table. What did he know about babysitting anyway? He would google how to do this, but the kid had his phone.

Kareem looked up from his perusal of Jackson's

photos. "How come you don't have a lot of pictures of other people in here?"

Ouch. "I don't travel with a lot of people."

"How come?"

"I just don't."

Kareem scratched the side of his nose. There were grass stains on his hands and something pink had spilled on his shirt. "You don't talk so much."

"I don't."

"How come?"

Jackson puffed up his cheeks. "I'm shy."

The boy wriggled. "How—"

"Do you like to cook?"

Kareem shrugged. "I dunno."

"Why don't we make something?" *And stop asking me painful questions.*

"Cookies?"

"Sure." Cookies he could make in his sleep.

It took Jackson a few minutes of rummaging, but he found everything he needed in Sadia's kitchen. He had Kareem cracking eggs and prepping the pan and chatting with him shortly.

So much chatting! But oddly enough Jackson didn't mind. It was good to take a break and create something with his hands while childish babble rumbled around him.

You have the most beautiful hands.

He concentrated on scooping flour.

"Uncle Jackson?"

So weird to hear that uncle in front of his name. He'd had no family for so long. "Huh?"

"You're Daddy's brother."

He folded the wet ingredients into the dry. "Yes."

"Can you tell me a story about Daddy? Mom does."

He had to swallow twice to respond. "What kind of story?"

Kareem leaned against the counter. Standing on a stepstool, he was almost tall enough to reach the counter. "Anything."

Jackson looked down at the bowl. He wondered if the boy knew how much wistfulness had been contained in that single word.

Jackson had been nineteen when his father died. He and the man hadn't had the most unproblematic relationship, but he grieved for Robert to this day.

Whatever his feelings about Paul, he couldn't imagine how this little boy had felt. "These cookies were our Grandpa's favorite."

"Grandpa John?"

Jackson frowned. How did the boy know about John Chandler? "No. Well, Grandpa John loved them, but it was Grandpa Sam who came up with the recipe. I made the cookies for this charity bake sale at school." Sadia had been running that fair, and she'd begged him to enter something. Without her urging, he wouldn't have exactly joined in. The last thing he wanted to do was call attention to himself, and years with his father had made it clear that cooking wasn't something the cool guys did. Business or golf, sure. Not baking.

"Some older kids walked by my booth and knocked the cookies to the ground. Your dad saw them."

Kareem's eyes grew wide. "What did he do?"

Jackson faltered. What Paul had done was grab the nearest one by the neck and punch him in the face. But somehow, he was pretty sure even the most lax childrearing expert would say that wasn't a good thing to tell a kid. "He gave them a lecture about how knocking things down wasn't nice," Jackson finished lamely. "And they got in trouble." Paul had gotten a suspension too, if he remembered clearly. Their mother had been livid, their father filled with barely concealed pride.

Jackson started dropping the cookie dough on the greased sheet. He'd forgotten that story. Paul had intervened with so many bullies for him, the same way he had for Sadia.

It's almost like you learned something from him.

"My daddy was really brave," Kareem boasted.

"Hmm." Jackson opened the oven and put the cookies in, then looked at Kareem. Now what? He didn't know how long Sadia would be out, and the kid needed entertaining. "What do you want to do now?"

Kareem tucked his hands into his pockets and stared up at him guilelessly. "We can ride your motorcycle."

Jackson's lips twitched. The kid was persistent, he'd give him that. "Maybe later." He'd have to go back at some point and fetch his bike from where it was sitting on the side of the road, but this was a safe enough town he wasn't too worried. Worst case, it might get impounded by the cops, but he could work that out later. "How about a movie? Or we can cook some more."

Kareem hopped off the stool. "Movie, but with popcorn."

"Done." That was easy enough.

Forty-five minutes of haggling over which movies were appropriate or not for Kareem, hunting down a stuffed bunny in the boy's room, and putting another batch of cookies in the oven, Jackson sat on the couch and reached into the bowl of popcorn, only to come back with kernels. "Did you eat all of these?"

Kareem licked his buttery fingers, his attention glued on the opening credits of the Disney movie. "Shh."

Jackson shook his head and shifted on the couch. Oh so casually, Kareem scooted, so he leaned against his side, and Jackson froze.

It wasn't a hug, but it was more contact than he'd had with the kid. Slowly, fearing the boy might move away, he rested his arm over Kareem's shoulder and cupped his head. His hand was almost as big as his whole head. So fragile.

To be solely responsible for one easily hurt human was no laughing matter. What kind of pressure must Sadia constantly be under?

They'd gotten about halfway through the movie when the front door opened, and Kareem sat up. "Who is it?" he called out, before Jackson could.

A pretty, stylish young woman appeared in the

living room archway, and her expression went from pleasant to stunned.

Ah hell. She was older now, but this was very obviously one of Sadia's younger sisters.

"Auntie Jia!" Kareem squealed, answering which twin this was, and launched himself off the couch. Jackson paused the movie and rose to his feet. "I haven't seen you in forever."

Jia caught the boy and hugged him close, then put him down. "Sorry, kiddo, I've been busy all week. I see I've missed some stuff." Her gaze was fixed on him, eyes wide. "Jackson?"

Jackson nodded. "Hello, Jia. You're looking well."

"Thanks. Uh, you too. I didn't know you were in town . . . ?"

"I'm here for a short visit." He had no idea what Sadia had told her family about him. Nothing, he assumed, if Jia didn't know he was here. Better to downplay things.

"Cool. I haven't seen you since I was like four-teen, I think."

When she was fourteen, he'd been thrown in jail. He could read her curiosity and speculation. "Yes, it's been a while."

"Well, I actually came over to see Sadia. She wasn't answering her texts and I wanted to make sure she got some help for her flat."

Kareem tilted his head back to look at her. "Uncle Jackson helped change the tire. The things were too tight for Mom."

Jia tugged on his hair with easy affection. Clearly she and her nephew were comfortable with each

other in a way he was not. "That happens sometimes, even for wondermoms. Where is she?"

"Sadia's not feeling well. She's resting in her
room. I was watching Kareem until she was better."

"We made cookies but Jackson said I could only
eat one when they were warm."

"Cookies! How cool." Jia smiled. "I can watch
Kareem for the rest of the night, if you'd like."

He wanted to say no, that he was enjoying sitting with Kareem, but that would have been more
words than he could string together.

Besides, this girl surely had more rights to their
mutual nephew than he did. "Very well."

Kareem surprised him with a hug when he
passed him, and Jackson awkwardly patted his
back, trying his best to temper his strength.

The boy rubbed his face on Jackson's shirt.
"Thanks for cookies."

"You're welcome."

Jackson stopped right outside the front door and
examined the chocolate stain on his shirt.

He couldn't contain his smile.

Chapter 11

Sadia woke in a panic, grabbing at her phone next to her, only there was no phone there. She sat up and looked around, confused. The room was gloomy, and she checked the time, stunned when she realized it was almost ten p.m.

The events of the afternoon came back to her and she scurried off the bed. Kareem. It was well past his bedtime. Had he been with Jackson all day? The boy didn't even really know his uncle well.

What kind of mother falls asleep and leaves her baby alone with a relative he barely knows?

She came out of her room to a soundless house. She crept through the hallway to Kareem's room and opened it a crack, giving a small sigh of relief when she spotted Kareem snug under the covers. She tiptoed closer. He was bathed and in his pajamas, his hair gleaming.

Okay. One worry down. She looked out the window toward the garage apartment. The lights were off in there, which meant Jackson was asleep, out, or in her home.

She slipped downstairs, the light coming from

the living room guiding her. The person sitting on the couch was not who she expected it to be.

Her stomach lurched. In relief, not disappointment. Or so she told herself. "Jia, what are you doing here?"

Jia put down the cookie she was eating and brushed crumbs off her bright green sweater. The color made her light brown eyes pop. "Hanging out. I heard you were sick."

This time the emotion she felt was definitely relief. Jackson hadn't revealed her panic attack. "Yes. The medicine I took was a bit strong."

Jia's face was sympathetic. "Headaches?"

"Sure. Yes." Sadia came to sit on top of the wooden chest that doubled as her coffee table. "Did you put Kareem to bed?"

"Yup."

"Thank you."

"No problem. He must have had an exciting day. He was pooped."

"It was exciting all right."

"I was worried when you didn't answer your phone after you texted us."

"Yeah." Sadia looked around. "I'm not even sure where my phone is."

"I put it on the kitchen counter, along with your purse."

"Thanks."

"So, like . . . I see why you haven't needed much help with Kareem this week." Jia tilted her head at the garage. "You got an old friend here."

Sadia's fingers curled. "Jackson's here temporarily. A few weeks."

"Kareem says he's working at the café too."

"It's not a big deal."

"Uh . . . okay. But I have so many questions. One, was he always super cute? Two, did he really not set that fire? Three, on a scale of one to ten, one being pretty cute and ten being a million degrees of cute, how cute do you think he is—"

"Okay, okay." Sadia held her hand up and prayed she wasn't blushing. "One, he's way too old for you to even be thinking of him like that. Two, yeah."

"He's your age! That's only six years older than me. That's not bad. Oh my God, how adorable would it be if we both married brothers—" She winced, obviously recalling what had happened to the elder brother. "I'm sorry. That was me being insensitive, wasn't it? Ayesha would smack me."

"It's fine."

Jia recovered. "Is he here to visit Tani, like Livvy was?"

"Not important." Sadia waved that aside. "Don't worry about the Kane family drama."

"But it's so interesting. We're positively boring compared to them. You married into, like, that family from *Dynasty*."

"How do you even know about *Dynasty*?"

"Reruns. Remakes. Rinse and repeat."

Sadia leaned back. "Listen, speaking of drama, let's keep this from the rest of the family for a bit, huh?" There was no need to get Noor or her parents worried over what Jackson was doing here. It would bring up bad memories for them. Her parents had been shaken when the Kane scandals had rocked the community.

What will people think? Her mother had exclaimed when Sadia had told her she wanted to marry Paul. *They say his father died while he was having an affair and his own brother was in jail for a felony. That will follow him around for the rest of his life, and your life too.*

It hadn't, not really. No one who had known Robert Kane believed he and Maria Chandler were in that car to run off together. Paul had never quite shaken all of his bitterness over losing the company, but she'd managed to live and raise her son in the shadow of Chandler's without constant gossip.

It had helped that so many people had liked Paul and the Kanes. She couldn't say the same thing would have happened if Jackson, who hadn't been quite as popular, had stuck around.

"Don't worry," Jia soothed. "I got my own stuff to worry about when it comes to the fam."

"Still thinking about going full-time, huh?" Sadia picked up a cookie from the plate next to her leg and bit into it, nearly gasping when chocolate and dough exploded on her tongue. "Whoa."

"I know, they taste better than the Chandler's ones. Jackson made them."

She finished the cookie in two bites, and went back for a second. They tasted like the Chandler's signature cookies because they were the signature cookies. Just fresh from the oven. She'd always been bugging Jackson to make these.

"To answer your question, I'm not just thinking about going full-time. I am going full-time."

Sadia tried to eat this cookie a little slower. "Have you considered that maybe you're making a rash decision?"

"No. I hate med school. And not in that way that everyone hates grad school. I watch Ayesha and even though it's hard and teeth-grinding, she finds everything we learn fascinating and exciting. I don't. I spend almost every class waiting to get home to my equipment or social media." She placed her hand on her chest, her eyes beseeching. "I've tried not to like this so much. I knew Mom and Daddy wouldn't approve. But I can't help it."

Sadia shifted, unable to resist making the parallels between Jia's passionate words and her own elopement with Paul so many years ago. Her parents and older sisters wouldn't have been okay with her getting married at twenty even if Paul had still been the heir to a fortune. She'd loved him so much, though, and when he'd pulled her close and begged her to marry him, telling her she was the only constant, stable thing in his life, what other choice had she had? While things may not have ended perfectly, she wouldn't change that decision. It had given her a number of happy years, not to mention her son.

But a livelihood and a marriage were still two different things. "Listen, if you do this, you're essentially going to be self-employed. I can tell you firsthand, running a business is not easy. It's sleeplessness and worry and constantly having the buck stop with you."

"I know all of that. But the parts you love make up for that, right?"

Uh, maybe for some people. But Sadia wasn't about to explain to Jia she hadn't exactly chosen the business owner life. "Ideally, yes," she hedged. "But it's hard."

"I know." Jia bent forward. She rummaged through her bookbag for a minute, and then pulled out a file folder, which she placed on the coffee table. "I don't have my head in the clouds. Here, I brought this for you to look over."

Sadia slid the file closer to her and flipped through the papers inside. There were pages upon pages of spreadsheets, along with letters from various suppliers and sponsorship offers.

"Those are all my earnings and projections. I have two sponsorship offers on the table that are going to be fairly lucrative, not to mention a licensing deal for an app game that wants to use my name. Right now, if just these things go through, I'll be grossing a million in a year, InshAllah."

Sadia blinked at the numbers. So Jia wasn't only going to be earning more than her . . . she'd be earning more than any of the sisters. She turned the page, stopping when she noted the letterhead on the crisp white linen paper. She read the short letter, stunned. "Jia . . . you'd be a spokesmodel for this makeup company? On television commercials?"

"Yes." Jia nodded, her hands clenched tight. "There's a reason they sent me their products.

None of you understand what I've done, how big it's grown. I love it. I'm proud of it. And I want to make it huge. I'm talking music, modeling, acting, maybe a book deal. A whole media company where I can call the shots." Her light brown eyes glinted with a fervor Sadia had never seen before. "I have an opportunity now girls like me don't get, Sadia. I have to take it. Please help me."

Sadia smoothed her hand over the paper. She wasn't unmoved, not in the slightest. She cleared her throat. "Give me some time to look all this over."

Jia bobbed her head. "Take it, yes. I can answer any questions you have."

"If I agree that this is a good idea . . . what do you need from me?"

"Ideally?" Jia's smile was sweet. "I need you in my corner. Talk to Noor and Zara. If all of you are on board, Mom and Daddy will come around."

Sadia started laughing before she realized Jia was serious. "Uh. You've met our sisters, right?"

"I know they're stubborn, but they listen to you."

"Jia . . . no one in this family listens to me."

Jia leaned forward, her sweet face earnest. "Of course they do. You're the peacemaker. Like the bridge."

If she was a bridge, it was one that needed significant structural improvements.

"I was hoping to quit school in the next couple weeks, actually." Jia made a face. "I don't see the point in taking exams that won't actually do anything for me."

"You want me to get our whole family over to your side in a couple of weeks."

Jia bit her lip. "I guess when you put it that way . . ." She looked down at her hands. "I just can't do this anymore, is all."

Sadia flipped through the papers. She had no idea what the right or wrong thing to do was here, but her baby sister was distressed, and she couldn't stand it. She made a quick decision. "I'll try to talk to Noor and Zara. I assume Ayesha is on board?"

"She's always on my side."

No surprise, when the twins were so close. "Okay then. Let's see what magic we can work."

Jia's lip wobbled. "Thank you. I knew I could count on you."

"Don't count on me yet." Sadia lifted the folder. "You've plotted expenses in here, right? Things like health care?"

"Of course."

"Retirement?" She didn't have a retirement stash, but that was no reason Jia shouldn't.

Some of Jia's smugness evaporated. "Um, no. I can, though."

"Good." Sadia polished off her cookie. "I require additional cookies."

"Those were the last ones."

She narrowed her eyes at her sister. "What the hell."

"Get your sexy houseguest to make you some more."

Sadia opened her mouth, then closed it. Now she knew she was blushing. Damn it all, she should never have had Jackson so close to her in her bed. Her only hope was that she hadn't said anything too wild to him while she was falling asleep.

Tomorrow she was working at the bar. She might have to go on the prowl and find someone who could take her mind off Jackson. "Too old for you."

"I can look, can't I?"

Jia might be able to. She definitely, absolutely, should not.

That train may have already left, friend.

Chapter 12

THAT TRAIN had definitely left.

Sadia came to this conclusion when Jackson opened the door to his little apartment shirtless, wearing nothing but a pair of low-slung gray sweatpants. With the café closed for the day, she'd spent most of her time with half her attention on whether Jackson was in his apartment or not.

She'd slipped away the second Jia had showed up to watch Kareem for the night. Her sister had leered at her when she said she had to run something over to Jackson. But a leer was entirely appropriate, because Jackson's chest was like a work of art, his pecs impressive, his stomach ridged with muscle. His nipples were two flat brown discs that made her mouth water.

He's Paul's brother. These are the wrong nipples for you to be intrigued by. Tonight, at the bar, you are going to find someone with nipples you can salivate over guilt-free.

"Sadia?"

"You have a lot of tattoos."

He glanced at his arm, like that was a perfectly

normal thing for her to blurt out. His half-sleeve consisted of thick curving and straight black lines, beautifully arranged in a pattern that embraced his muscles. Green palm fronds melted into the black lines and curled in a circle on his shoulder and chest.

"Not a lot." He touched his arm. "I got this one when I visited Maui. My father had a similar one."

She raised her eyebrows. In her memory, Robert Kane had always been in a suit, with a briefcase. "He did?"

"Yes." Jackson's eyes warmed. "We barely ever saw it either, but my mom blamed him for Livvy's interest in the art."

"Ah."

He widened the door. "Do you want to come in?"

So she could be in the same room as him with close proximity to a bed and think about their kiss last week? When he was tattooed and shirtless? "No."

Maybe that was too emphatic, but Jackson didn't react. He lifted his hand and braced it against the door frame, right at her eye level. "Is there something you needed?"

To lick you. "I wanted to thank you for yesterday. Your help," she said in a rush.

He only shrugged. "It was no big deal."

"It was." She struggled to speak. "The panic attack. How did you know what to do?"

"I didn't, really. But I had a sous-chef who had social anxiety, and I had to talk him through a couple of attacks. He had meds he took."

"I probably should, but I usually can't be incapacitated like that."

"Must be really hard. To be a single parent."

"I had anxiety before I became a single parent," she confessed, like it was a dark secret.

"Yeah, but adding all that stress can't make it much better." He glanced over her shoulder, toward the house. "And you're so good at it. Perfect."

Ha, what? She was the furthest thing from perfect.

"Sorry if I'm saying the wrong thing. Livvy said sometimes when I tried to comfort her, I made it worse. I'm just trying to tell you you're doing a really good job, even with everything going on."

Her heart softened again. "Thanks. No. You're fine."

"We never got to have dinner yesterday."

She fiddled with her earring, as flustered as a young girl out on a date. Surely there was nothing flirtatious in his words.

Whatever remaining anger she'd felt toward him had softened with his assistance yesterday. She was truly ready to try to be friends for as long as he was here. A friend who didn't lust after him, that is. "We'll do it some time this week. You can take a night off from cooking, we'll order out. Kareem would like to see you again. He can't stop talking about you now." From the minute he'd gotten home from school, it had been nonstop. Including when she'd taken him to visit Tani and Maile. "Maile says she saw you yesterday. So double thanks for helping me when you were dealing with your own shit."

He shrugged that off. "I was fine."

Maile hadn't given her any details, and Tani had been stone-faced in front of her grandson's excitement, but Sadia had the feeling everything hadn't been fine.

"Is that for me?" He pointed at the bag she carried.

She started when she realized she'd forgotten her errand in favor of staring at his ink and abs. "Oh, yes. Yesterday, I ran into . . ." she hesitated, loathe to even mention John. She'd never dared around Paul. Her husband hated any reminder of the company he'd lost. "John Chandler. He asked me to give this to you and to tell you he would love to see you sometime."

As always, Jackson's face was expressionless. He accepted the bag from her. "Thanks."

"I haven't seen him before this," she felt compelled to explain. "Not since . . . you know."

"I wouldn't judge you if you had."

"Paul would have been mad." The words slipped out before she could stop them.

"I'm not Paul. I never cared about losing the company as much as he did." Jackson's eyes grew flinty. "I cared about Nicholas making Livvy miserable, but John had nothing to do with that."

She swallowed. "For what it's worth, Livvy said John had nothing to do with stealing the company either."

He shrugged, and she believed him. He'd never really cared about the C&O.

She rocked back on her heels. "Well, I have to run."

His gaze trailed over her body, so quickly she might have missed it if she hadn't been attuned to him. "Working at the bar tonight?"

"Yes."

"Have fun."

She paused, feeling vaguely guilty. He couldn't know what kind of fun she was planning on having tonight, right? No, of course not. And even if he did, she had no reason to feel guilty. She nodded, and made her escape.

HAVE FUN?

Why had he said that? Now he was going to be consumed with thoughts of all the things that could fall under the banner of fun she could be engaging in all night.

Would she flirt with someone the way she'd flirted with him that first night, when she hadn't known who he was? Would she do more than flirt?

Goddamn it. All of the careful speeches he'd rehearsed had flown out of his brain when he'd opened the door to find her dressed in those tight black clothes.

I was worried about you yesterday.

More worried than I thought I would be for someone I don't love.

Let's dissect what that means.

Jackson grimaced. He sat down on the bed and weighed the cloth bag Sadia had handed him.

He pulled out the book inside, recognizing it instantly. Jackson's grandpa Kane had been a decent, robust guy, but he'd never met his maternal grandfather, Sam Oka. Sam and John were the ones who had cobbled together the beginnings of an empire, literally digging the first hole for what would become the C&O. Until it had burned down.

John had kept his best friend alive for Sam's grandchildren, telling them stories and passing down the man's traditions. It had been the only way they'd learned of the heritage from that side of their family, since Tani had never wanted to discuss her late parents. Paul and Livvy hadn't been as curious about Sam as Jackson had been, so naturally he and John had forged a solid relationship.

He traced the front of the journal. The leather was cracking in a few places, but John had kept it in great condition. Sam hadn't been the type of guy to keep journals, John had told him. There was this one, sporadically written in, and the letters John had meticulously saved.

He opened to a page at random. He'd read these entries so many times he could recite them in his sleep.

Tani was born today. I don't think anyone is more excited than John. He said we should betroth Brendan and her right now, so we can unite the families. I told him, not a chance. What if that boy grows up to be an asshole? He already has trouble sharing his toys.

Smart man, Grandpa Sam.

He flipped backward, to the entry about their first store.

Week four after our opening. Everyone's telling me to be happy with the one store, to stop working so hard, to figure out how to make this one a success and stop thinking of growing our business, but I'm seeing a chain. A nationwide one, a place where people come from miles just for the privilege of shopping with us.

John thinks it's about the money, and maybe it is, but no matter how much John says he understands, he can't. I want my family to be rich and powerful enough that they can fight the entire federal government if they ever need to. Money talks. Power talks. Nothing else can make the world sit up and take notice, not kindness or love or being good. I want my children to have every advantage I can buy for them. Enough so they're equal to John's children in the eyes of the law.

We help ourselves now. I can't quit, or rest. If I quit, it could all be over.

An undefinable swell of emotion filled Jackson's chest. Whenever John had done an interview after Sam's death, he'd been careful to stress that Sam had been the powerhouse behind the store, that without him, they wouldn't have thought big enough or grand enough to create the empire they did.

Jackson had sat next to John, wide eyed, while the man had told him the exact same thing, but these words directly from his grandfather, had always left him in awe, hammering home the measure of the man whose blood ran through his veins.

Harsh, proud, realistic.

All qualities Sam must have had to have to create a successful empire in an overcrowded market.

Nothing's over until you quit. He'd been six in John's kitchen when the man had first passed on Sam's favorite saying, then laughed, telling Jackson Sam had been considered quite the rebel in his family for being so headstrong and ruthless in his attitude.

Jackson turned the page, and something fell into his hands. A piece of paper this time. It looked like it had been read and read often, was almost as delicate as the paper in the journals.

He opened the paper and smoothed it out, but the handwriting here wasn't his grandfather's. It took him until the third or fourth sentence before recognition struck him.

His gaze flew to the bottom of the page and he inhaled sharply at Paul's signature.

He should put it away. This wasn't his to read.

But he couldn't. He braced his hand on the bed and bent his head.

> *Dear Grandpa John,*
> *I may have given up the right to call you grandpa by now—but it felt odd to address this letter as Mr. or only John, so bear with me. I'm not trying to soften you up.*
> *I'll keep this short. I was the one who set the fire at the C&O. I was angry and furious. I blamed you for my father's death, and my mother's grief. I blamed Nicholas for Livvy's pain. And finally, maybe mostly, I blamed all of you for*

taking the business away from me. The C&O was mine, and I felt robbed.

This isn't meant to be an explanation, or even an excuse. I have no excuse for what I did. I have even less of an excuse for what I did after that fire.

When I realized there was a witness who had mistaken me for my brother, I convinced Jackson to keep quiet and allow them to arrest him. I assured him I would get him out quickly, that the charges were false. I manipulated him. The hows and whys aren't important, but rest assured, it happened. And I knew he would do what I asked, because beyond anything, Jackson was a sweet kid with a heart bigger than his body.

It is pure dumb luck that witness recanted his story and Jackson's attorney—an attorney my aunt and sister got for him, because I was too blinded by panic and anger to even do that much—got him off. Or maybe it's not luck. If you were the one who persuaded that witness to recant, I thank you. From the bottom of my heart, I thank you for taking action when I could not.

I'm telling you all of this because I'm sitting in the hospital, watching my baby boy sleep on my wife's chest. They are so beautiful together my heart aches. I want nothing more for my son than the opportunity I had—to grow up with a father who is fierce and brave and loving and strong, and to maybe have siblings who are equally as strong and brave and protective.

I am not that strong, which is why I threw that

Molotov all those years ago. I am not courageous, or I'd send this to the police.

But I'm telling you, now, for two reasons. One, I want you to know that your son wasn't totally wrong to take the business. I can see now that I would have been a piss-poor person to run things by your side. Two, I want you to be able to take this letter to the authorities as a confession if you wish to.

I love my brother, and I used him, and I regret nothing more. I'll never forgive myself for that. I'll never forgive myself for the fire. It could have hurt someone. It seems like a just punishment that I have the threat of what you'll do with this letter hanging over my head.

Don't try to contact me. I won't respond, as usual. But I do love you. Thank you for everything you ever did for me, and my siblings.

Best,
Paul

I love my brother.
I used him.
I regret nothing more.

Jackson didn't realize how tight his grip had gotten until the paper crinkled in his hands. He breathed deeply and released his hold.

Fuck.

He sat there for God knew how long, turning the words over and over in his head. They made such little sense to him. Over the past ten years he'd imagined Paul gloating or stubbornly oblivious. He hadn't realized the man had actually hurt. He hadn't imagined he'd regretted things.

He hadn't imagined Paul still loved him.

In his head, he was back in their parents' bedroom of their old mansion, staring at Paul as the other man frantically paced the floor. *Tell me you didn't really set that fire,* he'd whispered, as if the police were actually in the house already. They weren't. They were on their way with a search warrant. Rumors were swirling of a witness who had placed Jackson at the scene.

Jackson's alibi was his family. He'd been holding his sister at the time. He hadn't left the house in weeks.

Paul had run his hands through his hair. *It's not what you think.*

I think you set the fire.

Their mother had been staring dumbly at the wall, but finally spoke up. *Jackson, if the police try to arrest you, go with them. You're innocent.*

But, Mom—

You're innocent. Paul is not. You have to protect your brother. We'll get you out quickly, I promise. And if we can't, then Paul will take responsibility for what he did.

He'd looked into his mother's eyes and believed her. And then Paul had uttered the sentence that had ensured Jackson would do whatever it took to shield his brother.

Jackson had sat quietly in a jail cell while reporters smeared his name and the district attorney gloated that they were going to hold a son of one of the two richest families in the county accountable. He watched circumstantial evidence pile up against him and held silent even with his own attorney, who while clever and competent, was also certain of Jackson's guilt.

He hadn't caved. He'd had to stay tough. He'd had to cover for his brother.

He carefully folded the letter up and held it in his hands. What was he supposed to do with this? He didn't doubt John had purposefully given it to him.

Paul was dead. If he wanted to, Jackson could go public. Clear his name in the court of public opinion, where it had, no doubt, been damaged. Maybe he might get punished for obstruction, but no one would think he was an arsonist.

He could stay here without fearing that every person he passed assumed he was a villain. But then everyone would know Sadia had married an arsonist who had thrown his brother under the bus.

He wanted to go see John, right this minute. But that wasn't an option. He couldn't drive up to the man's mansion and demand an explanation for why John had given this letter to Sadia—

His blood ran cold. Jesus Christ. Sadia could have read this.

JACKSON DIDN'T have to think about where he was going. He'd driven up to John Chandler's home too many times for him to recall. His own home had been right next door, separated by a small forest. Sam and John had been two peas in a pod and had built their homes close enough for their kids and grandkids to easily mingle.

Jackson pulled into John's circular drive. It was about seven, so later than most people would probably feel comfortable visiting someone, but Jackson couldn't wait. He needed to confront the man.

He rang the doorbell and waited, then rang it again, uncharacteristic impatience running through him. After another minute or so, the door opened and Jackson flinched. It was like looking at a ghost of Maria Chandler. Same round face, petite, chubby form, same dark hair and eyes. But this girl's hair was straight, not curly, and she had a form of self-possessed quietness Nicholas's mother had lacked.

Jackson tried not to think too hard about the night his father had died. He could only remember snatches of it. The sound of the policeman's radio squawking, his mother's screams, his sister's sobbing, his brother's raised voice.

At the same time the policeman had been at his door, another cruiser had been at the Chandler's door, to explain Maria was also dead.

No one knew why the two of them had been together in that car that winter night, and it didn't matter to Jackson. The last time Jackson had seen Eve Chandler had been before he'd gone to jail. Nicholas's sister had been thirteen then, younger than even Sadia's sisters. He braced himself. "Eve."

Eve looked far less surprised to see him than Jackson was to see her. "Hello there, Jackson. What brings you here?"

His fingers tightened around the book in his hand. "I'd like to see your grandfather."

She inclined her head, smooth as silk. "Let me see if he's receiving visitors. Why don't you wait in the library? I trust you know where it is?"

He nodded, feeling more than a little bit like he'd slipped into a surreal dreamscape. He waited for Eve to walk away, then drifted through the hallways of the home. The library had been his favorite room. He stepped inside and looked up and up at the stacks. There were a lot of books in here, but the place felt smaller than it had when he was young.

A framed photo on the wall caught his attention and he drew in a deep breath, prowling closer. Footsteps had him pausing when he was about to touch the frame.

"He'll be right with you," Eve said from inside the door, her tone neutral. "Can I get you—oh."

"This burned down." He knew his tone was harsh, but he couldn't help it. He looked at Eve, one hand touching the frame, the other holding his grandfather's journal. "What is it doing here?"

Her gaze went to the photo. It was old and black and white, of both of their grandfathers when they were little more than boys. It had been taken in front of the Oka's old supermarket in San Francisco, not long before Sam had been sent to an internment camp in Utah. "Grandpa tracked down the original photographer. There's a copy hanging in the flagship C&O again. Nicholas insisted before he left with Livvy that it be restored."

Jackson's chest felt tight. In all the days he'd been working at the café, he'd never once had the thought of going back inside the supermarket.

It was impossible for him to unlink what had happened with Paul and the fire to the company. He had no desire to set foot in that store, not for a minute. But if he had . . . Eve was saying if he had, he would have seen his grandpa. This picture he'd grown up looking at. His past, the man he'd come from.

His fingers tightened on the journal.

Eve cleared her throat. "I didn't know you were in town."

He turned back to her, the foreign emotions leaking past his defenses, making him sharper than he would have otherwise been. "I had to make sure your brother didn't hurt my sister again."

Her smile was reserved. Jackson had the feeling most things this girl did were as muted as her tasteful neutral pink pressed sheath dress. "Ah. You hate Nicholas."

"Very much so."

"Probably as much as I thought I hated Livvy."

His eyes narrowed. "How could you possibly hate Livvy? She didn't do anything to you. Nicholas is the one who fucked her over."

She raised a finely arched brow. "So it's my family that was the villain in every case?"

He opened his mouth, about to agree, and then he remembered what he was holding.

Paul's goddamn confession.

"My brother is a good person," she continued softly. "And so is your sister. I think it's time for both of our families to lay down our arms, hmm? There's been enough blood shed on every side."

His jaw tightened. "We'll see how good he is."

"I suppose we will. They'll be back tomorrow."

"Tomorrow?"

"Nicholas called me this morning." A smile touched her lips. "Mostly to make sure the business is struggling without him, which I'm sure is exactly what he wanted our father to see."

Nicholas had been in contact with his sister, though Livvy hadn't been in touch with him, beyond that damned voicemail.

Jackson tried to banish his unwarranted sense of jealousy. "Good."

"I hope it's good, and that everyone makes their transition back into the real world a smooth one." She raised her rounded chin and regarded him coolly. "You know what I mean?"

How old was this girl? Twenty-three, twenty-four? She was remarkably good at conveying a threat with only a look. "Do you work at the business?" She'd make a killer corporate type.

Her smile was sardonic. "No. I worked at the foundation, but I recently quit."

Maria's foundation. He'd donated money to the thing over the years. Just because he disliked the men of this family didn't mean he didn't like giving underprivileged kids a chance to go to college. Besides, Maria had always been kind to him.

The whir of the power chair had his gaze shooting to the door of the library. An elderly man entered.

John Chandler was older and seemed smaller than he had when Jackson was young and the man had taught him how to bake his grandpa Sam's famous chocolate chip cookies—so famous, that the cookie had been called Sam's Cookies at the old C&O. Who knew what the Chandler's called them now. Probably something boring. Like cookies.

He wore casual clothes, which wasn't new— John had always eschewed suits and ties for more informal plaid shirts and jeans, a quirk that had endeared the rich man to the locals.

John came closer, and Jackson could make out the lines and differences ten years had added. Jackson's heart was beating so loud he could hear it in his ears. This man had been a surrogate grandfather to him, but more importantly, he'd been a friend.

Jackson hadn't had many of those. Livvy, Sadia, and this elderly man who had let him be himself even when his own father had no patience with him.

The older man stared at him for a long moment, before a sad smile cracked his face. "Look at you. You grew up."

Jackson ran his hands over his jeans. "So did you."

John's laugh turned into a cough, and Jackson took a step before he could stop himself. His words had been glib, but he was rattled by how small

John seemed. Fragile. The man had once been larger than life, though Jackson had shot past him in height in middle school.

"Grandpa," Eve exclaimed, and came to stand next to his chair. She rubbed his back. "Are you okay? Do you want me to get some water?"

John glared at her, but patted her hand. "I'm not dying. I just inhaled wrong."

"Oh." Eve's shoulders relaxed.

"Give us some time alone, will you, Evie? I'll let you visit with your old friend Jackson here later."

He and Eve gave each other wary, measuring looks. They hadn't been friends when he'd left, not really, and there were slim odds they would be now when they were on opposite sides of the Livvy and Nicholas war.

The door closed quietly behind Eve, and John sat back in his seat. "It's good to see you, son."

It hurt to breathe. Funny how a simple word could take the air out of you, leave you starving for oxygen. Son. No one had called him a son in a very long time, and not with that air of paternal pride. He struggled with what to say. "You . . . too."

"You don't want to see me," John said gently. "I understand that."

"I didn't say that. I'm not good at talking."

John's eyes were shrewd but kind. "You never had a problem talking to me when you were young."

Because John hadn't minded him being quiet when he needed to be. While Livvy and Paul and Nicholas chattered at John, John would hand him a book or a cutting knife and fruit and set him to work on some solitary activity where he could be happy and quiet.

His mother had been much the same way. Unlike his dad, she'd never treated his lack of charm as a disappointment. "Things have changed."

"You look like your father."

He found his voice. "I know."

"Your grandfather, too. Around the eyes. The shape of your face." John ran his hand over the arm of his chair. "I'd ask for a hug, but you never liked being touched much."

Only from people he wanted to be touched by. Why did it have to be a strict either/or thing?

Jackson lifted the book in his hand. "I came about this. You gave this to Sadia."

"I did."

He pulled out Paul's letter. "You gave *this* to Sadia."

"Well, yes. I assumed you wouldn't want to see me, and I wanted to make sure you had it."

His earlier fear and anger came rushing back. "Sadia could have read it."

"Why don't you sit down?" Without waiting for Jackson to respond, he wheeled himself to the couch. "Over here. You always liked this couch, didn't you?"

He had liked that couch. Reluctantly, he walked over and sat down, unable to resist a direct request from his surrogate grandfather.

John ran his hand over his bushy white hair. "Where were we? Ah, yes. I knew Sadia wouldn't open the package."

"How did you know that?"

"I asked her not to."

Jackson's mouth dropped open. "That's it? That was your safeguard?"

"Sadia always was an obedient child. I was stunned when she eloped with your brother. Out of character for her." John shrugged. "I was fairly certain if I asked her not to look at it, she wouldn't."

Actually . . . that was probably a decent bet. Sadia did have a lot of respect for elders, and if John had told her not to open the bag, she probably wouldn't have.

There were a million ways she could have still seen it, but Jackson would try not to think about those. He couldn't handle the stress. "John . . ."

"I know. I know. It was risky. But I had to give it to you. I'm trying to get rid of stuff before I go instead of later. Have some more control over things this way." He nodded at the picture on the wall. "I was saving that for you and Livvy. I have a copy for each of you. One for Kareem, too."

His first instinct was to grab the photo and run, but then common sense prevailed. "I travel a lot. I don't usually carry things."

"Your sister said the same thing. You should consider settling down a little. It's nice to have a base."

"I can't make this my base." He thought of the café, and how nice it had felt to slide his hands over an oven he was intimately familiar with. "I have to . . . I can't stay here."

"Hmm. Why not?"

"Everyone thinks I burned down your store, for

one." Harriet's reaction hadn't been repeated, but it could be.

"It was *our* store, and we both know you didn't." John nodded at the letter.

Jackson stared at John's placid face. "How can you be so calm about it?"

"Insurance paid for everything. And it was an accident."

Jackson shook his head. Paul hadn't intended that level of destruction, but he'd deliberately thrown that cocktail through the grocery store's window. "It wasn't."

"Listen, Jackson. You and I, we're going to talk about that letter exactly once, right now, and then we're never going to discuss it again. Yes, your brother burned down our store. Yes, I understand he persuaded you to go along with the police. Yes, I understand he did something terrible. I also understand that you were both barely old enough to vote and reeling from the death of your father and your world turning upside down. Sometimes, people do dumb things, and they should be forgiven for those things. I forgive Paul, forgave him a long time ago, but it's not my job to forgive Paul for you. It's your decision, what you want to do with that confession. Use it to clear your name, shout it from the rooftops, let everyone in your family read it, whatever."

"What would you do with it?"

John's eyes gleamed. "Burn it. But again, that's not my call." He sat back in his seat.

Jackson glanced around the empty room. "Did you pay off that witness?"

"No. I did not."

There was a finality in John's voice that made Jackson believe the other man. He nodded.

"Can I ask you, son? Since this is the last time we'll talk about this. What made you do it? Did he only have to ask?"

Jackson swallowed, and he was back in his mother's bedroom, a scared nineteen-year-old kid. "Yes. But then he made sure I couldn't say no."

"How did he do that?"

Jackson looked into John's kindly blue eyes, the secret bubbling up. The secret only he, Paul, and their mother had known. The secret Sadia could truly never know. "I can't tell you."

"Fair enough. What's the other reason?"

Jackson rubbed his forehead, the conversation moving too quickly. "What?"

"What's the other reason you can't stay here?"

"I—I just can't."

"Then why are you here at all?"

He pressed his lips together tightly. "I came for Livvy. That's all."

"She's not here."

"I'm helping Sadia until Livvy comes back and I can make sure—" He remembered at the last minute that Nicholas was this man's beloved grandson, and out of respect, cut himself off. "Uh, make sure she's okay."

"That's the only reason you're here? Out of obligation?" John shook his head. "Do you know who you remind me of?"

"My father."

"Oh, no. Not your father or your grandfather, actually. Your grandmother's older brother."

Jackson had never met Sam's wife, Lea. His grandmother had died when Tani was young. "I didn't know she had an older brother."

"She didn't like to talk about him much. And I'm afraid I was always so busy telling you kids about Sam that I didn't give Lea enough screen time. I should have."

Jackson settled deeper into the sofa. When he was young, there had been nothing he'd loved more than listening to John's stories.

"When Sam was in that internment camp in Utah, Lea and her brother were sent to a place in Arizona. Michael was a quiet boy, like you. A baker, as well. Sam learned that cookie recipe from him." John's lips turned down. "Michael didn't think they'd have to be held there for long, that everything would get sorted out. It didn't. So he grew convinced he only had to prove his loyalty to the government. He signed up for the army as soon as it was permitted."

Jackson placed the journal in his lap, hating that he knew where this was going. "He died overseas."

"No. No. Took a bullet in the leg and came back home." John's frown deepened. "But he was different. Disillusioned. He shut down. Isolated himself. And eventually, he killed himself."

Jackson had to swallow. "I never went to war, and I'm not suicidal."

"Oh, of course not. I don't mean to minimize either of those things, either. But you were hurt, weren't you? Deeply hurt. So you powered your-self down so you wouldn't be hurt anymore by the people you love."

Jackson stared at him. He couldn't speak.

John nodded, like he knew. "It's worth it to power yourself back on, Jackson. Trust me."

Those colors in his heart, flickering to life one by one. How good it had felt to tell Maile he loved her. "I can't—"

John raised his hand. "You know, I used to use that word a lot. Can't. Your grandfather broke me of the habit. He used to say, 'Can't or won't, John?' And the answer was almost always won't."

Jackson closed his mouth. He'd heard this saying before, of course, but it rang true suddenly in a way it hadn't before. *Nothing's over 'til you quit.*

"Won't," he admitted softly.

"Because you're scared. Nothing wrong with protecting yourself, son, unless you get to a point where you're actually hurting yourself."

The room had grown steadily darker, but they hadn't turned on the lights. Maybe it was the gath-ering dusk, or the comfort of sitting in this room again, with this man, but Jackson confessed his deepest fear. "I don't think I know how to love anyone. Not anymore."

"You haven't loved anyone since you left here?"

He was about to say no, but then he thought about Ariel. The team he protected, who protected him. He couldn't deny that he felt something for them. "Not like I did before," he finally responded.

"Well, son. You don't just decide to love and suddenly everything is fine. Love takes practice. Love isn't passive, it's active. A verb." His hand pressed over Jackson's on top of the journal. "Your past is scary. I understand you were hurt. Facing it is painful, but it could be worth it. For you and for the people you love."

"This is all a . . . lot." And he'd grown used to shoving things aside so he wouldn't have to think about them too deeply. He'd lived in the present. Gotten through each day one at a time, never daring to look back.

John released him. "Go on then. Go home and think about things for a bit. Maybe you could come back and we could talk some more."

His tone was so hopeful, Jackson didn't have the heart to disappoint him. All of these people wanting to see him again. It was so weird. "Maybe."

"You heard Livvy and Nicholas are coming back tomorrow?"

"Yes."

John's smile was faint. "You don't sound happy about it."

"I'm happy Livvy will be home."

"I understand your animosity toward Nicholas. But you know his father put some pressure on him back then to end the relationship, right?"

"He was a grown man. He could have resisted the pressure."

"He could have. But at the time, despite his faults, Nicholas trusted his father. He believed the man would harm his sister. He is and always has been a protective brother."

Jackson shifted, not liking to think he and Nicholas had a single damn thing in common.

"Can you imagine that Jackson? Can you imagine doing something that hurts you to your very core because you care about another person so much?"

His eye twitched. "Well played."

"Nicholas has changed. So have the circumstances. I believe he adores your sister. I think this is the healing step we need. As a family."

"We're not a family."

It was the cruelest thing he could say to John, but the man kept that tiny smile on his face. "We haven't been, in a long time. But if your sister and Nicholas can make things work this time around, we could be."

"That was always your dream, wasn't it? No one was happier when the two of them started dating all those years ago."

John shrugged. "Can you blame me? Uniting the families would take care of a great deal of problems."

"Except there's no families to unite anymore."

John's eyes were sad. "That doesn't have to be the case."

Love is active.

Goddamn it. "I'll try not to punch him in the face when I see him." Again.

"Can't ask for more than that."

Chapter 13

He was back.

Tucked away in another booth at O'Killian's, with his baseball cap pulled low, big body hunched over like there was a chance in hell he could be invisible. This shouldn't be like it was two weeks ago. Knowledge of his identity should dampen Sadia's desire, but that wasn't what was happening.

She might not be sex-starved, but could she be Jackson-starved?

Her brain immediately shied away from that thought. It implied she'd held some sort of seething desire for Jackson. Which was ridiculous. She was quite capable of being friends with someone and not wanting to have sex with them. Hell, Livvy was gorgeous, and she'd never entertained the thought of kissing her.

Once, only once had she considered Jackson in a non-platonic way, and it had been the night he'd taken her as a pity date to their junior prom. She'd been so swoony over how romantic and handsome he'd looked in his perfectly tailored tux and the red rose corsage he'd gotten her, she'd kissed him on his cheek when he dropped her off at home.

But nothing had ever come of those silly stirrings, and not long after, she'd fallen hard and fast for Paul.

Right now, though, her heart was accelerating, her palms growing damp. She wanted nothing more than to walk over there and not know who he was and hand him a drink. Flirt. Take him to a hotel.

Right place, right time. Wrong man.

"Is something wrong?"

She smiled automatically at the blonde in front of her. She'd had a one-night stand with the pretty woman a few weeks ago. The girl traveled a lot for work, and she wasn't from here. "Nope."

The woman leaned forward, her breasts plumping up. Sadia would have normally spared a glance. "You look preoccupied." She tipped her head. "Stressful day?"

Sadia knew the woman was saying that as a precursor to offering to relieve that stress, but she couldn't work up the interest right now.

Argh. Mentally, she kissed her chances of getting laid tonight goodbye. There was no way she'd be able to find anyone else attractive when her brain was so terribly focused on Jackson.

She finished assembling the drink and placed it in front of the woman with a kind smile. "I'm fine, thanks. Hope you have a great night."

The woman accepted the drink and the gentle decline of companionship with a rueful wink. "You too."

Sadia wiped down the bar to give herself something to do. Monday nights were rarely very busy, unfortunately.

Her body felt tingly, like every nerve ending was exposed and alive. She knew he was watching her, but every time she glanced up, his head was averted.

He wasn't imagining her naked or thinking about the fact that he'd tucked her into bed last night. He hadn't relived their kiss a million times in the past week.

Except he had returned that kiss.

The little devil on her shoulder cackled. *That means he's interested in you, you should probably have lots of sex with him. Lots of it. Until you're weak and can't move and sweat's dripping down your body and maybe you're aching in all those secret, dirty places.*

She blew out a breath. Nope.

She'd go say hi, and that was that. Jackson being here was no different than him being in her home. Either way, he was utterly unsuitable for her short-term needs.

She contemplated her liquors. Finally she settled on a bottle of gin.

Her heart beat was so loud when she approached him, she feared he could hear it. His head lifted slowly.

She placed the drink in front of him. "This was created by one of the first woman bartenders in the country, pre-Prohibition." Sadia wiped her hands on her apron.

"What's it called?"

She could feel her cheeks turning red. "Hanky Panky. They, um, had interesting names for drinks back then."

"They did." He took a sip, then another one. "It's good. I can't drink much, but it's good."

"Alcohol still gives you a bad reaction, huh?" For all that she loved bartending, Sadia wasn't much of a drinker. Jackson wasn't either. He'd never managed to have more than a couple of beers without getting sick.

"Very much so." He drummed his fingers on the table and it was then that she noted the strain around his mouth. Libido temporarily dampened, she leaned against the table, concern filling her. "What's wrong?"

He shook his head, his eyes shifting. "Nothing."

"Something's wrong."

"You know me so well?"

"I do." As she said the words, she felt that kick of relief, of connection at knowing someone so well. This was one thing she couldn't get from her bar conquests, this familiarity.

He pulled off his baseball cap and placed it on the table, raking his hand through the short strands. "I saw John today."

"Oh."

He twisted the glass around. "You didn't look in that bag he gave you, right?"

"No. He told me not to."

He took another sip of his drink. "You're a woman of your word."

"I was honestly busy."

"It was only my grandfather's journal."

She'd seen Sam's journal before. She didn't think having it would wind Jackson up like this. "Do you want to talk about it?"

Before he could answer, she got hailed by her fellow bartender. She raised her hand. "I'll be right back."

AFTER HE'D left John's house, Jackson had dropped Paul's letter and his grandfather's journal off in his apartment and then driven around aimlessly for a while, trying to sort the chaos in his brain. He finally found himself pulling into O'Killian's. He told himself it was because he wanted a drink, but truth be told, he wasn't much of a drinker.

No, he wanted to see Sadia. That was it.

He assumed he'd sit in a corner booth, order a ginger ale, and sneak glances at her, the same as he had before she'd spotted him a week ago. Oddly enough, it wasn't that satisfying this time around. Maybe it was because he'd realized how good it felt to do more than watch her. To be with her again. Touch her.

Kiss her.

He watched her walk away. She was poured into a skintight black shirt and pants that cradled every curve of her body.

A plain cotton T-shirt shouldn't be so sexy, but she'd ripped the collar and the ragged hem of her V-neck pointed straight down to the shadowy valley between her breasts. He wanted to push the fabric aside and lick the mound, down the valley. He wanted to know what color bra she had on today. Was it lace? Cotton? Satin? Red?

His gaze dropped to her ass, but someone blocked his view and he had to bite back a sound like a wounded bear.

Did he want to talk about John? No, not really. He felt off-kilter and jacked up, filled with a buzzing anxious energy. But the thought of talking made him want to claw at his eyes.

He took another sip of his drink. It was loud in the place, and he felt anonymous, the same way he did whenever he was in some big foreign city. No one here was looking at him. He was free to watch Sadia and the ease with which she interacted with the patrons.

I started bartending downtown today as a way to pick up some extra cash. Paul said I should be a waitress at the café if I wanted to work in service so badly, but I can't imagine working and living together. I mean, I love the guy, but I'd kill him.

Besides, I like bartending so far! My boss said I'm good at it, and it's kind of like chemistry or cooking, but I'm better at it than I was at either of those things. Plus, I get to meet all sorts of interesting people.

Jackson studied his drink. She'd talked about O'Killian's a lot after that, until Kareem was born, and she'd stopped. He'd assumed that meant she'd decided to stay at home with him instead of continuing.

She was good at this. Not only at the mixing drinks, but at smiling and talking with each guest like she cared. He'd worked with enough bartenders to know that the successful ones were genuinely interested in people.

He didn't realize he'd finished the drink until he was frowning at the empty glass. He was about to ask Sadia for another one, but someone clapped him on the shoulder, making him jump.

He swiveled his head, and came face to face with a couple of guys he vaguely recognized from high school. They were blond and handsome enough, in the preppy, posh way a lot of people he'd grown up with had been.

Most kids had fallen into two camps. They'd either recognized the Kane's wealth and power and cozied up to the family, or they'd hated them for it. Even the ones in the first camp had mostly ignored or mocked Jackson, though. He'd been far too weird for them.

"Holy shit," one of them said. "Jackson? I thought it was you, but Eric couldn't believe it." The man beamed. "It's me, Zach."

He stared at them blankly, hoping they would take it as a clue that he truly didn't want to talk. His fingers twitched next to his baseball cap, but it was too late for disguises now.

At his continued silence, Zach's smile disappeared. "Slumming it tonight like us, huh?"

Jackson glanced around the bar. It wasn't the nicest place, but they were exaggerating. "It's not a slum."

Eric leaned against the table. Jackson had always disliked him more. "Well, not for you, I suppose."

Ah yes. Jackson hadn't stuck around to watch but the other moderately wealthy people in town had surely seen the fall of the Oka-Kane's fortunes with barely concealed glee. Tani had never socialized much but how had Paul stood it?

Don't think about Paul.

Anyway, Jackson was certain he had more money in his bank account than either of these fools, but he also had nothing to prove.

Zach cleared his throat. "Your sister-in-law works here, right? Man, your brother was lucky. She's hot."

Eric nudged Zach. "We should go say hi."

A flash of anger ran through him at these men so much as thinking about Sadia. "Or you could not."

Zach's eyes flashed, like he scented blood in the water. Sharks, yes. Cold-blooded, waiting for their chance. "Now, now. We just wanted to come over and say hi. No need to take any offense, jailbird."

Before he could answer, a shadow fell over all of them. "Now that you've said hi, you can head on out, boys. I'm about to have a drink with my friend here."

A muscular man with dark auburn hair and a

matching beard nudged them aside and slid into the other side of the booth, placing a half-finished beer on the table. He was dressed casually, in a flannel shirt and ripped jeans. He gave them all a big smile, the laugh lines around his eyes crinkling.

"Well, well," Zach said snidely. "If it isn't the charity case, here to save the weirdo. Feels like high school all over again."

Gabriel Hunter's smile grew bigger, and Jackson wondered if the two idiots standing next to the table could sense the edge of menace in the friendly expression. Gabe had been their housekeeper's son, but he'd attended school with them, had been a year ahead of Paul and Nicholas.

Gabe cocked his head. "If it was high school again, I'd be kicking your ass outside, Zachary."

Jackson had had enough. There was a reason he'd never gotten along with many men—these absurd power plays were too foolish. He straightened to his full height and stopped hunching. Even sitting, he was easily bigger than Zach. And Eric. Combined. "The weirdo doesn't need defending," he said flatly. "You two should head on out of here, since you're so tired of *slumming* it." *And never ever talk to Sadia.*

Eric opened his mouth, but Zach took measure of him, and hustled his friend away.

He and Gabe were left alone. Jackson half-expected Gabe to get up and leave, but the man leaned back against the padded seat, his grin turning genuine. "Jackson, son of a bitch. Jesus, look at you. You're the spitting image of your brother."

Jackson barely refrained from cringing. He and Paul had used to joke about that. His brother would grab him in a headlock. *Just 'cause we're the same height and color everyone thinks you and I are twins.*

Especially that witness, outside the C&O that night. He'd definitely mistaken the two of them.

"How are you doing?"

"Good, thanks." He was genuinely happy to see Gabe, but he'd give anything to get out of this conversation. Small talk. Kill him. "You?"

"Fantastic." Gabe hooked his thumb over his shoulder at a table. "I'm waiting for my sister, she's visiting. She made an app. Lives in San Fran now."

"That's great." Jackson wrapped his hand around the empty glass. "And your mother? How's she?"

Fondness softened Gabe's face. Mrs. Hunter had been their housekeeper from before Jackson was born. She'd been a kind, no-nonsense woman who had run their large household with brutal efficiency. "Good. Travels a lot, likes to see the world. She's in Chicago right now."

"Great." He cast around for something more to say. He and Gabe had grown up together, but the man had been closer in age to Nicholas and Paul, so the three of them had naturally hung out together more. Unlike a lot of people, Gabe had never been snide or frightened of Jackson.

Not quite a friend, because he hadn't had many of those, but not an enemy either. Gabe had been in California when Robert had died, but he'd flown back for the funeral. Jackson had wondered once or twice what had happened to their lifelong housekeeper after Tani had sold their big house and downsized. He was glad things had worked out for her.

"I didn't know you were in town," Gabe said.

"Yeah. I heard Livvy's been working at your place?"

"She's amazing. People come from all over to get ink from her. A few weeks ago, a guy flew up from D.C."

His chest inflated with pride. He'd always been proud of Livvy, merely for surviving, but it had been a while since anyone had related her accomplishments to him.

"I guess she's back together with Nicholas though, huh?" Gabe shook his head. "Man, that stunt he pulled for her. Life works out in weird ways, I guess. Good for them."

At some point, he might want to know exactly what amazing thing Nicholas had done in order to seduce his sister back into his web. Later, maybe, when and if the man actually proved himself to Jackson. "You still know Nicholas well then?"

Gabe's smile was bittersweet. "No. I haven't talked to him in years. I got Paul in that custody battle."

"There was a custody battle?"

"After what happened? Sure." Gabe braced his hand on the table. "Lines were drawn. I don't think Nicholas would have minded, but you know how Paul was. If you were his, you were his alone. Besides, it would have been strange, talking to one without the other. I was one of the few mutuals who didn't also work for C&O—uh, Chandler's—so it wasn't such a hard decision for me."

He'd forgotten how much Gabe . . . talked. "I see."

"I'm sorry about Paul's passing. It's still hard to believe for me. I can't imagine what it's like for you."

Jackson spun his empty glass around in a circle. Friends they might have been, but clearly they hadn't been close enough for Paul to tell Gabe that he never spoke to his little brother. Or why. "Yes." What was the proper response to an expression of condolence? He'd been too grief-stricken to remember what had happened in the aftermath of his father's funeral, and no one had consoled him for Paul before. "Thank you."

Gabe blew out a breath, looking away for a second, thick eyebrows knitted. When he looked back, his smile was sunny. Kind. "So how long are you going to be here for?"

"Not long."

Gabe cast a glance behind the bar. "You're hanging out with Sadia?"

There was no judgment in the question, but still Jackson stiffened. "Uh, yes."

"Good. I've tried to stop by and see her every now and again, and she seems wound tight. More family couldn't hurt."

Family. Family didn't think about each other the way he thought about Sadia. They definitely didn't run their hands all over each other the way he wanted to run his hands all over her. "Right."

"Are you drinking here alone? Do you want to join me and my sister? She'd love to see you."

"Uh." The hair on the back of his neck stood up. He shot a look at the bar to find Sadia's dark eyes on him. They were assessing. He turned back to Gabe. "No, I should . . . uh." This was why he didn't talk to people. He never knew how to turn them down or end a conversation without seeming abrupt or rude.

"Gabe, hi." A feminine voice came from next to him, and suddenly Sadia was there, next to his elbow. She'd taken off her apron.

"Sadia!" Gabe came to his feet and pulled her in for a hug. It was a platonic hug, but seeing the man's tattooed, muscular arms around the smaller Sadia made Jackson's stomach clench. "How's my favorite bartender doing?"

"How many bars do you go to that you have a favorite bartender?" Sadia pulled back.

"Too many. Don't tell my mama." Gabe beamed at him. "You know why this place is so busy, right? Word's got around about Sadia and her famous cocktails."

Sadia rolled her eyes. "Not famous."

"She gives the history of every drink she serves. It's the cutest damn thing."

Jackson waited for Sadia to blush, but she merely looked tolerantly amused at the heavy-handed flirtation. "I have a few old mixology books. Might as well use them."

"How's Kareem?" Gabe gave Jackson a conspiratorial smile. "Isn't that kid a firecracker?"

Jackson froze, but he didn't answer because Sadia was speaking. "He's fine. I'm not, thanks to that annoying drum set you got him."

Gabe sniffed. "It's an honorary uncle's job to spoil his nephew."

Jackson stiffened further. He was the kid's real uncle, and he hadn't spoiled the boy. He could have bought Kareem stuff from all over the world.

He'd thought about it. Sometimes he'd see something pint-sized and be tempted, but he'd always left the store empty-handed.

"Try to spoil him with something quieter next time," Sadia said dryly, and turned to Jackson. "I'm sorry to interrupt your reunion, but Jackson, can you give me a hand with a box in the back?"

Jackson nodded eagerly. He never turned down a socially acceptable exit. "Yes. Sure."

"Nice to see you, Gabe. Give your sister and mother my love," Sadia said.

"Nice to see you too." Gabe grinned at Jackson. "If you ever want to grab a drink while you're in town, I'd like that."

There was nothing but sincerity in the other man's voice. Jackson dipped his head. "Uh, thanks."

He followed Sadia past the crowded bar and into the back hallway, which also happened to be crowded. She bit her lip, cast a glance over her shoulder, and crooked her finger. "This way."

He grew confused as she wound around between the people and through the back door. They stepped out of the building, the cool air slapping him in the face. The door to the building clanged closed behind him. "What did you need help with?"

"Nothing. I'm on my break. You looked like you needed one too." Her hand disappeared into her pocket and she pulled out a cigarette, handing it to him. He accepted it, surprised. "My co-worker smokes. You've been wound tight since you walked in and you didn't exactly look comfortable with Gabe."

Jackson rolled the cigarette between his fingers, both confused and touched. How had she known? He'd thought he was so subtle. "I quit smoking." He broke the cigarette in two and stuffed it in his pocket, to toss later.

"Since when?"

Since he'd realized it aggravated her asthma, but he couldn't tell her that. "I've been meaning to quit for a while."

"Hmm." She tucked her fingers into her jean pockets and leaned against the door.

He cautiously braced himself against the brick wall next to her. They stood there in silence for a while, the muted music and conversation carrying out to the alleyway. Slowly, the tension eased from his shoulders. He could shelve worrying about his brother and that letter and John and his mother and Livvy for now.

This was what he had come looking for. No one was as good as Sadia when it came to calming him down. She knew what to say and more importantly, what not to say, how to be silent and give him time to process and think things through.

She'd always been able to read him, better than his twin, even.

She stirred. "Gabe's been good to me, since Paul died. Always stopping by. He and Paul were fairly tight. But I know he can be a bit much."

"Gabe wants to be my friend."

"If it helps, Gabe wants to be everyone's friend. He's like a puppy. A large, tattooed, flannel-wearing puppy."

"That doesn't make me feel better. I don't understand wanting to be everyone's friend at all."

"It's an extrovert thing, or so I understand."

"Anyway, thanks for the assist. I'm not good at ending conversations."

A faint smile played around her lips. "I remember. You were never really great at starting or continuing them either."

"He saved me from talking to those other guys though."

She wrinkled her nose. "I was busy with customers or I would have rescued you from them, too. Ugh. What are their names? Eamon? Zeke?"

His mood lightened. "Eric and Zach."

"Whatever. Most of the bros we went to high school with were all the same."

"They asked me if I was slumming it."

She snorted. "Did you tell them that if the place was good enough for the Banksy of restauranteurs it was good enough for them?"

His cheeks heated. A reporter had come up with that name, and he'd immediately hated it. He wasn't an artist. "You googled me."

"About five seconds after you told me what you did. You're a big deal."

"Nah."

"You travel the world being a famous chef and a crusader for human rights."

Jackson scowled. He cooked and pitched in as a large warm body when the occasion required it. "Don't make it sound more glamorous than it is."

"Now I wish you had responded to my emails, so I could have lived vicariously through you. You must have had so many adventures."

He shot her a quick look, gauging if she was angry or being sarcastic, but she really only looked bemused. "Do you want to travel?"

"Yes. I went to Pakistan and England when I was young, but my parents hadn't wanted to juggle five kids through multiple international trips. The domestic ones were chaotic enough."

"Why don't you travel now?"

"Money."

"That's the only reason?"

She lifted a shoulder. "I mean, I'd need someone trustworthy to watch the café. But yes. It's the money."

"I'd give you money."

He made the offer casually, and she received it in kind. "Thanks. But no. I'm not taking your money."

"Proud."

"You know it." She shrugged. "Tell me about your travels sometime. That'll be enough for now. Google can only give me so much information about you."

He imagined telling her about all the places he'd been and seen. It should have exhausted him, the thought of all that talking, but instead he experienced a sense of excitement. He wanted to tell her. He wanted to see the world again through her eyes. "Will you tell me everything about you that I missed?"

She scraped her foot over the concrete. "You know what you missed. I was writing to you."

She didn't sound as bitter over those unanswered emails as she had before. "Those gave me the outline of your life. You could fill in the details. I don't know everything about you, do I?"

"What you see is what you get."

"Somehow I doubt that."

The air turned taut. "What do you want to know?"

He inched closer. His eyes had adjusted enough to see her, but they were in darkness here, the bulb above the back door burnt out, the light from the street only illuminating a small triangle in the alley. "Whatever you want to tell me."

She inhaled. "I don't want to shock you."

"I doubt I would be shocked."

She snorted. "You say that now."

"I mean it."

Her eyes were unreadable. "What do you think of when you look at me, Jackson?"

Perfection. "I see a remarkable woman."

She went still. "What?"

Had he said the wrong thing again?

She stepped closer. "Say that again."

"I see a woman?" he said, this time with a

question, because he wasn't sure what she wanted from him.

She opened her mouth, but a high-pitched laugh interrupted them. Jackson moved instinctively to shove her behind him at the perceived threat, but he needn't have bothered.

It was only a man and woman, both tipsy, judging by the way they tumbled into the alley from the street. Jackson tensed, ready to intervene if something was amiss between the couple, but the woman shoved the man up against the wall and plastered herself on him. "Kiss me." Her voice carried easily along the fall breeze.

"Gladly," the man muttered, and then their lips were locked. It was messy and crude and graceless.

It was exactly how he wanted to kiss Sadia. Full-on, open-mouthed, tongue rubbing against hers.

The man was tall and muscular, the woman curvy and half his size, but she held him against the wall easily. Her blond hair gleamed in the moonlight as he tunneled his hands through it, gripping the strands.

She gasped and tilted her head back so he could kiss his way down. Her neck arched and she looked directly at him and Sadia. Jackson's muscles tightened. Sadia was behind him and therefore hidden, and they were standing in enough darkness that his features were most certainly unidentifiable to the couple, but he was poised for anything.

However, the woman gave a throaty laugh instead of a gasp of outrage. "Darling, looks like we're being watched."

The man licked the hollow of her throat. "Do you mind?"

"You know I don't," she said in a loud whisper. "Let them see everything."

Jackson turned his head slightly to look over his shoulder. He expected Sadia to crack a comment about the amorous couple, but she was frozen. Her eyes were wide, locked on the man and woman.

Curiosity. Interest. Lust.

"Do you want to go inside?" he asked quietly.

He waited for her nod, but her lips parted. His arm shifted back and he brushed his pinky over hers.

Slowly she turned her hand and rested her palm against his. Her body came closer, so she was pressed against his back, her breasts flattened against him.

His breathing stuttered. "Do you want to watch?"

Now. Now she would say no. But instead, this time . . . he got a nod.

Heaven help them both.

He turned his head back to face front. Once when he was in Vienna, he'd gone to a party that had swiftly turned into an orgy. He hadn't participated. But he liked to see everything, process it, turn it over in his own brain, so with permission, he'd sat and watched. It had been the most erotic experience of his life, though no one had touched him.

It *had* been. Watching this random couple kissing with Sadia's hungry gaze on them was going to probably top that.

Watching anything more than a kiss . . . he didn't know if he'd be able to survive.

But he was about to find out.

The man twisted and pressed the woman against the brick wall, his fingers dancing over the back of her neck and the tie to her halter dress. With one tug, the fabric fell, and she was topless, her firm breasts and pink nipples exposed to the night air.

The blood rushed to Jackson's cock. Sadia's breasts were larger. Were her nipples as big? Were they a light brown color, or a darker shade?

The man dipped his head and took the nipple in his mouth, and Jackson rubbed his thumb over his own lips. He wanted to do that. Open wide and swallow as much of Sadia as he humanly could. He wanted to own her nipples, make it so she never felt anybody or anything but him.

The woman cradled the man's head to her breast and tipped her head back, her breath coming in deep sighs. "Fuck me," she whispered.

The man kissed his way up her neck, licking and sucking, while he jerked at the fastening of his pants.

He grabbed the woman's leg, hoisting it up to his waist. The fall of her dress hid them from view, but Jackson could tell by their matching groans when he pushed inside of her.

A brush of sensation came against his palm. Sadia's finger, stroking up and down, mimicking the man's body.

It was only her finger and he had to close his eyes, fearful he might embarrass himself.

"Jackson," she whispered, and there went his resolve. He'd never heard her whisper his name like that, needy and wanting.

"Yes," he whispered back.

"I need something."

As always, he was helpless to not give her what she desired. "What do you need?"

The anonymous woman's cries were swallowed by the music and the crowd inside. The man started fucking her in earnest, his hips moving like a piston back and forth, her bare breasts jiggling.

Sadia's other hand coasted up his arm, leaving fire in its wake. "It's wrong, what I need."

Yearning. "Nothing's wrong."

"Yes, this is. It's wrong."

He kept facing forward, fearful of breaking this sultry, seductive spell. He was bouncing from cushion to cushion again, trying to stay off the lava on the floor. That lava would hurt him. "Tell me."

"You said I was perfect, and I'm not."

He *had* said the wrong thing to her, earlier tonight. How to explain she was perfect to him?

"I've tried to be perfect. I've worked really hard at it, and never really quite succeeded. Tried to be the best mom and the best wife and the best daughter and . . . I never get to be . . . average old me."

He was fascinated despite his raging arousal. He hadn't seen Sadia display this glimpse of vulnerability since they were young.

Average? Ha. She was so beyond average.

Her laugh was razor sharp. "I was going to pick someone up tonight to screw. I've done it before. I only do it here, at the bar, where I can find people who don't know me. Where I can take an hour or so and indulge my needs while my son is safe and taken care of." Her chest rose and fell against his back. She rested her chin on his shoulder and her breath tickled her ear. "What do you think of that? Are you shocked?"

He was aroused. He shook his head.

"What if . . ." Her words were almost a whisper. "What if I said I've been thinking about doing things with you?"

Jackson had been punched a time or two, right in the chest. That's what this felt like, like someone had slammed their fist into his solar plexus, knocking the air out of him.

What did he say? He wanted to give her everything and anything.

Because you love her.

The realization didn't come on him like a thunder clap, but with a gentle whisper, because the love had always been there, lurking under the surface, even if he'd been terrified of verbalizing it.

He'd lied to himself. He hadn't traded his heart in for a black-and-white model, he'd just unplugged the cord. Coming back home had plugged it back in, and now each color was flickering alive one by one.

Love is an addiction.

She had only said she wanted him, not loved him, but this . . . this changed everything. Because even if she never loved him, now he could give her something no one else could.

Fuck waiting and lingering and brooding. *Love is active.*

Adrenaline and exhilaration ran through him.

They were healthy and single and consenting, and except for their own baggage, there was no reason for them not to lust after one another. Or love each other for that matter, but right now, he'd deal with the lust she'd admitted to.

He released her hand and turned around. He grasped her waist and backed her up against the door.

"Jackson, I want to—"

"Shh." It took a second to hoist her up his body, mirroring the other couple in the alley. She automatically locked her legs around his waist and he groaned at the way his body nestled into the cradle of hers. "You want to get off." His voice was low and guttural. She deserved hearts and flowers, not crassness, but all she had was him, and he was crass.

She whimpered.

"What have you thought about doing with me?" He had to know.

The woman's cries rose, punctuated by the man's grunts and the slap of flesh on flesh. Sadia's cheeks darkened, her gaze darting between him and the scene over his shoulder.

"Like that?" He rocked his hips, so she could grind against his dick. "Have you thought of me fucking you like that?"

"Yes," she whispered. "I've used my vibrator and imagined it was your cock inside me."

He almost came, right then and there. "Use me like she's using him," he murmured. "Use me like you'd use whoever else you'd planned to pick up tonight."

"What do you mean?"

He didn't tell her, but showed her, moving his hips in a circle. In the darkness, her gasp joined the chorus of ecstasy behind them.

"Oh don't stop. You're so big," the other woman moaned, and Sadia's eyes locked on him. She rubbed herself against him and nodded, as if she were agreeing. The zipper of his fly might leave an imprint on his dick, he was so hard.

He pressed his palm over her ass and used his grip to slowly move her up and down. The woman's voice cried out behind him, and he rocked Sadia harder, savoring the dazed pleasure in her face. He wanted their clothes gone and their bodies bare. He wanted to shove himself inside her, hard and deep.

He couldn't do that, not here in this alley, but he could give her something. "Come on my cock," he murmured, and adjusted his grip so he was pressing tighter against her, his entire body tense with the need to fuck her. He pressed his lips against hers, and nothing about this kiss resembled their lip lock on the stairs last week. That had been a tentative, exploratory kiss. This was so she'd have a place to scream. She came shuddering in his arms, as the woman behind them cried out in orgasmic bliss.

He left her lips slowly, regretting that they wouldn't have more time right now to talk, and . . . well, whatever people did during a seduction, but he didn't want either of them spotted or recognized by the couple. He released her so her legs dropped from around his waist. His cock was nearly bent double, but he'd take care of it later. "Go inside." He kissed her on her forehead.

Her breath was still coming too fast to talk. She stared up at him with dark, troubled eyes. He tried to head off her panic. "Don't stress about this. It's not a big deal. I'll see you tomorrow."

He gave her a push when she didn't seem in a rush to move, and she finally budged, scurrying inside, casting confused looks over her shoulder.

He braced his hands on his hips, keeping his back to the couple until they stumbled away, laughing. He hadn't felt this good in a long time.

He'd deal with the implications of her having been married to his brother and his complicated history with the man later. Now that he knew she wanted him? Now that he could finally, finally voice his desire for her, even if only in his own head?

He'd have her.

Chapter 14

SADIA'S PARENTS had never allowed her or her sisters to watch much television, so children's programming had been something she'd had to sneak when she was a kid. She tried to limit Kareem's television consumption to a healthy amount, but if he watched an extra hour here or there, she didn't mind. Especially if she got to watch it with him.

Sadia pressed a kiss on her son's forehead, inhaling the scent of laundry and little boy. Kareem was snuggled tight next to her. They'd been watching television since he'd come home from school an hour or so ago. She knew at some point she needed to get up and do productive things and have him get started on his homework, but she'd savor this for as long as possible.

She'd never quite appreciated how much she enjoyed staying home with her son until she'd had to rely on her support system of sisters and in-laws to take care of him while she worked. Sometimes she found herself becoming jealous of the people who got to see Kareem when she couldn't.

And her ability to stay at home now was due solely to the six-foot-plus slab of muscle currently working in her café.

How could she have told Jackson that she wanted to have sex with him? Or that she regularly picked people up at the bar and banged them at all?

How could he have reacted like he did? Accepting, eager? His reaction—and the orgasm he'd given her—had ensured she'd slipped into a dreamless sleep last night after she'd come home. After staring at his dark apartment for a while.

She'd woken up this morning determined to avoid Jackson until death. Positive reaction notwithstanding, she didn't know how she could ever look at him again without her face catching on fire.

He hadn't let her ignore him. From the moment she'd walked into her office, he'd forced himself in. First dropping off an apple danish and coffee for breakfast, then an off-menu poke bowl that he'd introduced for lunch—which had, of course, been a big hit.

He hadn't talked much either time, but when he had, his eyes had been warm and he hadn't shied away from touching her. Little touches, on her arm or her shoulder, but each one had sent a wave of excitement through her. So much so that she'd been useless for the hours in between his drop-ins into her office.

It had been a relief to escape the café and go pick up her son.

Kareem pressed his face against her side, as if he

could tell she was growing agitated. She and Paul had somehow managed to raise the most empathetic little boy.

The doorbell rang, and she looked down at Kareem. "Were you expecting someone?"

He took her seriously and shook his head. She got up. "Let's see who it is then."

When she opened the door, she could only stare.

Livvy gave her a sheepish smile. Her best friend and former sister-in-law was dressed in laced-up combat boots, frayed jeans, and a pink button-down. Her hair was vivid blue now and pulled on top of her head in a messy bun. Livvy had always favored a punk goth look, which had somehow never failed to look perfectly appropriate on her tiny frame.

Sadia crossed her arms over her chest, so she wouldn't give in to her automatic urge to hug her friend. She couldn't help it. She was still annoyed Livvy hadn't said one word about her affair with a man they'd grown up with. Not to mention her running off without so much as a phone call. "Well, well, well—"

"Hey, Aunt Livvy." Kareem shouldered around her and gave his aunt a sweet smile. "Mom said you went on a vacation. Did you get me anything?"

"Kareem," she scolded. He was far too used to her sisters spoiling him with presents whenever they traveled.

Livvy squinted. "Um, as a matter of fact . . ."

Livvy reached into her bag and rummaged for a second before she pulled out a pack of gum with an air of triumph.

Kareem looked down at the half-finished pack of gum, then up at Sadia. "I like gum."

She sighed. "You can have it."

He snatched it from his aunt before she could finish speaking. Objective achieved, he turned to run away, back to the T.V. "What do you say?" she prompted him.

"Thanks, Aunt Livvy."

After he ran off, she pursed her lips at Livvy. "I'm pissed at you."

"You should be." Livvy nodded so hard her blue bun wobbled. "I'm so sorry."

Sadia dropped her voice. "I can't believe you kept the fact that Nicholas and you were seeing each other from me. I'm your best friend. Even your mother and aunt knew, and I was totally in the dark. And, and! You left without telling me anything about where you were going. I had to rely on getting updates from Mom and Maile. Every gossip in this town has been asking me what's going on with you."

Livvy bit her lip and Sadia almost relented. Almost, but not quite, because she was still annoyed as fuck.

"My mom and aunt don't know everything."

Sadia sniffed. "Don't think I'll forgive you because you give me exclusive dirt."

"Okay, but . . . Nicholas and I have been seeing

each other for a decade. We'd get together on my birthday every year."

Sadia stared at her for a second, and then opened the door wider. "Do you want coffee or tea?"

A half-hour later, the two of them sat in silence after Livvy finished relating the somewhat abbreviated saga about her and Nicholas.

"Huh," Sadia finally said. Her affronted outrage had dissipated quickly, replaced by fascination.

Jia was right. The Kanes and Chandlers really were like a soap opera.

Livvy linked her hands around the mug and leaned forward. "I really am sorry I didn't tell you. I didn't tell anyone . . . Mom and Aunt Maile just found out. I didn't know how to talk about Nicholas. He was my dirty secret for so long."

"Don't worry about it. We're cool. How are things between the two of you now?"

Livvy's eyes glimmered. "I think . . . pretty good? It's too soon to tell, but we've spent every spare moment over the past couple weeks talking things through."

"Do you think you'll stay here?" She tried to not inject her own desire into that question. More than anything, she wanted Livvy within driving distance. She'd always been in Sadia's pocket, there at the push of a button, but nothing beat having Livvy close at hand.

"For now. Nicholas is figuring out his work stuff and I'm tired of traveling so much."

Sadia nodded. Paul had always been a little

jealous of how both his siblings had ditched everything and roamed the world. If she was totally honest, Sadia had been too. She'd always dreamed of having the freedom to travel and see the world and have some adventures. Flying far and having the security of knowing she had a home and roots waiting for her for whenever she was ready to go back.

"What happens if you get restless?"

Livvy's lips twisted. "I didn't travel because I was restless. I traveled because I was trying to find . . . I don't know. A home?" She rested her hand on the kitchen table. "Some place I belonged with people who belonged to me."

"You always had me," Sadia said gruffly.

"I know." Livvy's eyes were shiny. She sat back and picked up her mug. "So what's up with you?"

Nothing much.

Same old, same old.

Working a lot.

All acceptable responses. So she was shocked by what came out of her mouth. "I made out with your brother."

Livvy didn't bat an eye. "I assumed you created Kareem some way, but I'd rather not think about it, thanks."

Ugh. In for a penny . . . "Not that brother." Sadia ran her hand through her hair. "Your other brother. Jackson."

Livvy very slowly put her mug back on the table. "Wait. What?"

"I made out with Jackson."

"Hang on." Livvy shook her head. "What?"

Sadia bit her lip. "You're freaking me out."

"I'm freaking *you* out?" Livvy's eyes were so wide, Sadia could see the whites all around the pupils. "Okay okay okay. Let's . . . let's take a minute here. Jackson's still *here*?"

"Oh. You didn't know?"

Agitated, Livvy released her hair from its bun. "No!"

"He's actually, um . . . he's staying with me."

"What?"

"You keep using that word."

Livvy bundled her hair up, and let it fall loose again. "Because you keep surprising me."

"He's helping out at the café and staying above the garage."

"Is he home now?"

"No, at the café."

"How long has this been going on?"

"Since about a week after you left. I needed a chef."

Livvy's nostrils flared. "Jackson's a chef?"

Sadia blew out a breath. "I feel like you need to have a separate talk with him."

"No shit."

Sadia made a mental note to have the bad language talk with Livvy later.

"And you made out with *Jackson?*"

"Shh." Sadia glanced at the open doorway of the kitchen, but the cartoon was still blaring, which meant Kareem was still occupied. "I didn't mean to. Jackson—"

"Whoa, I can't deal with this." Livvy screwed her face up like she'd tasted something vile. "You can't call him Jackson. The only way we can discuss this is if you change his name. Call him, like, Bob."

"That's silly."

"How would you like it if I talked about making out with one of your sisters?"

Ehhhh. Sadia nodded. "Okay, yes, I totally get it when you put it like that. I never really thought about . . . Bob . . . like that before. I don't understand it. It's like he came back and I'm suddenly seeing him in a whole new light." Maybe things would have been different if she hadn't spent a week lusting after him. Like, if he'd just walked up and knocked on her door instead of lurking in her bar.

She thought about his body and hands and knew that was false.

Livvy's lips turned down, but she admitted, "Bob does come from rather attractive genes. You really never felt anything for him before?"

"I felt lots of things for him, but they weren't sexual. I was with Paul."

"Let's call him Carl."

Sadia rolled her eyes, but she played along. "I was dating Carl, and then I was married to him. I couldn't have been attracted to his brother at the same time. That's . . . terrible. I'm not built like that."

"Okay but Paul's been gone for over a year, Sadia. You're not betraying him by hooking up with Jackson."

Since Livvy had dropped the silly aliases, Sadia did too. She puffed out her cheeks, debating whether she should tell her friend everything. After another glance at the door, she leaned forward and spoke even more quietly. "Paul and I were separated before he died."

"Oh."

"That's why he went on that hike alone. We always went on our anniversary, and you know what a creature of habit he could be. Even though that trail isn't meant for solo hikers—" She cut herself off. She couldn't bear to think of Paul dying on the trail they'd climbed together. She didn't want to imagine what his final hours had been like.

They said he'd fallen, that his injuries had been too severe, and he'd died instantly. She still couldn't quite believe that. Paul had been so sure-footed.

Livvy made a sympathetic noise. "I'm sorry."

"No one knew. It made things complicated. I still grieved for him."

"Of course you did. You should have told me, if only so I could help you."

"I didn't want to put you between me and Paul."

"Saint Sadia," Livvy said, with affection.

Sadia sighed. "Not a saint."

"You gotta look out for yourself too, sister." Livvy rested her hand on hers. Sadia turned her palm up so their fingers could link. "It's okay for you to feel however you feel about Paul dying and your marriage and kissing other people now."

"I wasn't conflicted about kissing anyone new until Jackson."

"And why him?"

"Because our history is so complicated, I suppose."

"Yeah. I know all about complicated histories." Livvy's smile was sad, but understanding.

"I worry I've made things terribly weird."

"It hasn't been not-weird in a long time, Sadia."

"True."

Livvy's expression was sympathetic, but not pitying, thank God. "Is it only your past that makes this rough?"

"I don't want a relationship right now." She couldn't fall in love with someone again. Not now, maybe not ever.

"You think he does?"

"I don't know." They sat in silence for a minute. Sadia shifted. "He's a good uncle. Kareem likes him."

Livvy brightened. "He's a good man. That hasn't changed."

Sadia thought of the way he'd stayed in town to help her even though it would be uncomfortable for him. The way he'd taken care of her when she'd had the panic attack.

The way he'd taken care of her in the alley last night.

"Yeah." She exhaled so deeply it came from the soles of her feet. "I was so mad at him, you know. I kind of wish I could go back to being mad at him."

"Sometimes anger is a simpler emotion than love."

She opened her mouth, ready to reject the notion

of love and Jackson, but she did love him. She loved him in so many ways.

She simply couldn't be *in* love with him.

She also wanted to keep touching him every second he was within touching distance.

Argh. "Life is hard."

Livvy grimaced. "Yeah. I'm sorry, I wish I could give you an easy answer here, but I don't see one."

Neither did Sadia. She sat back in her chair. "Enough about me and Bob. Tell me everything about the love nest in Paris you and Nicholas ran away to."

"Paris?" Livvy's forehead scrunched up. "We were at a cabin twenty miles away."

Chapter 15

JACKSON CLIMBED the steps to the tattoo parlor two at a time. Livvy had texted him earlier that she was back in town, along with a paragraph below it.

> OMG I just came from Sadia's and you're here? How could you not tell me you were still here??? And you're a chef? WTF Jackson you don't tell me anything. I have to go to work rn but I'll come over after and we are going to have a talk, mister.

The threat of a conversation should have unnerved him, but instead he was kind of excited. He wanted to see his twin. He wanted her to hug him and, hell, he even wanted to talk to her.

He also wanted to make sure she was still standing and gauge how badly he needed to punch Nicholas in the face. Again.

The bell jingled above the door as he walked into the quiet shop. He braced himself to have to deal with friendly Gabe, but the place was deserted, the waiting room neat and tidy. A curtain hid the back room from view.

"Hello?" he called out.

"Jackson? Ack. Hey, hang on." The curtain rustled, and then his sister was there. Her hair was streaked with some ridiculous bright blue, and piled up high on top of her head in a topknot.

From her exasperated text, he couldn't tell what reaction he would get, but her face split in a big smile when she laid eyes on him, and she gave a whoop of joy. Then she ran straight at him. He had to think fast to catch her and lift her up so she could hug him.

He closed his eyes. It still felt awkward, this hugging business, but Livvy didn't seem to mind. "Hey."

She lifted her head from his neck and beamed up at him. There was a glow to her skin. A less cynical man might say it was love, but he figured she'd been catching the last dying rays of the fall sun while she was off with Nicholas. "You stayed."

"I did."

"I didn't think you would."

He ignored the sting. "I know."

"But you did." She squeezed him again before separating.

The curtain moved and Nicholas walked into the waiting room, lowering the sleeve of his shirt. Jackson caught a glimpse of a Sharpie-drawn princess, but then it was gone.

Like a junkyard dog scenting fresh meat, Jackson drew up, laser focused on Nicholas. "You."

Nicholas's face was expressionless, the cold robot in place. He finished buttoning his cuff, and then came to stand a foot away. "Jackson. I'm happy to hear you decided to stick around."

"No, you're not." Jackson paused. "Nicky."

Oddly enough, Nicholas smiled. What the fuck? He didn't want Nicholas smiling at him. "Ah yes. You and Livvy are definitely twins."

Livvy cleared her throat. "Okay, guys. Let's play nice. I don't want to have to clean up any blood on the tile."

Jackson didn't need to make Nicholas bleed. He just needed him in pain. "I didn't realize he was here," he said to Livvy. "I can come back later."

Nicholas rocked back on his heels. "I was actually leaving. I have to get to work."

"Surprise, surprise," he muttered. Nicholas and Livvy both ignored him. Jackson gritted his teeth at the stars in his sister's eyes. She'd looked at Nicholas like that when she was younger, too, until he'd broken her heart.

Granted, the other man had a similarly sappy look on his face. *That doesn't mean anything.*

Some love wasn't selfless. Some was selfish. Manipulative.

Nicholas pulled Livvy in tight. Their kiss made Jackson's hand curl into a fist. When he came up for air, Nicholas gave him a measuring look. "You okay, Jackson?"

"Yes," Livvy said firmly. "He is."

"No, I'm not. I don't like this. You're going to hurt her."

Nicholas returned his gaze evenly, not backing down. Jackson was physically larger than the other man, and had spent his adult life in some of the nastier areas of the world. Fighting dirty wasn't new to him. If Jackson didn't dislike this man with a raging fire in his gut, he might respect Nicholas's lack of fear. "I won't this time."

"You can't be sure of that."

"I can be sure we have no secrets from each other this time around. I can also be assured I'm in love with her."

At that Jackson sneered. He knew what love was, true love. He'd given everything up for it. Nicholas had given up Livvy.

"You don't believe me?" Nicholas said.

"It doesn't matter," Livvy bit off. "Jackson, quit it."

They both ignored her. "No, I don't believe you. You loved her before. What's different now?"

"The difference now is I'm no longer a child."

"You weren't a child then, any more than I was. If I'd gone to trial, I would have been tried as an adult."

"Because arson isn't child's play—"

"Nicholas!"

Nicholas immediately stopped and glanced down at his girlfriend. Then he took a deep breath and turned his attention back to Jackson. "Apologies. Livvy is certain of your innocence when it comes to that fire, and I told her I'd trust her."

Except he couldn't. Jackson could see the truth in Nicholas's eyes. Nicholas would always believe Jackson had set that fire. Save for the women in Jackson's family and Sadia, no one would one hundred percent trust that Jackson hadn't burned down Nicholas's family legacy.

Jackson's skin crawled. He wanted to hide under a rock somewhere, but he couldn't. At his silence, Nicholas continued, his tone subdued now. "I know we have a painful history, but I don't want to be at odds with anyone in Livvy's family. That includes you."

Livvy nudged Nicholas. "Why don't you go on to work, Nico? Let me talk to my brother."

Nicholas smoothed his hand over her back and nodded. With one last, measuring look at Jackson, the other man walked away. Nicholas paused at the door and shot him a warning look. "Don't upset her."

Jackson's lips twisted. "I'm not in the business of hurting Livvy." *You are*, was the unspoken accusation.

A muscle ticked in Nicholas's jaw, but he didn't say anything more, merely closed the door quietly behind him. The bell hadn't stopped jingling when Livvy smacked Jackson in the chest.

He rubbed the spot. "I have had it with you Kane women hitting me," he growled.

"Then stop acting so hittable. Quit glaring at Nicholas."

Jackson snorted. He'd discovered the first night he was here that his and Livvy's rapport was far too easy to slip back into. Half-bickering, half-annoying, with odd flashes of heartfelt emotion and protectiveness. He was louder when he was with his sister, and talking came easier, her blunt personality easing him.

He wasn't about to let some robot in a suit fuck his sister up. "He's lucky if all I do is glare at him." He couldn't count the number of tears Livvy had shed after Nicholas had dumped her. Or how many makeshift weapons he'd collected from her room, lest she hurt herself. Or how many hours he'd stayed awake on the floor of her bedroom, terrified he'd missed some sharp implement or pills.

His sister put her hands on her hips. She looked like their mother, though her bright blue hair was distracting from that resemblance somewhat.

He flicked his finger on that wobbly bun, mostly because he was certain it would annoy her, and sure enough, she swatted him away. "What did I tell you? Nicholas wasn't to blame for my depressive episode back then. Or my suicidal ideation."

Jackson flinched away from that word. "You told me that."

"It's true."

"Uh-huh."

"It *is*."

"Last time I saw you, you said you weren't ready to risk getting into a relationship with Nicholas."

"He convinced me things would be different this time."

Jackson couldn't contain his snort. "And you believed him."

"I did. He's not the same boy he was all those years ago."

"There's no guarantee—"

"You're right, there isn't. There's no guarantee on anything. But we're talking, and I think maybe, we could try to make this work this time. I want to try, Jackson. So badly." Pain and need mingled in her tone as she spoke. "I love him."

He shoved his hands in his pockets. "I didn't come here to fight."

She stuck her chin out, clearly peeved. "Why'd you come here then?"

I couldn't stay away. Only he wasn't quite ready to say that. He glanced around the shop, thinking quickly. "You told me no one inks me but you. I'm in the market for a tattoo."

Quicksilver in her moods, Livvy brightened. "Yeah? What do you want?"

He said the first words that came to his mind. "A rose. Red. Crimson."

"Right now?"

"If you have the time."

"I got the time."

He hadn't really been eager to get another tattoo, but now the idea was in his head, he couldn't get it out. Besides, a Livvy Kane original was nothing to laugh at. "Let's do it."

"Follow me."

Within minutes, he had his shirt off and was ensconced in Livvy's chair. "You trust me to freehand it?" she asked, fiddling with her tools.

"Yeah."

"Why a rose?"

He thought of Sadia. That dress, that corsage. "No reason."

She finished whatever she needed to do and moved over to his shoulder, touching the palm frond there. "What's this for?"

He shrugged.

She looked over his half sleeve critically. "It's cool that you were able to replicate Daddy's tat so well." She tapped the tattoo on his shoulder. "A rose would look good over this, I could work it in really nicely, but if you want it somewhere else . . ."

"No. Do whatever you want."

Pure giddiness crossed her face. "Oooh, hooray, magic words. Okay, lay back."

He closed his eyes while she prepped his skin, not budging even when the needle started entering his skin.

"So you're helping Sadia?"

"Yeah."

"She still hasn't found a chef yet, huh?"

"No." Two men had applied. He'd reviewed both resumes, then thrown them in the trash. Sadia had been out, so she didn't know.

It wasn't that he was deliberately keeping qualified staff from her. They'd both been inexperienced, amateur cooks. He wasn't about to waste her time or the goodwill he'd built with the customers. If someone competent applied, he'd happily pass them along.

"How about Kareem? Isn't he a cutie?"

Yes, damn it. The kid was cuter than a fucking button. "Yeah."

Livvy cleared her throat. "Feel free to elaborate on any response."

He opened his eyes and stared up at the ceiling. "I don't want to distract you."

"I can talk and be super competent at my job."

But he could barely talk.

"I didn't even know you were a chef."

"I am." *Elaborate.* "I do pop-up restaurants."

"What kind of food?"

"Comfort food." He hadn't even known that was a category of food. Ariel handled most of the branding for their operation, and it fit what he cooked. Hearty, simple, hot meals inspired by places all over the world. Fancy foodies flocked in, but normal everyday people liked what he made too.

"Well now, that's super cool. When you gonna cook for me?"

He had a kitchen now. He could cook for his sister. "Whenever you want."

She kept her gaze down. "Nice. And where are you staying again?" she asked, far too casually.

He narrowed his eyes. "You know I'm staying at Sadia's place. Or you wouldn't have asked."

"She might have mentioned it."

Ah-ha. He'd always been able to read his twin. "What else did she mention?"

"Nothing."

Too quick. "Tell me."

"No. I'm not getting in between you and her."

So Livvy knew there was something going on between him and Sadia. His cheeks heated. He wanted to get up and walk right out, but there was a needle driving into his skin. "What did she say?"

"Nuh-uh. Not. Talking." She gave him a stern

look. "We aren't in high school. If you want to know what's on her mind, you ask her."

He'd wanted to, damn it. He'd spent all morning at the café treating her to his clumsy heavy-handed wooing. He'd cooked for her. Hovered around her. Even spoken to her. Why couldn't that be enough?

Livvy's expression softened, but she didn't shift her focus from her work. He was impressed with her multi-tasking capability. When he cooked, he didn't really want to register anything else in the world.

"I'm a little worried about you, Jackson," she said.

"Don't be."

"I don't want you hurt."

"I won't be."

She was silent for a long time, the tattoo machine the only sound. He was lulled into a false sense of complacency, which she shattered with a single sentence. "Are you in love with her?"

He opened his eyes. "Yes."

"And what if she doesn't love you back?"

His heart seized. Sadia *had* said something to her. "Now you have to tell me. Did she say she doesn't love me?"

She pressed her lips tightly together and shook her head so her bright blue bun wobbled. "But she did say she's not looking for a long-term relationship right now."

Jackson stared at Livvy, expressionless. He had not honestly thought as far as a relationship. He barely knew how to love someone. He wasn't even sure he could sustain a relationship.

From all signs, though, Sadia wasn't averse to a short-term relationship. Could he have her temporarily? His gut screamed no, but his practical side shrugged. If he could have her at all, he would take her. A week with Sadia would be worth a year with any other woman. "Thanks for telling me."

Her forehead creased. "I'm worried about you, brother."

"Don't be."

"I think you need a support system, like I did."

"I do not need a support system." No one had ever taken care of him. He definitely didn't need them to start when he was in his thirties.

"It's kind of nice to have. I know I feel better with you here. To see you and hear you and touch you . . . it's like a dream come true."

He shifted his feet. He wasn't anyone's dream, not at all. "Yeah." He should have figured out some way to meet up with Livvy over all these years. He'd come back to the States every now and again, but not for long. "Uh, same."

She beamed up at him. "I love you too."

He grunted. "Yes. Good." Another reason he wasn't sure if he could have a relationship. He could barely admit he loved Sadia to himself. Surely women wanted that sort of thing verbalized, yes?

"Have you seen Maile or Mom?"

"Yes. It was fine," he lied. "Mom and I were civil. It was good to see Maile again."

"I'm surprised our aunt's not hanging around you like a necklace."

"I think she's giving me space."

"Hmm." She continued her work on his shoulder. "Will you come with me to Paul's grave?"

Oof. The twists and turns of Livvy's thoughts had never used to feel quite so painful. "I don't think that's a good idea."

"I have to make my peace with never making my peace with him, so to speak." Her words tripped over each other on their way out. "I haven't been to his grave since his funeral. I should go."

"You can go."

"Jackson—"

"No, I don't think so. I can't."

Can't or won't?

Maybe both.

Not all memories were created equal. It was one thing to face his past when it came to John or Maile or Sadia or even his mother, but he couldn't think about Paul. If he thought about Paul, he'd have to think about that confession that was sitting on his nightstand, tucked away in that journal, and he wasn't ready to do that. Not yet, maybe not ever.

"Okay. No pressure." She continued working on him. She had a gentle touch.

"Thanks."

"Anything for you."

Jackson looked away, unable to hide his emotions. His heart flared, the black and white turning bright and colorful. *Anything for you.* Just like he'd do anything for her.

He still didn't think he needed a support system, but she was right. Knowing she was in his corner was pretty fucking amazing.

Chapter 16

AFTER HER talk with Livvy, Sadia found herself glancing at Jackson's apartment far too many times. Finally, she bundled her son up and came to the café. The time after-hours was ideal to get some paperwork done, and Kareem loved having the run of the empty business. He could actually wander around and not get scolded for poking around the kitchen or the office or the front.

Plus, she needed to do all the work she hadn't gotten to today while Jackson had been hovering around her feeding her.

That had been the plan, but it had been compromised. Sadia glanced around the table. She'd made the mistake of telling Noor where she was when her older sister had called. The next thing she'd known, Noor and Zara had shown up on the doorstep. Noor had tossed Kareem her phone, and he was ensconced in another booth, playing with whatever games she kept on there.

They said they were here to discuss their parents' anniversary party, but Sadia was suspicious.

There was no need for them to have not brought Jia and Ayesha unless . . .

Noor leaned forward, her hands cradling her mug of tea. Her lightly draped shawl brushed the table. "We need to talk about Jia."

Sadia inwardly groaned. "What's to talk about?"

Noor huffed. "This ridiculous idea she has about dropping out of medical school."

In the midst of her own tumultuous life, Sadia had almost forgotten her vow to help Jia. She'd reviewed the girl's finances, and she honestly saw no reason for her sister not to follow her dreams. The girl was raking in cash with her YouTube videos, way more than Sadia had expected, and she had a solid five- and ten-year plan.

Sadia tapped her planner. Clearly, no one cared about her list, and she was going to have to be the one who dealt with the tiny details remaining for the party, but whatever. This was a great opportunity to fulfill her promise to advocate for her sister. "Do you know how much she's earning?" Sadia rattled the numbers off from memory.

That made Zara pause. "Wait, you can earn that much showing people how to paint their faces and put on a hijab?"

Good thing Jia wasn't there, or she would have hissed at that description. "She's a personality. People like her. She has plans for a book deal, modeling, acting."

"Whoa." Zara frowned, considering all of this. Mostly the money, probably.

"It's nice she's earning that much now, but we all

know how fleeting this stuff is," Noor said sternly. "I won't have my sister bankrupt at thirty because she put all of her eggs in the Internet basket."

Sadia's eye twitched. She'd considered filing bankruptcy in the early days after Paul's death. It was still an option on the table. She didn't need to wonder how her family would view that. "It's not all her eggs. It's what she loves to do."

"She can do stuff she loves in her free time."

Sadia rubbed her hand over her face. "How much free time do you have, Noor? What about you, Zara? What hobbies do you have?"

Both her older sisters drew up tall like outraged crows. "We have tons of hobbies," Zara said. "We're just busy with our careers and our children."

"And if Jia has a family like you two, she'll have to put her hobbies on the back burner." Sadia spread her hands in front of her. "She's twenty-four years old. Let her have a couple of years. If she hates it or if it tanks, she can always go back to medical school."

"I suppose leaving wouldn't stop her from going back," Zara conceded.

Noor scowled at Zara. "You're not seriously buying into this madness?"

Zara tapped her manicured fingers on the table. She must have come straight from work, because she still wore an elegant black pantsuit and a lavender blouse. A pair of chic sunglasses were perched on her head, holding her hair back. "She's earning a lot of money. More than us."

"It's not about the money. What will people say?"

"Who cares?" Sadia said with more bite than she intended. But honestly, who cared? "She's a grown woman. Let her be happy."

"Mom and Daddy won't support this. I'm trying to save her that pain. You know firsthand how Mom reacts when she doesn't support something, Sadia." Noor gave her a pointed look.

"Yeah," Sadia said slowly. "I know exactly how she would react. I also know she probably wouldn't have reacted that way if either of you had stood up for me back then."

Whoa. She wasn't sure which one of them was most surprised by her saying that.

Zara recovered first. She removed her sunglasses and placed them on the table. Psychiatrist that she was, she adopted her most soothing tone. "Sadia, are you blaming us for how Mom and Daddy reacted to you dropping out of school?"

Her first instinct was to smooth everything over, make them forget what she'd said. She glanced over at Kareem sitting in the furthest booth, but he was absorbed in the phone and out of earshot of their conversation. "Not blaming you, no."

"I don't know what you think we could have done," Noor huffed. She was visibly annoyed. "We told you to wait to marry Paul and finish school."

"Right, well, telling me I shouldn't have done the thing I got cut off for isn't really supporting me."

"You weren't cut off. I mean, of course, Mom and Daddy weren't going to financially support you after marriage, but—"

"I didn't care about the money."

The financial part had hurt the least. It had been difficult to go from having money to living paycheck to paycheck, but that had been a harder transition for Paul than her.

No, it had been the rest of it that had killed a part of her soul. For someone who craved and needed family, like her, it had been hell to be at odds with her parents like that. "I couldn't come to dinner. I couldn't stop by and have coffee with Mom. I couldn't . . ." She waved her hands over her planner. "I couldn't plan anniversary parties."

Noor drew herself up. "You made the decision not to do all those things, Sadia. Mom and Daddy never told you that you couldn't come back to the house."

"You don't have to formally disown a child to make them unwelcome in their own home. How would you feel if you brought Rohan home and everyone ignored or scowled at him instead of welcoming him? Paul was my *husband*." Sadia shook her head. Now that she'd opened this can of worms, she couldn't stop herself. "Yes, I was rash. Eloping with him was probably the most reckless thing I ever did, and the fact that I was doing it at all should have made it clear how badly I wanted it and how sure I was that I loved him."

"You're blaming us for our parent's actions," Zara said, her tone gentle. "That's not fair."

"No, I'm blaming you for not being my big sisters." She closed her journal with a shaking hand. "All you had to do was support my decisions, even if you didn't agree with them. That's what we're

going to do for Jia. We're going to support her and
be happy for her and console her if it fails, and
we're not going to tell her we told you so or—" She
cut herself off before she said too much about her
own marriage and her fears. "Or at least I'm going
to. You two can do whatever you want."

"Okay." Zara fiddled with her earring. "Things
are getting heated here. Why don't we all take a
time—"

"I don't need a time-out. I've said what I need to
say. I'll handle all the details for the party. You can
go home." Sadia came to her feet, just as the front
door to the café opened.

Three sets of eyes darted there, and Sadia mentally sighed. This was really shitty timing on Jackson's part.

Or maybe it was perfect timing? She was so
mad, she could probably handle this really assert-
ively right now.

Jackson came inside and closed the door behind
him quietly. His eyes met hers, and she caught the
flare of surprise and consternation there. He took a
step back, but then his gaze swept over the booth,
and back to her. His shoulders squared, like he was
bracing himself.

He walked toward the booth and nodded at her
older sisters. "Noor. Zara. Good to see you."

"Jackson?" Noor said finally. "What . . . what a
surprise."

"Yeah. Sorry for coming in so late. I didn't think
anyone would be here." He shifted the bag in his
hands. "I came in to try a new recipe."

"Try a new recipe?"

Jackson was silent, and she realized he was waiting for her to answer. "Jackson's been working here for the past couple of weeks. Rick left. I needed him. He's staying at my home too." She kept her explanation short and to the point. Sadia nodded at Jackson. "Feel free to come in whenever. It's your place as much as it is mine."

He studied her for a minute and nodded. "This bag is getting heavy," said the man who looked like he could easily bench-press cars. "I'll get out of your way."

He walked away but then slowed as he noted Kareem's presence in the booth closest to the kitchen. He paused in front of him. Kareem beamed. "Hey."

"Hi. Do you want to help me in the kitchen?" he asked gruffly.

Kareem put Noor's phone down and looked at Sadia for permission. Sadia cleared her throat. "You can help him."

Her son brightened and scrambled out of the booth, pausing only to drop Noor's phone off on their table, before running behind Jackson.

As soon as the two were out of earshot, Sadia whirled on her sisters before they could speak. "Yes, I know he was arrested for arson. He was never convicted. He's innocent."

"I didn't say anything!" Noor exclaimed.

"You were thinking it."

To her credit, Noor looked guilty. "Maybe. Sadia, let's talk."

"I can't." Sadia fisted her hands together. "You

need to leave. We need to think about all of this. Or rather, you do, if you don't see why I'm so upset."

Her older sisters did, at the least, look chastened and regretful, but not enough.

She shut and locked the door behind them. She should go to the office and calm down first, but the smells and noises coming out of the kitchen were so intriguing, she followed her nose.

Her spirits lifted as soon as she walked in. Kareem was standing at Jackson's side on a step stool, a massive apron tied around his waist. His face was already covered with a streak of white, and he was carefully grating a block of cheese under Jackson's watchful eye.

By the way Kareem was chattering, one would think he'd known his uncle forever. "And then the girl said she wouldn't go to school 'cause she was sick, but she wasn't sick—she was faking."

Jackson hummed and corrected the way Kareem was holding the grater.

"Kareem?" Sadia stepped inside the kitchen, letting the door close behind her. "Do you mind giving your uncle and me a minute to talk?"

"Yeah." Kareem glanced at Jackson. "Uncle Jackson, you got any games on your phone?"

"Uh. I have a calculator."

Kareem blinked up at him and then turned to her. "I'm gonna go play on your computer, Mom."

"Okay, love."

She waited until he was gone and opened her mouth, but Jackson beat her to it. "I hope I didn't make things hard on you. I didn't know how much your sisters knew about me being here." He didn't look back at her, but continued working, and she was glad. She didn't think she'd be able to function under that intense gaze. Not when he used words like *hard*.

"No. It's fine. You have every right to be here."

At that, he did look at her, a narrow, even glance out of the corner of his eye.

"You do." She changed the subject before he could argue with her. "What are you making?"

"Mac and cheese, but I'm still messing with the recipe. Kareem asked for hot chocolate, though. It's ready."

She'd ordered pizza for her and Kareem, but that delivery felt very long ago now. Her stomach grumbled, and she drifted closer. "Oh."

He grabbed a mug and ladled up a serving of thick, liquid cocoa. He held it out to her. "It's not super cold out yet, but you used to like this all the time."

She accepted it, the scent of chocolate teasing her nose. "You're feeding me a lot today."

He lifted his shoulder. "It's something easy I can do for you."

"You're already doing a lot for me."

He grunted.

So about last night . . . "Livvy's home," she said instead.

"Yeah, I saw her."

She waited for him to continue, but got nothing more. "Ah."

"Nicholas, too." His motions became rougher as he grated cheese.

"Ahhhh." Well, Jackson had always cooked when he was upset. "You didn't punch him, did you?"

"No. Not today."

"Good. Let's keep it that way."

"Were your sisters annoying you?"

She recognized a change in subject when she saw it, but she was still teeming over with enough emotions to allow it. She bit her lip and perched on the stool, cradling the hot chocolate. "Jia wants to quit med school. My parents won't be happy. Noor and Zara were thinking of ways to get her to do what my parents would want and avoid the drama instead of supporting her and I guess it triggered something in my brain."

"About how they treated you when you married Paul?"

She hesitated. "How'd you know that? I never said anything about it to you."

"It's what you didn't say. You would have talked about them, and you didn't, not until Kareem was born."

She swallowed, thinking back through her emails. She supposed he was right, but the fact that he'd known her so well was a little absurd.

Jackson swiped his arm over his forehead. "I was happy you seemed to reconcile with them. You need your family."

"I really do. I couldn't have done what you did."

He stopped what he was doing and turned to face her. "What do you mean?"

"You left all of us behind."

"Do you think that was easy?"

"No, I don't." She made her voice soothing. "I know you were traumatized by the arrest—"

"It wasn't the arrest that traumatized me."

She paused and placed her half-full mug on the counter. "Then what?"

His face was so hard it could have been carved in granite. "Never mind. It's not important."

"Tell me. If it wasn't the arrest and the gossip, what could have made you leave us like that? Was it something your mom or Paul or I—"

"Not you." He closed his eyes tight and shook his head. "Never you."

But he hadn't denied Paul or his mother's involvement. Since he'd been in sporadic contact with Livvy, at least, she assumed his sister hadn't done anything to him.

She eased from the stool and approached him carefully. Pain radiated off him. It made her heart seize up. "Jackson? Did something happen between your mom and you before you left?"

His nod was so subtle she might have missed it. Unable to stand the sight of his hurt, she placed a hand on his chest. "And you and Paul?"

Another nod.

"Was it a fight or . . . ?"

He released the breath he was holding in a shudder, then placed his hand over hers and squeezed tight. His opened his eyes and looked down at her. "It doesn't matter."

"It does."

"No. The past is over. I don't want to think about it." He ran his thumb over the back of her hand,

and just like that, the air in the kitchen grew very heavy. "I'd rather think about the present."

She looked at his finger, the single, blunt digit, and couldn't fight the blush on her cheeks. "Jackson—"

He lowered his head, until his lips were a hairsbreadth from hers. "Hmm?"

"We shouldn't do this anymore."

"Do what?"

"Touch. This attraction . . . I don't know where it came from."

"It doesn't matter where it came from." His breath tingled against her lips.

"I'm not . . . I'm not looking for a relationship right now, Jackson."

"Do you say that to all the people you pick up at the bar?"

Her face turned redder. How could she have told him that? "No. But they know anything we do isn't serious."

He tucked a strand of her hair behind her ear, then that blunt, calloused finger slid down her cheek and over her jaw. "Why does it have to be serious with us?"

"Because—because of who you are and who I am. Our past and our family and . . . Kareem . . ."

Before she could continue, he brushed his lips against hers. God, he was such a good kisser. She responded before her brain could issue a proper warning.

When he drew away, she could only blink up at him. "I don't think of any of those things when I kiss you."

Neither did she, and that was a problem. "This isn't right."

"You always do what's right?"

"Lately, yes." She had to. She had too much at stake to indulge herself.

"I'd be the safest wrong thing you could do." He ran his hand down her arm, then up again. "You said you want me. I want you too. The attraction between us isn't going anywhere."

A disbelieving laugh slipped out of her mouth.

He frowned in reaction. "Is it funny?"

"No, sorry." The no-nonsense, blunt approach to seduction was exactly Jackson's style though.

"I don't want to feel like I'm using you."

"I want to be used. If you need anything physical from me, you can take it. I'm willing."

"But you're Paul's brother," she whispered.

"Doesn't matter."

"But—" Her phone beeped and they both looked at her pocket. She sighed and reached inside and pulled it out, glancing at the screen. "Oh, shoot."

"What is it?"

"I forgot I told another bartender I would cover their shift tonight." She'd meant to ask Noor or Zara if Kareem could stay the night with them, but she'd been so annoyed, she hadn't bothered. "I don't have anyone to watch Kareem."

"I can watch Kareem."

"Hmm." She glanced up at him.

"If you want me to, that is."

"I want to stay with Uncle Jackson!"

At Kareem's shout, Sadia took a huge step back

from Jackson, though they weren't doing anything inappropriate. "Uh—"

"Please mom?" Kareem looked up at his uncle. "Can we make the cookies again and can I have more than one?"

Jackson rested his hand on the boy's shoulder but waited for her cue. She grimaced. She didn't particularly want to work tonight, but their conversation right now was effectively over with Kareem hovering. It may be good to have some time apart, where her hands and her brain could be occupied with other stuff. "You can make the cookies and you can have two."

"Good."

She was startled at the curve of Jackson's lips. It was almost . . . almost! . . . a smile. A tiny one, but a smile.

She hadn't seen him smile in so long. She craved it, almost as much as she craved his body. And now she'd been told she could have the latter, even if she couldn't—wouldn't—have the former.

I want him.

He wants me.

I love him.

I can't fall in love with him.

Complicated. So freaking complicated.

Chapter 17

SADIA CREPT inside her silent house. She'd had to stay at the bar a little late tonight, and resented every second. Jackson was capable of handling her son for a few hours. She hadn't been anxious. She'd simply wanted to join them.

Well, join them for fun and to watch their bonding. Join Jackson after for . . . something else.

I want to be used.

She'd texted him twice during the night, and each time he'd responded that everything was going fine. Which made sense, because Jackson was a responsible adult and Kareem was a sweet, generally obedient child.

If Jackson was finally willing to connect with his nephew, she wanted to give him the full opportunity to do so. Kareem deserved to have his uncle in his life.

The light was on in the living room. She walked inside and came to a dead stop.

Oh. My. God. This is the cutest thing I've ever seen.

A mountain of pillows and blankets were piled high in one corner. Toys were strewn everywhere.

Books were scattered around the sofa like someone had knocked over a tower of them.

Anyone else would say the place was trashed, but after years of being a mother, she knew what she was looking at.

Fun.

Her smile spread when she took in the sight on the couch. Jackson was dead asleep on his stomach, head pillowed by his arms. Kareem had fallen asleep right on top of him, his cheek pressed against his uncle's shoulder blades. He was being raised and lowered by Jackson's deep breaths.

As gently as she could, Sadia picked up her son. He was a heavy weight, but she cuddled him close, walking down the hallway and up the stairs to his room. She laid him on the bed, grateful that she'd had the foresight to get him in his jammies before she left for work.

Kareem's lashes fluttered open when his back hit the bed. "Mom?"

"Shh." She sank down next to him. "Go back to sleep."

"I love Uncle Jackson," he said sleepily.

Her heart gave a little kick. Kids fell in love so easily. *Jackson, please don't forget this boy when you leave.* "Yeah?"

"Yeah. We had fun."

"I'm glad."

"We made a fort."

So that's what that pile of pillows was. She made an interested sound.

"He's shy."

She almost laughed at anyone using the word *shy* to describe Jackson. He wasn't shy. He was big and rude and could probably pick her up with one arm and—

And he also hated to meet new people and ran away the second he met a stranger and melted into the shadows when there was a crowd.

Maybe he was a little shy.

"Kareem, you may be right."

"I know. He told me so."

She smoothed his hair, curious now what they could have talked about. "What else did he tell you?"

"He told me about my Grandpa Sam. He was Grandpa John's best friend."

Her smile spread. She'd been around the Oka-Kanes long enough to know the history of Sam Oka, but she hadn't told her son much about it. Jackson had been the only one of the three siblings interested in their heritage. She could only give her son rough outlines of his father's people. Jackson could fill in the blanks.

"He said my Grandpa Sam and Grandma Lea were put in a jail cause people were scared of the way they looked."

Her smile faded. She wasn't sure if internment camps were an appropriate topic for a six-year-old, but Lord knew if there was a good age to learn about them. "I see."

He scooched closer, and now she knew why he'd woken up to talk to her. Her baby couldn't sleep when something was on his mind, and his worried frown was clear. "I'm a quarter Japanese."

"You are. A quarter Japanese-American, a quarter Hawaiian, half Pakistani-American." She leaned down and nuzzled her nose against his. "All you."

"Could someone put me in jail even if I didn't do nothing?"

Sadia hid her instinctive flinch and placed her hand on her son's cheek, tracing her thumb over his soft brown skin. "They'd have to get through me first," she said lightly.

Think of all the evil in the world, all the danger that waits for this boy. How are you going to keep him safe, all by yourself?

She batted away the panic rising in her chest. No. She couldn't fail at this. And she wasn't alone. "Me, and your grandmas and grandpa, your aunts and uncles and cousins. There are lots of people who would protect you."

"Uncle Jackson too. He's big. He could fight anybody."

Not everybody. Some things were bigger than muscles. But her baby needed to sleep now. "Yes." She slid her thumb over his nose and stroked the bridge of it, between his eyes. The rhythmic stroking always made him sleepy, and this time was no exception. Within a few moments, he was breathing deeply.

She sat there and watched him, the minutes ticking by. He was almost seven. In ten years, he'd be leaving for college. If he wanted to go to college.

She fisted her hands to still their shaking. He'd be on his own, away from her protectiveness and control.

Which was scary but also natural and normal, and as it should be, she reminded herself.

She rose from the bed and made her way out of the room and to the living room. She expected to find Jackson still asleep, but he was crouched next to the toy chest. He glanced up, in a white T-shirt and sweatpants, half his hair sticking up, eyes still bleary, a Pokémon toy in his hand.

He'd never looked so sexy. "Leave it," she said. "I'll get it later."

"I don't mind." He put the toy away and started gathering Lego pieces.

She perched on the arm of the couch. "Thank you for watching Kareem tonight."

"It was my pleasure."

"He told me you talked about your grandfather."

Jackson grimaced. "Sorry if it was too heavy. I mentioned Sam, and he asked me to tell him a story."

"No. He should know his own history." She crossed her arms over her chest. "I'd love to keep all the worst parts of the world away from him, but things don't work that way."

Jackson nodded, a dark shadow moving over his face. He'd traveled the world, and she imagined he'd seen some of the nastiest parts of humanity along with the most beautiful. "Yes."

She ran her hands up and down her thighs. She was nervous. "Do you want a drink?" She popped up before he could respond. She didn't keep much alcohol in the house because she didn't like to drink by herself, but there were a few beers in the fridge. She grabbed two and made her way back to Jackson.

He'd made headway on cleaning up the toys and was busy folding the bedding. "A fort, Kareem said." She handed him the drink.

"Exactly." He put the comforter on the couch and sat down. She settled in next to him, her legs curled up under her. She'd go change out of her bartending uniform in a second or two, after he left, but right now it felt good to simply sit with him in the quiet.

He took a sip of the beer. "No fancy drink this time?"

"I don't keep liquor in the house."

"Don't want to bring work home with you."

She smiled. "Something like that."

"You're good at it. Bartending. Coming up with those old drinks."

She relaxed into the couch. She hadn't done this in so long, the whole decompressing with someone after work thing. "You know I always liked history. I got this old mixology book, and the customers get a kick out of me putting together something new. It's silly."

"It's not silly. Not if you like it."

"I do like it."

"You should do it more often."

"Ha. Yeah. What would I do with the café?"

He cocked his head. "You could turn it into a bar."

She started to laugh, and then realized he wasn't joking. "I can't do that."

"Why not?"

"Alcohol isn't what Kane's is famous for."

"So change what it's famous for. You're the owner now. You can do that. Make it a café/bar. Only serve specialty drinks in the evening, not beer and wine. Unlikely you'll get a lot of drunkards. And it might be profitable."

That made sense. Paul would have never so much as changed the menu, let alone changed the character of the café by turning it into a nighttime bar. Only Paul wasn't here anymore.

But . . . "I feel like it would result in more paperwork for me."

His gaze was a little too astute. "You don't like owning the café, don't you?"

"What? No."

"Yeah, you don't. That's okay. Not everyone wants to be a business owner."

She tried to work up the energy for more protests, but she couldn't really find them. Finally she sighed. "I should love it. Running a business is perfectly respectable." It was something that, if she excelled at it, could make her a legitimate success.

He stretched out his legs in front of him. "You don't *have* to love anything. It's okay to be good at something and want to do it even if it doesn't make a ton of money."

"I could probably support Kareem and myself on my bartending money," she admitted. It was the café and its loans that were the drain.

"So you make some good tips?"

She responded to the ghost of a tease in his eyes.

"I said I liked it for a reason. That's one of the reasons."

"What are the others?"

"I feel like myself there. I can talk to people and chat with them. It's good to keep my skills sharp."

"What else?"

He knew. He was remembering what she'd said, about picking up bed partners at the bar. Her breathing grew shorter. "I . . . you know."

"Tell me again." He placed his barely touched beer on the coffee table.

Use me.

"The . . . the sex. I can find people there who don't know me."

"I know everything about you."

"Maybe not everything."

"A lot."

"Yes," she whispered. "That's why I told myself it was wrong to—"

He took her beer and placed it on the table as well, then moved closer, so they were sitting hip to hip. "Wrong to what?"

"To need you like this."

"It's not."

There was no one and nothing to interrupt them right now. Nothing that could stop her.

She wanted him. It was unwise and complicated, but she didn't know how she'd survive if she couldn't have him.

She'd regret it forever, and she lived with enough regrets.

"Ground rules."

"Yes?"

She traced his nose. He was completely frozen as she ran her finger over his lips, and then his eyebrows, his cheeks and his ears. She took her time, examining every feature. She had to relearn him. This wasn't the boy she'd known. He wasn't the man she'd created in her imagination, reading her letters miles away.

He was new, and so was she.

"Sadia. The rules?"

Oh yes. She stroked his neck, the thud of his pulse against her forefinger. "No matter what happens between us, you don't disappear again. You can leave this town and you can avoid me, but you'll be there for Kareem. He needs an uncle like you in his life."

He stared at her for a long moment and slowly, the corners of his lips pulled up. The lines around his eyes crinkled, and his teeth flashed.

A smile.

She drew back. It was there and gone so quickly she might have missed it, but she clutched it close to her.

"I would be honored to be in Kareem's life. But I'm not going to disappear again."

She didn't know if she could believe that second part, but so long as he agreed to the first, she would somehow muddle along. She leaned forward and pressed her lips against his. She ran her hands over his skull and down to his thick neck, scraping her fingernails over it. They kissed lightly, learning each other.

Finally, she pulled away. "Do you want to go to my bedroom?"

He glanced around the living room, his gaze stopping on the framed family photo on the bookcase. She flushed.

There was no graceful way to get around the fact that she'd shared a bed with his brother, so she'd sacrifice grace for bluntness. "Paul and I were separated. We hadn't slept together for almost a year before he died. The bed in my room is new." It was an offer and an explanation.

She expected a million questions about their separation, but other than his thoughtful frown, he didn't ask, only nodded. "Maybe next time. This first time, though . . . I want you somewhere with no memories." He extended a hand. "Come with me?"

JACKSON HAD to wait for Sadia to go to her room and grab her phone, which gave her access to the monitor in Kareem's room. She avoided his gaze the whole time, though he didn't think it was because she was embarrassed.

No, she was aroused. He could see it in the flush of her cheeks, her rapid breaths. "Here," she said, after she locked up the house, and handed him a foil packet.

He closed his fist around it, understanding why she'd gone to her bedroom. He was operating on pure lust and adoration now, every drop of blood from his brain redirected to his dick. And his heart, which was pounding so loud, he feared she could hear it.

He paused on the third porch step. She glanced at him. "What's wrong?"

He tested the step. "Something's wrong with this one."

"I know."

"I'll fix it," he promised.

Her eyes gleamed in the near darkness. "Later. Fix it later."

Yes. Later.

He led her to the garage, and she started laughing. "Jackson, we're not going to . . ."

"What?" He opened the passenger side door, shoved back the seat as far as it would go, and got in. The car was newer, less than a couple years old.

He didn't want to be with her anywhere that she and Paul had also been. It would be too weird, too steeped in reminders he was doing his damnedest to avoid.

"I haven't had sex in a car—well, ever."

"Then you should start with me."

Her lips curved. There was enough light from the car's interior for him to make out her features and body. She put her hand in his, and he hoisted her over him, onto his lap. Her lips slicked over his. He closed his eyes and let her sample him, each long drag making his hands tighten on her waist. He tugged at her shirt, pulled it up and over her head, tossing it somewhere in the back. He undid her bra and tossed it as well, too consumed with licking her nipples to care about where it landed.

He kissed up her neck, and she stilled on him, her breath catching as he caught her ear between his teeth. He tugged at the flesh before sucking on it and she gave a broken cry, arching her back, her crotch rubbing against his.

"Here? You like this?" he whispered in her ear, and for response, she traced her nails over the back of his neck and pulled him closer. He sucked and licked her again, dipping his tongue inside her ear before switching sides. "Tell me what you like," he insisted.

"I like—that. What you're doing."

"What else? What do you fantasize about?"

The corner of her tongue touched the corner of her mouth. "Everything."

"Give me specifics."

Her long fingers dropped to his crotch. She rubbed him through his sweatpants and he inhaled, unable to stand the sensation of the cotton abrading him. "This."

"My cock?"

She shuddered at the word. "Yes."

"When did you fantasize about my dick, Sadia?" That was a totally unfair question. She hadn't dreamt of him the way he had of her.

Her eyes darkened. "After we kissed."

"You said you used your vibrator."

"I did." The words were a purr. Her nipples were dark brown, the points long and puffy. He committed them to his memory, fearful he'd never see them again. Her hand moved over him, again and again, stroking him lazily.

His body jerked, his erection swelling. Her lips parted.

He imagined her fucking a vibrator in her bed, dreaming of him. He shoved at her pants, and she raised herself up so she could awkwardly wrestle them off in the tight confines of the car, along with her pink cotton panties. The dim interior light painted her body with a hint of gray-green.

Her body was perfect, her thighs round, her belly soft. A small vee of hair shielded her pussy from him. "Use me like you used that vibrator," he ordered, his voice guttural. Like she'd used him in that alley. Only naked this time, so he could feel how wet and slick she got.

Her nostrils flared. She worked his cock free of fabric while he ripped open the condom. She accepted the latex.

The sight of her fingers on his cock was almost too much to bear, but it wasn't like he could not watch her roll the condom down his length. His stomach clenched when she shifted and pressed his dick between her legs. Her head tipped back and she moaned.

She rubbed the tip of his erection against her clitoris, in a tight circle. He was a captive audience. He wanted to write a treatise on how to please Sadia. "That's how you like it," he muttered, and placed his hand over hers, squeezing tighter than she'd dared, keeping up the motion she wanted. "What else? Do you fuck yourself with that vibrator?"

She swallowed. "Sometimes."

"Show me."

Her heavy breasts swayed when she shifted forward, and he had to give each nipple a suck. Her body jerked against his. "You're making me lose focus."

He caught the tip between his lips and tugged before releasing her. "Is that bad?"

"You want to fuck me, don't you?"

The filthy word on Sadia's angelic lips made his entire body tense. "Yes."

She fitted his cock to the opening of her pussy. "Say please."

If she thought he wouldn't beg, she didn't know him at all. He'd waited his whole life for this moment. "Please."

Her dark eyes narrowed and she moved, just the head of his cock sinking inside of her. His chest worked. She shoved his shirt up greedily. He expected her to delicately stroke his chest, but she scraped her nails over his hard belly, making his body arch. Another tiny inch sank inside her. "Ask me to ride you."

He gritted his teeth. He never cared who called the shots in the bedroom, so long as he and his partner walked away happy, but he adored Sadia taking charge now.

There was no doubt that he was giving her exactly what she needed. "Please ride my cock."

Her nails kneaded his chest, like a pleased feline. "Good," she sighed, and sank down on him.

It was heaven. Nirvana. His eyes slitted, but he couldn't close them. He couldn't lose a single second of watching her grind her soft, long body on him. Her brown skin glistened, concentration and lust tightening her face. Her fingers tunneled through his short hair and grasped at his skull as her hips worked faster and harder, each tight contraction drawing his balls tighter.

He couldn't be a spectator for long. He arched his hips up, fucking her in short, shallow strokes until she was gasping and crying out, unrestrained in a way she hadn't been in the alley. Her hands traveled over his shoulders, and he grunted in pain when she brushed against his new tattoo, hidden under his shirt and a bandage. He adjusted her grip so she would avoid the tender flesh. "What do you need?"

In answer she grabbed his hand and brought it down to her pussy. "My clit," she whispered. "Touch—oh." She leaned back to give him greater access and he watched his cock penetrate her while he fingered her clit in tight circles, her wetness making him gleam.

"Look at us," he ordered.

Her hair slipped over her shoulder and tickled his chest when she glanced down. He pressed his forehead against hers while they both stared, their breathing matching. He made his strokes slower and more explicit. "You're so pretty. Look at that pink pussy. How greedy it is."

"I need to come. Harder."

He leaned forward, wrapping one hand around her waist so he could control her better. He kept his other thumb on her clit. "Whatever you'd like."

He shafted her hard and deep, holding her close. When her cries became louder, he latched onto her ear, sucking hard. She shivered and came on his lap, small, broken noises falling from her lips.

Her pussy gripped his dick so snug and tight he came with her, every part of him seizing and releasing.

He wanted to stay here forever, but eventually she moved to the other seat. She got dressed in silence, murmuring a thanks when he retrieved her shirt and bra from the backseat. He only had to take care of the condom and pull his sweatpants back up.

He winced when his leg creaked. He was too old for sex in a car.

He half-expected her to run away or to turn shy once she was put to rights, but instead she awkwardly hopped into his seat again and snuggled up in his lap. Stunned, he automatically put his arm around her.

"Can we keep doing this?" she asked.

Oh, thank God. "Yes."

"I know you're going to leave for New York soon. And who knows where after that."

He didn't know if the reminder was for him or her. Maybe both of them.

It didn't matter. They could have this even if they had nothing else. He'd learned this lesson before, knew how much love could hurt, and he'd probably limp when he walked away from here, but the bright flaring colors in his heart would make that pain worth it. He wanted to taste those colors for as long as humanly possible. Love truly was addictive.

There was no surprise he'd been willing to take on a felony charge for her. He'd done it for Paul yes, but it had mostly been for her. Not that she could ever know that. "C'mere." He pulled her tighter against him, and didn't answer her. He would do his best to keep her safe and keep her from being hurt. If he got battered, that was fine. He'd been battered before. He was still standing.

He feared he was holding her too tight, but she didn't complain. Yes, even if he hurt, he'd take this for now.

Chapter 18

H‌E WAS here tonight.

Baseball cap pulled low, slouched in a booth in the darkest corner of O'Killians, away from the crowds. Friday nights were always busy, but she'd been on the lookout, so she'd registered his presence the second he'd slunk in.

She wanted to hop the bar and go running at Jackson, but that might call more attention to them than either of them wanted. Besides, she was still working.

She placed a drink in front of the customer who had ordered it. "Enjoy."

The guy peered up at her. "No history lesson tonight?"

"Um." She racked her brain for the name and year of the creation she'd made. "It's . . . turn of the century, and um . . ."

Out of the corner of her eye, she caught Jackson shifting, his legs widening.

Actually, it was already five minutes past her shift. Time to go.

"It's good," she finished. "Try it."

She moved away before he could demand anything more from her poor brain. She stripped her apron off as she walked, pausing only to speak to the other bartender. "I'm going to take off now, if you don't mind."

Jason nodded. "No problem."

After making sure no one was paying attention to her, she headed over to the booth in the corner. His smile was visible, even with his disguise. She'd grown used to his tiny smiles over the past couple weeks.

She was going to miss them when he was gone. The day he'd leave for his job in New York was rapidly approaching. She didn't know what would happen after, but she assumed he'd be back for Livvy and Maile, who he'd seen a few times now. Not to mention Kareem, who followed him around like a tiny shadow. They'd bonded so tightly every other word out of her son's mouth started with "uncle."

And hopefully, he'd be back for her, she not-so-secretly hoped. For sex or for friendship. Though she'd be sad when this off-the-charts sex ended. She'd had good sex before, but Jackson was so eager to do whatever she wanted.

Sadia shivered. So. Eager.

She stopped next to his table, every nerve ending prickling in anticipation of his touch. "Here again, huh?"

"Can't stay away." He glanced up at her, that sideways glance that never failed to make her heart pound. "You didn't make me a special drink tonight?"

She'd been in such a hurry to get to him, she'd forgotten. "Let me get you something."

He caught her wrist before she could go. "No. It's okay. I'd rather be sober when I'm inside you."

She flushed and automatically glanced around, but no one was paying attention to them. "Jackson," she hissed.

His eyes warmed. "Is that not what we're going to do?"

"You know very well it's exactly what we're going to do." She flipped her hand around so she was the one holding him and tugged. "Come on. It's time to go home."

He obliged and they left the bar together, the noise cutting off as the door closed behind them. She inhaled the apple-scented air. "Winter's going to be here soon."

"Mmm. Have you been to New York City around Christmas?"

A chill that had nothing to do with the weather ran through her. "No."

"You should go."

Ah, okay. This wasn't an invite. It was a suggestion.

She wasn't disappointed. She would have had to shoot down an invite. An invite would have been way too relationship-y. She'd been so careful not to fall in love with him so far. She'd succeeded.

Have you?

Yeah. Sure she had. "Someday I'll go." She stopped

next to her car. He slid his arms around her waist and walked her backward, until her butt met the vehicle.

Jackson rested his forehead against hers, his fingers brushing her shirt up so he could stroke the strip of flesh above her pants. "How did Lucy work out for you today?"

Her smile was more of a grimace. Lucy had shown up yesterday morning, a bright young chef fresh out of school with glowing recommendations and a sweet attitude. Jackson had been the one to find her, through his mysterious contacts in the culinary world. Lucy had easily fit into the kitchen and after hovering behind her all day yesterday, Jackson had left her alone today as a test.

"She didn't do well," he guessed, misinterpreting her grimace. "My friend can find you someone else."

"No, no. She's great. I like her a lot." The problem wasn't Lucy. The problem was what she represented, yet another reminder Jackson was leaving. She twined her arms around his neck and tugged. "Let's stop talking about work, huh?"

His thumb stroked her side. "What do you want to talk about instead?"

"I don't want to talk." Or think.

His lips met hers, and he kissed her like he understood that desire completely. His hands roved over her back and tugged at the hem of her shirt, pulling it up so he could skim over her back and up to her bra.

His fingers found the clasp, but before he could

undo it, a loud whistle came from behind them, followed by drunken laughter.

He pulled away, his body blocking her from whoever was behind them. She noticed he did that a lot, using his body to shield her. "I like watching, but I hate being watched," he said. "We should head out."

Her face flushed as she remembered the way they'd watched the graphic real-life porno play out in the back alley. That had been hot as hell, but she was on the same page with him about not being the actors in that sort of scenario. "Let's go."

He released her and stepped back, waiting until she was inside before walking around the car to get into the passenger side. It was getting too cold for his bike. He'd parked it in the garage. Which was not any kind of sign of permanence, she reminded herself.

She drove home with his hand on her thigh, his thumb stroking her skin through the thin material of her black pants. The tiny circular motions tightened the crank of need inside her, so much so she shuddered in relief when they pulled into the garage. The dim light from the overhead lamp highlighted the curves of his face.

She licked her lips. "Where?" She didn't need to elaborate. They'd had sex almost everywhere, except inside her house.

His touch went a little higher, flirting with the crease at the top of her thigh. "Your choice."

How was she supposed to think when he was so big and strong and . . . and . . .

His pinky dipped between her legs and rubbed. Her thighs clenched, trapping his hand between her legs. "We might end up in the car again," she warned.

"Wouldn't be the first time." His fingers curled in the tight space she'd created, finding her clit and plucking it. It was like Jackson had taken a master class on what she liked. "Is that what you want?"

"I don't know."

He wedged his hand tighter against her. She'd been right. He could play her like a violin. "I'll do whatever you want."

"Will you?"

"Sure. You know, maybe everything tonight should be your choice."

The blood rushed out of her head and her breath came faster. She clamped her hand over his to still him. His face was utterly innocent, but he couldn't fool her. She knew what most people didn't.

The man was a gentle giant in the street and a freak in the sheets.

"Upstairs. Let's go upstairs." They'd had sex in his apartment before. She'd wondered if it would be difficult for her, but her brain had apparently now deemed it Jackson's place.

He released his buckle, the click loud in the silence of the car. She swallowed before speaking again. "I'll give you a couple minutes. Get naked and wait for me."

There was that tiny smile again. The sound of the car door closing behind him made her jump, though she was expecting it.

She waited a few minutes, taking the time to apply an extra layer of lipstick and adjust her breasts in her low-cut shirt. When she'd dallied all she could, she got out of the car and made her way to the garage apartment.

She was about to knock, but she decided to go full-on aggressive and shove the door open. The sight inside made her knees weak. She shut the door behind her and simultaneously closed out the outside world and her own too-active brain. All she wanted to focus on was touching him. Wanting him. Lusting with and for him.

He sat on the edge of the bed, totally, gloriously naked, the only light coming from the dim over-head fixture in the bathroom. His fists were braced on the bed behind him, his biceps standing out in sharp relief. His golden, smooth skin was a smorgasbord of muscles and bone and sinew, all knit together to create a perfect vision of manliness.

His tattoo caught her eye as always. The geometric lines on his arm, the leaves draped over his shoulder, and Livvy's newest addition, a beautiful red rose that popped so lush and real it took her breath away. He said it wasn't tender anymore, though she'd been careful to avoid the healing wound. She'd asked him what it signified, but he'd only shrugged.

The ink highlighted the muscles of his arm and chest, but the rest of him deserved equal appreciation. His stomach was a ridged slab, his thighs massive and flexed. He had his feet planted flat on the floor, legs spread. His penis jutted between his thighs, a thick, long, delicious length that she'd felt now between her legs and in her mouth and against most of her body.

She wanted him to kiss her like he'd kissed her before, like he was going to die if he didn't crawl inside her and taste her. Or strip her clothes off and take his time studying her body. Or fall to his knees in front of her and lick her like he'd never get enough. Or hold still while she did the same to him.

So many possibilities. So she did what she always did, and made a mental list.

Sadia unbuttoned her pants and shimmied them down her legs, aware of his hot gaze on her. She stripped her shirt over her head and dropped it on the ground, and then her bra and her panties. He made a motion to grasp his cock. "No." Her tone was sharp.

He froze and his hand fell back to the bed to clutch the bedspread.

A rush of power swept through her. "Come here."

He stood and walked toward her, the muscles in his legs bunching and releasing. She wanted to write odes to those muscular thighs.

He stopped in front of her, waiting instruction, that massive cock brushing against her belly, leaving a wet trail. She wanted to fall to her knees and explore it with her mouth, but she had a list now, and she wouldn't stray from it. She rested her hands on his arms and breathed in deep, taking in the scent of spices and warm bread. He smelled like her kitchen. She wanted him to smell like her, a strange possessive thought she'd never had before. "Kiss me."

She expected him to kiss her passionately, but instead he cradled her cheek, tilting her face up. His breath ghosted over her skin, and then he was pressing chaste, tender kisses against her forehead, continuing over her nose, down to her lips. He sipped from her lips and her breath caught.

Pampered. Cared for. It was an illusion, but one she'd happily buy into.

"You are so perfect," he whispered.

She opened her mouth to speak and closed it again, oddly shaken at his repetition of this praise. She was a mess. A failure. "I'm not. What I am is tired," she confessed, and a stab of shame hit her. She didn't complain. She never complained. Complaining was also a form of failure.

Jackson wouldn't chastise her, though. His hand trailed over her shoulder, her arm, down to her waist. "Let me make you forget how tired you are."

If her body hadn't been wet before, it would have immediately softened at that offer. Her head tipped back as he drew her closer, until she could feel the hard length of his penis. He was thick and so enticing she pressed harder against him.

"Tell me what you want me to do."

"There are so many things."

A stroke on her side. "Use me for all of them."

She paused. She hadn't thought anything of him uttering that word *use* before, but now it left a vaguely bad taste in her mouth.

"What's wrong?"

"I don't want to use you." Not like she'd used other people she'd slept with. That had been a mutual using, an itch to scratch.

Jackson was different. Even without their complicated past, he'd be different.

"But I like it. I enjoy it."

Sadia cupped his head. "How about we say we're enjoying each other then? That sounds better."

He processed that. "Fine. But you can still act like you're using me." His smile was bigger and more than a little wicked. "It's hot when you take what you need."

Whimper. "In that case, kiss me like you mean it."

His lips descended on hers and he complied, working her mouth. The kiss was filthy, wet and rough, giving her a preview of what was to come. She wanted that tongue all over her.

She pulled away and leaned back against the door, arching her body and spreading her legs. "Get on your knees and lick me."

He was on the floor before she could finish the sentence. She kept meaning to groom or shave or something—she wasn't keen on yanking out her body hair unless someone else was going to appreciate her efforts—but he didn't seem to mind so it was low on her priorities. His fingers combed through her pubic hair, the crinkling noise magnified in the dimly lit room.

Two fingers opened her up, and his breath puffed over her wet folds. He blew, gently. She cried out. His laugh was low and deep. His laughs were rarer than his smiles, and the noise almost distracted her, but then his tongue swiped her flesh and her knees buckled. His hands wrapped around her, fingers digging into her ass.

He licked her again and again like she was a delicious treat, only taking breaks to suck on her clitoris. Even if she wanted to move, she couldn't, he held her so tight. She might have bruises tomorrow, but she didn't mind. Not when he was sampling her body so luxuriously. Climaxes had become a perfunctory act in the past couple of years, to be achieved as quickly as possible so she could sleep or go about her life. Jackson was lazy with his mouth.

He sucked her harder when she grew restless and pressed one finger inside her, then two, and hooked them, rubbing against the bundle of nerves hidden inside her. His hand moved faster as she moaned, not ceasing that perfect pressure. She came with a shudder and a groan of pleasure.

He gave her a chance to come down off the high, his touch light on her sides and bottom. She looked down at his dark head between her thighs, catching her breath enough to speak. "Good boy."

He nuzzled her. "How good?"

She ran her hand through his short hair. "So good you deserve a treat."

His tongue ran over his teeth. "Yeah?"

"Oh, yeah." She tugged at the strands. "Stand up and go sit on that chair." He got to his feet and turned. Feeling playful, she slapped his ass. He froze, then glanced over his shoulder.

"I liked that."

She'd just had an orgasm, but her body readied for him again. "Did you?" She slapped his other cheek, and then stroked over the hard flesh. She'd happily touch his ass all day, but then again, there was that list.

"The chair." She tapped him.

He went to the chair and sat down, his cock demanding her attention. She sank to her knees in front of him, then grasped his erection in her hands. She sucked him deep into her mouth, but pulled away when she felt his hands in her hair. "Nuh-uh," she said firmly. "Keep your hands to yourself."

His eyes gleamed in the near darkness. "Will you tie me up if I don't?"

Funny how verbal the man could be when he put his mind to it. She imagined him tied up in her bed, patiently waiting for her to do everything that lurked in her dirty imagination.

Next time she'd bring some of her silk scarves. "Yes. I will."

Jackson clasped the arms of the chair. She twisted her hair around her hand and tossed it over her shoulder so it wouldn't get in the way, then sucked his penis into her mouth again, making him nice and wet.

He groaned when she released him. "Don't stop."

"I call the shots, remember? And right now . . ." She grasped his cock in both hands, and stroked the hard, wet flesh. "I want to massage this cock of yours."

"Massage . . . oh God." His hands tightened into fists as she rubbed him. She alternated the motion with her mouth, keeping him wet and slick as she manipulated him with her hands until he was groaning.

"Let me fuck you," he finally gasped.

She licked his cock. "Why?"

"What?"

"Why do you want to fuck me?"

"Because . . . because you're the most beautiful woman I've ever seen."

Awww. "There are more beautiful women than me."

His brow furrowed. "No."

Just that. A simple no. She scraped her nails up the side of his hard thigh. "Stay here."

She rose to her feet, and as she walked to the bed, she did feel like the most beautiful woman in the world. She arranged herself on the bed, appreciating his tortured moan when she got on her hands and knees, her back arched.

She rested her forehead on her stacked hands. "Fuck me now."

He bolted out of his seat like she had cut the cord on some invisible leash. His cock brushed over her bottom as he leaned over and grabbed a condom from the drawer in the nightstand.

She had a moment to prepare herself before he shafted inside her, fucking her hard and deep. Her fingers curled into the bedding, and she rested her forehead on the bed. In between the bursts of pleasure, one thought rose up. "Don't stop."

"I won't." He fucked her harder, pulling her hips up higher.

She whimpered, her disquiet fading in the heat of the moment. The coil of tension tightened inside her and she came with a great rush, her body weakening and softening all over his.

He grunted and went rigid. He caught himself on his arms so he wouldn't collapse on her, then rolled to his side.

They were both breathing hard, momentarily satiated. He drew her close and she rested her hand on his chest, right under the healing red rose. Her cheek brushed his chest and she studied the Japanese characters written on the inside of his bicep.

When his breathing slowed, she spoke. "What does that mean?"

He lifted his head and looked at the characters. "Translated, it means once in a lifetime, or never again."

"Oh." She'd been asking what it signified to him, but she doubted her favorite clam would tell her that.

He kissed her forehead, then rose from the bed. She winced at the bright light from the lamp he turned on. "I'll be right back."

She smiled and leaned back on the pillows, watching his ass flex as he moved to the bathroom, trying to avoid the odd sadness inside her. They'd fucked plenty over the past week, but cuddling had been limited. Which was fine. She hadn't asked him for cuddling. If she had, he would give it to her.

She didn't want to be cuddled, she told herself firmly. She was fine. *Fine.*

She rolled over and noticed that the nightstand drawer was still open. Sadia leaned up on one elbow to shut it. She wasn't sure what caught her attention, but her gaze went to the leather-bound book inside, sitting there like a hotel room bible. This must have been what John had given him. Sam's journal.

Her love of history and nostalgia had her picking the thing up. She flipped through a couple of pages, rereading words she'd read long ago. Sam had been a no-nonsense, determined man. She wished she could have met him, though John had tried to keep him alive for all of them.

She turned another page and a folded-up piece of paper fluttered out of the book onto the bedspread. She sat up and retrieved it, opening it.

Dear Grandpa John . . .

She didn't realize she was crying until the letter was pulled from her hands. She looked up, Jackson's rigid face appearing wavy and distorted to her wet eyes. He'd put on his boxer briefs and jeans.

She shook her head. "No," she said, and that was all she could say. "No, no, no, no . . ."

He put the letter on the nightstand carefully, like anyone needed to be careful with that. "Sadia . . ."

"No!"

"Listen to me." He tried to place his hand on her shoulder, but she scrambled backward.

"That's not real. Tell me that's not real."

His eyes darkened. "It's not real."

"You're lying to me." She dug her palms into her eye sockets, like that could make her forget what she'd read.

Her husband, the man she'd adored and married and had a child with, had not only committed a felony, he'd then persuaded his younger brother to keep his mouth shut when he was arrested.

Sadia swallowed, struggling to keep her nausea under control. "All this time, I thought it was an accident, or someone else did it, and you were a scapegoat. And you were a scapegoat, only it was my husband who made you into that scapegoat."

"Please don't be upset."

"John knew. Did anyone else?"

"My mom."

"Of course." She nodded, hysterical laughter bubbling up inside her. "I knew you must have had a reason to cut them both off." Everything made sense now, like someone had turned the lights on in her dark world. She still carried wounds over her sisters not standing up for her a decade ago. How must Jackson have felt, when his brother had actively urged him to take the blame for a crime he hadn't committed. "I can't believe this is real."

"I'm sorry. I never wanted you to know."

"You don't have to be sorry. Oh god, I'm sorry."

"If I don't have to be sorry, neither do you."

"I was married to him. I should have known." She couldn't begin to reconcile the man who had held his infant so gently with a man who could lie to get his baby brother into jail.

"How would you have known?"

"I . . . I don't know. But either way, he was my husband. I'm responsible for his actions."

He twisted so he could look at her more fully. "That's absurd."

"How did he get you to agree?"

"It's not important."

"Tell me, damn it!"

"He told me you were pregnant!"

It was the first time Sadia had ever heard Jackson raise his voice. He pressed his lips tight together immediately after, as if to recall the words.

Too late.

"Pregnant?" she whispered. "I wasn't pregnant." She and Paul had always been super conscientious about birth control. It had taken a year of active attempts for her to get pregnant with Kareem.

"I know. He told me he lied after I was released."

Slowly the truth dawned on her. Paul had manipulated his brother. Because Jackson would have willingly gone to jail if it meant Paul could stay with her and their unborn child.

People. Quality. Fairness.

"Oh my God. How you must hate him." A thought struck, and horror swamped her. She grabbed the sheet and yanked it up to cover her body. "Fuck, is that what this was? You and me? Were you . . . getting some sick sort of revenge?"

His eyes opened wide and he shook his head. "Oh no. No, not at all." He grasped for her hands, but she couldn't let go of her death grip on the sheets.

"He was dead, but I was here, is that it?" Nausea rose up in her throat. "You could punish me—"

"No. Never. I slept with you because . . ."

"Because why?"

"Because I love you."

Her hand tightened, an involuntary reflex. "Like a friend," she said faintly.

"No. More than a friend. Paul wasn't dumb, he knew I'd do anything for you. I've always loved you, from the moment I saw you on that playground, wearing that rose red dress. I always will."

There was no air left for her. It was all gone, grabbed away. Her lungs worked. Her gaze drifted to his new rose tattoo.

The silence in the room stretched between them, absorbing every soughing breath she took. "What—always?"

"Always."

There was no room to misinterpret his words or think he was kidding. This was real. He really had always loved her, romantically.

She opened her mouth, but nothing came out. Her brain was scrambled. Even as she tried to come up with something, anything, she watched Jackson shut down. First it was his eyes, shuttering, then his lips tightening. Finally, he rose from the bed and stuffed his hands in his pockets. "I'll go."

"Wait." He paused, but she could only shake her head. "I need some time."

He nodded. She thought he understand what

she was asking of him—hold her, comfort her, let her work this out and they could talk—but instead, he grabbed his shirt and shoes from the floor and walked soundlessly out the door. Leaving her absolutely alone with all the ghosts of her past.

Chapter 19

JACKSON BLINKED open his eyes to a whistled tune he couldn't identify. Waking up was never difficult for him. He'd spent enough time in enough bedrooms all over the world that he'd lost the sensation of disorientation most people suffered.

Today, though, he stared up at the white ceiling, taking a second to get his bearings. His eyes were crusty, tired from a lack of sleep. He craved both coffee and a cigarette.

The latter craving he'd ignore, but he could probably bum the former. He rose up on his elbows and peered over the back of the sofa. Nicholas was standing in front of the round mirror in the living room, adjusting his tie. Their eyes met in the mirror, and Nicholas jerked, spinning around. "Jesus fucking Christ. Jackson. What the fuck?"

"You kiss my sister with that mouth?" Jackson scrubbed his hand over his face. He wasn't sure what had possessed him to come here in the middle of the night. He'd left Sadia's and gone to O'Killian's and had a couple of beers, which was more than enough to get him drunk. He didn't even remember giving the taxi driver this address.

"I do, indeed," Nicholas said grimly. "What did I tell you about breaking into my house?"

"Then stop making it so damn easy." Jackson vaguely recalled picking the lock and peering at the alarm panel. "Your mother's birthday this time? I told you to change it from Livvy's to something harder to guess."

"I kept forgetting the random numbers."

Jackson sighed. "If you have Livvy staying here, I need you to take better care of your security." Nicholas's eyes narrowed and Jackson swung his legs over the side of the couch, coming to his feet. He was spoiling for a fight. Maybe that was why his subconscious had led him to Nicholas's place in the wee hours of the morning.

"Jackson? What are you doing here?"

He shifted his gaze to the arched opening to the room, his aggression vanishing. Livvy was wearing loose gym shorts and a boat-necked T-shirt, no makeup, her blue hair loose. She looked like a teenager, not a fully grown woman of thirty.

He slipped his hands inside his pockets, but couldn't speak. What could he say? There was no excuse for him to have come inside Nicholas's place last night, except Livvy's car had been parked outside.

He needed his sister.

He wasn't accustomed to needing anyone, and Livvy had always needed him, not the opposite.

People had always looked at his big, hulking body, his capable hands, and assumed he was more than self-sufficient.

And he was. Except in this. His heart was bruised and battered.

Her face softened as the silence stretched and she spoke to Nicholas. "Nico, why don't you make us some coffee?"

"Livvy, I won't have your brother breaking in whenever he feels like it."

"It's not like he's making a habit of breaking in."

He and Nicholas exchanged a look, and Jackson waited for Nicholas to out him, but the other man only grunted and exited the room, his feet stomping slightly louder than necessary.

Livvy walked over and grasped his arm. "Sit down."

"Your boyfriend is right. I shouldn't be here."

"I think you're exactly where you need to be," Livvy said firmly, and tugged at his arm. "Now sit down."

He allowed her to push him down onto the couch. "I wasn't certain if you'd be here or not."

Livvy made a face. "Mom's still not keen on Nicholas and me. We had a bit of an argument after dinner, and I came here."

He couldn't imagine his mother was super on board with Livvy and Nicholas hooking up. Forget the fact that Nicholas's father had taken over the company. His mother had died with her husband. Seeing Nicholas's face couldn't be easy for her.

"She's going to come around," Livvy continued

with more optimism than he could handle without coffee. "I'm sure of it."

"Don't expect us all to sit down for dinner anytime soon," he warned Livvy.

Her gaze drifted away, and he knew she'd been imagining exactly that. "Livvy—"

"I know! I'm a marshmallow." She glared at him. "Don't remind me."

"You and Nicholas went away and worked through your issues. It's going to take everyone else some time."

"And some people may never come around, I know," she said quietly, and he knew she was thinking of Nicholas's father. She pasted a bright smile on her face. "Enough about me. What's up with you?"

He scrubbed his hand over his face. "I told Sadia I loved her last night and she didn't say anything back." As the words fell from his lips, a part of him stood apart, horrified.

He was naked, vulnerable. But Livvy didn't look alarmed or confused or surprised. She pursed her lips. "Ah."

He linked his hands together between his knees. "Actually, I said a lot before that too."

"Tell me."

He was so tired. "Paul set the fire at the C&O."

She blanched, but she didn't look totally surprised. "I wondered," she murmured. "People were always confusing you and him. It wouldn't have been absurd for a witness to have mistaken him for you."

He had also been the more believable villain.

Paul had been loved by the town, the future heir to the family fortune. No one had wanted it to be him. "Yeah."

"He asked you to go with the police, didn't he?"

"Yes. He said there was no real evidence against me." He left out their mother's role in persuading him. "And when I was still on the fence, he told me Sadia was pregnant."

Livvy drew back. "Uh, she was not pregnant back then."

"I know. He lied. When I got out, he told me, and we had a massive fight." He glanced up at her. "He was scared I'd tell everyone he did it. I was scared he'd tell Sadia the truth. I was ashamed, too, that he knew I was in love with her. I'd been so careful not to let her see."

"Why?"

"What?"

"Why were you so careful not to let her know how you felt about her back then?"

"Because she was with Paul."

"Not always," Livvy pointed out. "You were friends with her way before Paul fell for her."

"I was . . . I don't know." He thought about it. "I guess I was scared. I told myself later I was only saving her the burden of knowing, but it was also for me." He wouldn't have to face the consequence of rejection if he never tried.

Can't or won't.

He curled his hands into fists, recognizing the truth. He had been scared. He'd always been scared.

"I've tried not to care for anyone. It gets me into trouble."

"No. Caring for people isn't what gets you into trouble. You're, like, super good at caring for people." She placed her hands over his. "I can testify to that. The problem is, you're a marshmallow."

His lips curved up. "You're the marshmallow."

"Yup," she said cheerfully. "We are a package of two marshmallows. Someone pokes at you, and you feel it, don't you? You dent and bruise."

"I don't understand where you're going with this analogy."

Her smile faded. "I'm saying Paul hurt you by lying to you. He used your love for Sadia against you, and that was cruel and mean, and it sucks that you can't yell at him. He dented you hard, and you ran to protect yourself. But marshmallows spring back, and I think that's what you've been trying to do, coming back here. You've been trying to regain your shape."

He released a shaky breath. "I don't know what I'm doing."

"I think there's a difference in not caring for anyone and being careful in who you love. Sadia isn't Paul. I'm not Paul." She paused. "And as many problems as I had with the guy, Jackson, I don't think the Paul who died on that trail was the Paul who hurt you."

Jackson thought about that letter Paul had sent to John, confessing his sins. *I love my brother.* "I don't . . . I don't know."

"It's hard to make your peace with someone who isn't around anymore. Or more accurately, to make your peace with never making your peace." She smiled sadly. "But sometimes it's the only thing you can do."

A scrape from the doorway had them both looking up. Nicholas was watching them, his lips pressed tight together, two mugs in his hands.

Shit. How much had the man heard?

Livvy had stiffened next to him as well. Nicholas walked over and handed him a mug, and then handed Livvy hers. She looked up at him, and he cupped her cheek. Then he glanced between the two of them. "If you two don't mind, I'm going to propose that what was said here never gets repeated again. Not outside the family, at least. As far as I'm concerned, and my statement if anyone asks, is that Jackson was totally innocent of any wrongdoing."

Livvy closed her eyes, and then opened them again. Nicholas wiped her tear away. "Thank you," she whispered.

The look Nicholas gave Livvy was so tender and filled with love, Jackson had to find something else in the room to study. "Don't thank me," Nicholas said. "I cared about Paul, too, and there's no need to poke that hornet's nest again. The only ones who would pay for it are you and Kareem and Sadia." Nicholas turned to Jackson, and this time his expression was stern. "Jackson, I know you don't like me, but speaking of Sadia, I'd really advise you to get your shit together and go talk to her."

"But—"

"She found out she was one of the reasons you went to jail, discovered her husband committed arson, you told her you loved her, *and then* you walked out when she didn't reciprocate fast enough. Is that right?"

Fuck. When he put it like that, the night sounded worse than he'd even thought. "I—"

"She's the best thing that ever happened to you or your brother. She was understandably upset yesterday. Give her some room, then make your case as to why she should give you the time of day."

"Just like a Chandler," Livvy said affectionately. "Bossy as hell."

Nicholas smiled, and it was supremely un-robotlike. "Just like a Kane," he returned. "Giving me hell."

"I can't handle this foreplay," Jackson muttered, and rose to his feet. He looked Nicholas in the eye and stuck out his hand. "Maybe you're not all bad."

"High praise." Nicholas accepted his offer. "Sorry I thought you were a felon."

"I understand." And he really did.

"Do me a favor, though," Nicholas added. "Please stop breaking into my home?"

Chapter 20

SADIA CRACKED an eye open when she heard the feminine voices coming down the hall toward her bedroom, but even that was too difficult, so she closed them. Her eyes were crusty and hurt. She was exhausted but hadn't slept.

Her son snuggled closer against her side. It was Saturday, which she hadn't realized until Kareem had come tumbling into her bed a few hours ago, telling her Ayesha had already left the house. She'd forgotten her sister had slept over, too.

Sadia had handed Kareem her phone, and he'd been well occupied watching videos and playing games. She needed to feed him and get dressed and check in on the café, where hopefully Lucy had showed up to cook like she was scheduled. She didn't know if Jackson would be there or if he'd left town already. Maybe after she'd stumbled out of his apartment and gone to her home to cry soundlessly in her shower, he'd come back and packed his things up to leave.

I love you.

She screwed her eyes tighter, as if that could block out everything that had happened last night.

"Sadia? Are you still in bed?"

She opened her crusty eyes to find all four of her sisters filing into her room, carrying large garment bags. Weird.

Kareem looked up from his video for a split second. "Hey, aunties."

"What are you all doing here?" Her voice was hoarse, and she must have sounded worse than she looked, because they exchanged silent looks.

"You told us to come here in the morning so we could make sure everything would run smoothly for the party tonight, remember?" Zara's words were slow and measured. "You sent us lists."

Fuck. Her parent's anniversary party. She didn't want to go or organize anything or even think about moving today.

What will people say?

What did it matter?

Noor hustled over and laid a hand on her forehead. "You don't have a fever. Are you sick? You're never in bed this late."

Sadia listlessly shook her head.

Her sister's gaze drifted over the wooden box on the empty pillow next to Sadia's. She picked it up. Sadia couldn't work up the energy to stop her.

Noor stared down at the rings and Paul's photo for a long minute before snapping the lid shut. Sadia flinched from what she saw in her sister's expression.

Pity.

Noor rallied. "Ayesha, can you please take Kareem to get cleaned up and ready?"

"He hasn't eaten yet," Sadia managed.

"I'm not hungry," Kareem interjected, his gaze locked on her phone.

"We'll see if we can find you something," Ayesha said brightly.

Sadia's arms felt empty when Kareem scrambled away, taking her phone with him. It was fine. She didn't need it today. Their schedule was already fucked.

She squeezed her eyes shut tight, trying to block out her remaining sisters. Perhaps if she couldn't see them, they would leave her in peace.

That was a silly hope. The mattress shifted as the three of them took places, one on either side of her, one by her leg.

A small, smooth hand stroked over her brow. Zara. "Sadia, what's wrong?"

"Nothing."

Jia's fingers snuck into hers and tightened. "It doesn't look like nothing's wrong."

"Kareem—"

"Kareem's fine," Noor said, and her touch came on her shoulder. "Ayesha will take care of him."

A tear snuck out from the corner of her eye. "I can't believe I didn't feed him breakfast."

"A child missing one meal is not the end of the world. Or a reflection of your parenting." Zara's soothing strokes continued. "What's wrong?"

She couldn't tell them. There was no way she

would be able to ever let anyone know about Paul and the fire and Jackson, not even her family. She rolled her head to look at perfect, pristine Noor.

Sadia wasn't perfect, and she was so exhausted. She wanted to smear herself in front of them as much as she was able, to destroy whatever image they had in their heads about her. "Jackson loves me," she said flatly.

Noor raised her eyebrows. "Your brother-in-law?"

"Yes."

"*Love* loves you?"

"Yes. He came home, I had an affair with him, and he told me he's in love with me."

"My." Noor pursed her lips. "You do have a type."

"Noor," Zara snapped, but her tone softened when Sadia looked at her. "That's okay, Sadia. Grief sometimes makes you act out and—"

"It's not grief. What I did with Jackson had nothing to do with grief. I slept with him because I wanted him." She studied them, but none of them looked particularly shocked.

"But you don't love him back?" Jia asked.

Sadia hesitated, confused by their lack of scandalized horror. She'd slept with her former brother-in-law, and they were all looking at her like that was a perfectly normal thing for her to do. "It doesn't matter whether I love him, or not. I can't have a relationship with him."

Noor cocked her head. "Why not?"

Don't say it. It wasn't worth it to get into all of this. She should climb out of bed and end this therapy session. "Because I'd fail. I'm a failure," she blurted out.

Jia screwed up her face. "What?"

Noor drew up tall. "No."

"Why do you think that?" Zara questioned.

Another tear leaked out. "My marriage failed."

"Your husband died, love." Zara's voice was very gentle. "That's not your failure."

"No." She hated this, but she couldn't stop now. "It failed before he died. We were going to get a divorce. That was why he went alone. Otherwise I would have been on that trail with him . . ." She stopped talking, eyes widening. Oh, god. She hadn't realized how her brain had linked the two of those things. "He wouldn't have died," she finished in a whisper, her tears coming in earnest. "Kareem would have his father. I'm the reason . . . oh god, I'm the reason he doesn't."

"Oh, no." Zara shifted, gathering her close as she started to sob. "No, my love. That's not true at all."

She pressed her hand against her chest, praying that familiar tightening would stay away. She couldn't handle a panic attack right now, not on top of this emotional destruction. She took Zara's comfort, absorbed Noor's careful pats on her back, took strength from Jia's murmured crooning.

When her tears had slowed, Zara spoke. "Sadia, did you see that psychiatrist I recommended after Paul died?"

"I had a few appointments. He just gave me some medication and didn't really seem interested in talking. It felt like a waste of time."

Zara didn't look pleased by this. "I'll find you someone else. In the meantime, let me tell you, quite certainly, you had nothing to do with Paul's death."

"But I—"

"If I got a divorce tomorrow, would you call me a failure?"

"No."

"What about Noor?"

Sadia sniffed. She could see where Zara was going with this. "No."

"What about any other woman?"

"No."

"Then why are you crueler to yourself than you'd be to a stranger?"

The rationale made sense, but she couldn't banish the crushing sense of failure that lingered over her. "I'm a mess in every way, though. I can't take care of Kareem by myself and I can't run this business and I can't get up for this party and I—I can't do anything."

Noor tapped her knee. "You take care of Kareem fine. You're a better mother than me."

"That's a high compliment from Noor," Jia added, in a deliberately light tone. "She thinks she's the best at everything."

Noor snorted. "Oh please. I know I'm not the best. And I know you're not a failure, Sadia. You're simply an anxious perfectionist like the rest of us."

Sadia swiped at her nose. "I have panic attacks."

"Me too," Zara said, stunning her. Her older sister smiled faintly. "Love, we are all different, but Noor is right. We're also all basically the same. I've had to work at not setting standards for myself I can't possibly reach, because when I don't meet them, I feel like a disaster. I used to have an anxiety attack if I ever got a grade that was less than perfect."

"I threw up every morning in residency," Noor admitted gruffly. "If I ever got chastised, I was certain I'd screwed up everything."

They looked at Jia, who scrunched her nose sheepishly. "Whenever I post a photo, I obsessively refresh it until I get a certain number of likes. It's why I can't post anything too close to bedtime."

Zara smiled. "Noor and I have been talking about this a lot this week, haven't we, sister? About how we're all different and how success can mean different things to each of us? And we should be allowed to pursue our own dreams?"

Noor let out a rough exhale at the pointed words. "Yeah." She nodded at their youngest sister. "Jia, I want every piece of financial information you have on this silly—I mean, on this business you want to start."

Jia started. "Oh." Her eyes widened, Noor's words sinking in. "I wasn't expecting this right now, but yes! I will. I'll send it to you."

Zara tapped Sadia on her cheek to get her attention. "Do you see? You did that. You're our moral compass and our organizational whiz and our heart, Sadia. If you're looking for what you're truly good at, that's a great example right there of your success."

A trickle of warmth lit her chest, easing the tightness that had threatened.

"If I ever made you feel bad about yourself, I'm sorry," Noor pulled her close in an awkward hug. "You were right. We should have supported you in whatever decisions you made instead of telling you they were bad decisions."

Sadia could count on one hand the number of times Noor had ever apologized. To anyone, let alone her. She hugged her back, then sat back against her pillows. "Thank you."

Noor glanced at her watch and came to her feet. "You don't have to go to this party, if you don't want to, Sadia. But could you please tell the rest of us what we need to do?"

Sadia ran her hand through her hair, encountering knots. "I have to go to the party. What will people say?"

Noor rolled her eyes. "Honest to god. Who cares?"

Chapter 21

Livvy had been exactly right. It was impossible to make peace with a dead man.

Jackson found Paul's grave easily. It was near their father's and their grandparents'. Someone had been taking care of them. All of his family members' stones were free of weeds, with fresh flowers in little vases.

Jackson first went to Robert Kane's tombstone and laid his hand on it. The wind was picking up force, cutting through his leather jacket, dead leaves whirling around him. He pressed his palm against the cold marble. "Hey, Dad. Sorry I haven't visited in so long." He'd never visited, actually. Not after his father's funeral.

He stroked the marble, weathered now after a decade. He hadn't had the closest relationship with his father but they'd loved each other. Part of him was glad he hadn't visited this grave before. He'd rather have the image of his father as a big, boisterous man than this cold stone marking his last place.

Jackson stood there for a second, then made his

way to Paul's stone. It was smaller than their father's. Jackson crouched down to tug at a tiny weed encroaching on Paul's space. "Hello, brother," he said quietly. "I'm so mad at you."

As he said the words, his shoulders lightened, like he'd shed a weight he'd been carrying for a decade. "I'm mad at you for telling me nothing would happen to me. I'm mad at you for lying about Sadia. I'm mad at you for knowing I loved her. But most importantly, I'm pissed as hell that you went and died before I could tell you any of that." He tugged harder at the weed. A part of him had been certain that one day he'd see Paul again. That they'd fight and scream at each other, and then they'd be back to where they'd been before that horrible day in his mother's bedroom. "You wrote a letter to John, of all people, you dumbass. You couldn't write a letter to me? You couldn't tell me you loved me directly? What is wrong with—" He took a deep breath, realizing he was yelling at a grave. "I'm even mad at that letter. Because you managed to tell me you love me, and I—I'll never be able to tell you I love you."

He knows.

For a second, he wondered if someone had whispered the words, but then he realized they were coming from inside him. "He didn't know." All his brother had known was that he coveted the man's woman.

You were ready to take on a felony charge for him. For Sadia, yes, but also for him. He knew.

Jackson closed his eyes. He wasn't a man given to praying, but he prayed that was true. He prayed his brother had known he'd come back eventually, that he'd loved him unconditionally. He really needed his brother to have known that.

"Jackson?"

He opened his eyes and looked up at his mother. Tani was holding multiple bouquets of flowers in one hand. Her cane wasn't in sight. She came closer. She was walking with a slight limp.

"You're out here alone?" he asked gruffly. He came to his feet and took the flowers from her. She let go of them, but reluctantly.

"I always come alone. A broken hip wouldn't stop me from that."

He stepped back and let her circle her son's grave. When she started to painfully get to her knees, he held her arm. "Let me help you, please."

He assisted her to the ground, and she removed the older flowers from the vase and held out her hand. He placed the bouquet in it and watched as she carefully, methodically arranged the flowers. "I am surprised to see you here," she said quietly.

"Livvy said I needed to make peace with Paul."

"That sounds like something Livvy would say. She's been speaking like some kind of therapist since she got back."

The words were a criticism, but the fondness underlying them couldn't be hidden. Livvy and their mother had always had some sort of odd, half-critical, half-kind relationship he'd never been able to parse. Growing up, his mother had never sniped at him about his weight or his eating habits or hygiene, so he assumed this was some sort of mother-daughter thing he didn't fully understand.

He crouched down next to his mother, hating the way she flinched. He kept his gaze on Paul's grave. "You don't have to be scared of me," he murmured. "I'm not . . . I was mad at you. Maybe a part of me still is. I thought I was your favorite, but you chose Paul so quickly. You backed up his lie about Sadia. And then you didn't come see me when I was in jail, and I was scared. But I'm trying to get over that mad. I'm hoping I can, someday, and we can have some sort of relationship."

There.

He started to rise to his feet, but his mother placed her small, trembling hand on his arm. "Have you ever driven through a thunderstorm? When the rain is pounding down on the windshield and the wipers are working overtime, but you can't even see the car in front of you?"

At his nod, she continued. "That's how I felt in the weeks after your father died. I don't completely remember every minute of it. Livvy asked me last week if she thought I was perhaps having a depressive episode, and maybe I was, I don't know."

"We don't have to talk about this," he interjected.

"We do. Because I remember the panic of Paul confessing what he'd done, and about the man who saw him. I backed him up about Sadia, because I believed him at the time. I didn't know until later that she wasn't actually pregnant." She took a deep breath. "I asked you to go with the police, Jackson, because I honestly thought it would be resolved in a day or so. It shouldn't have taken as long as it did."

"None of us really knew the law, so that makes—"

"I knew the law," she countered crisply. "That witness kept upping his price. It took me a couple of weeks to liquidate the cash necessary to pay him off."

He reared back. Instinctively, he looked all around them, but the graveyard was empty. If there was any place to confess secrets, this was it. "What?" He shook his head, as if that would clear his hearing. "Wait, what?"

Tani sighed, and adjusted a flower that didn't really need adjusting. "There was no way in hell I'd let either of my boys go to prison. Luckily, I had Brendan's money for the shares in the C&O, though it took a while for all of that cash to clear. You ask me why I don't regret selling that place? For one, it made it possible for neither you nor Paul to pay with your lives for one moment of reckless passion."

"Mom. Jesus."

"Don't take the Lord's name in vain," she said primly, this woman who had covered up arson. "All of this is between the two of us, of course. And it's no excuse for my not coming to see you or talking to your attorney. But driving through that rain and fog while trying to raise enough money to pay off that man? That took all of my resources then. I had none left to spare on making jailhouse visits. And I'm sorry about that."

He didn't know what to say. He was generally a

champion for fairness and justice, but who would benefit from him chastising his mother for bribery? Nicholas and John had already said they didn't care about what Paul had done. Paul was dead. Nicholas's asshole dad was the only one who might stand to benefit from this revelation, and Jackson wasn't about to go snitching to him.

And in an odd sort of way, he was touched. He knew better than anyone what shape Tani had been in then. It must have taken all of her spoons to get up out of bed and . . . commit a crime.

He exhaled roughly. No one had ever said his family wasn't dysfunctional as hell. "Are we done with secrets? Is there anything else we should tell each other?"

"You could tell me what you've been doing all this time."

"It's a long story."

His mother rose to her feet, and he assisted her, coming to his feet as well. "I have time," she said.

He needed to figure out what to say to Sadia, but he couldn't turn down this offer. These sorts of second chances came too rarely. "We can go home. I can make lunch for us and give you a quick rundown. Maybe you can help me too."

"With Sadia? What happened, did you upset her?" She smiled at his surprise. "Yes, I assumed there was a reason you were staying with her. A fool could see you loved her when you were young. Paul would be happy."

"Are you sure?"

"Your brother loved Kareem and Sadia more than

anything. To have someone like you in their lives? When you've already proven how willing you are to sacrifice for that woman? He'd be ecstatic."

"I hope so."

"I know so." His mother wasn't an expressive person, but she seemed lit up from within, her skin glowing. There was no hesitation when she took his arm.

And there was no hesitation when he put his hand on hers.

Chapter 22

AFTER A couple of hours with her sisters, Sadia felt well enough to attend the party. Not because she ultimately cared what people thought, but because she truly didn't want to miss it. Her parents would never have this party, this anniversary again. Her sisters had helped her get dressed, Jia wielding makeup magic so she didn't look quite so exhausted.

The house was loud, packed with guests who had known the doctors forever. Sadia did her best to smile and nod and mingle, even when she felt like running away and going home to see if Jackson had packed up his apartment.

I love you.

She blew out a breath, still unsure of what to think about that. Maybe she wasn't a total failure, but she still had no guarantee everything would work out perfectly. He'd left her before, what was to say he wouldn't leave her again?

There were extenuating circumstances then.

"Hello, Sadia." Her father appeared at her side. He was dressed in a suit that she was certain he'd had tailored for the occasion, but it still hung a little limply on him.

"Daddy. You look so handsome." She straightened his tie, though he didn't really need it.

"I still don't see why I had to wear a suit," he grumbled.

Sadia leaned in close. "It's because Mom likes to see you dressed up. She thinks you're handsome, too."

His cheeks darkened. "Hmph. Nonsense." He paused. "Did she tell you this?"

She allowed herself the first real moment of amusement she'd experienced all day. "She didn't have to. I've seen the way she looks at you."

Tall as he was, Mohammad was able to easily search the crowd for his wife, his face softening when he spotted her, dressed in her pretty new blue shalwar kameez. "I suppose there is something to dressing up now and again."

"Indeed."

Mohammad turned back to Sadia, expression warm. "Thank you for throwing this party. Everything is perfect."

"Oh, we all organized it together."

"Sadia, I know my daughters." Her father put his arm around her and gave her a quick squeeze. "When you were young and we would go on trips, you were the only one who didn't make me feel like I was herding five cats." A reminiscing smile played on his lips. "You had lists and then lists for your lists."

Sadia's smile was genuine. "I'm glad you're enjoying yourself."

He pressed a quick kiss on top of her forehead. "I am. MashAllah, I am a blessed man."

Warmth spread through her. She cleared her throat, wondering if one of her sisters had said something to their father. He wasn't normally enormously demonstrative, though he'd always been affectionate enough for a man with a demanding profession and five children. "Why don't you go compliment your bride?" She leaned over to the nearest hightop table and pulled a white rose out of an arrangement. "Give her this. Be smooth."

He accepted the rose. "That is why your mother married me. Because of how smooth I am."

Sadia watched him make his way across the room, grinning when he bowed in front of Farzana with a flourish. Her mother tittered and blushed, glancing around them at their guests, but then she accepted the rose with a secretive grin.

Sadia turned in time to catch Kareem scurrying past her. She grabbed his arm before he could disappear, tsking over the juice he'd already spilled on his shirt. "Kareem, really." She blotted at the stain with the napkin she held.

"Mom, come on," he whined. "I wanna go play."

His usual refrain when he was around his cousins. She rolled her eyes and stood. "Fine. Go." All of the kids would have more than juice stains on their shirts by the end of the night, of that she was sure.

He ran off, then stopped and pivoted. "Is Uncle Jackson coming?"

She swallowed the sting of pain, her mood dimming again. "I told you, he's not coming tonight."

Kareem's disappointment was palpable, but he darted off, the lure of his cousins too bright to maintain pouting.

If only *she* could not pout about this.

She drifted through the crowd and she was sure she said all the right things, but it was hard to know for sure when her brain was barely there. It was firmly stuck on the man who'd managed to worm his way into her mind and heart in barely a few weeks.

I love you. I've always loved you.

"Where's that nephew of mine? I have some more gum for him."

Sadia's shoulders relaxed and she turned to face Livvy. "You came."

"Of course." Livvy had toned down her look for the party, bundling her dyed hair up in a neat updo, and wearing a simple black dress and flats.

Sadia had invited Livvy last week, but she hadn't been sure the other woman would attend. "Is Nicholas here?"

"No. We decided he would be too distracting."

That was a good call. Chandlers tended to draw attention no matter what, and Nicholas and Livvy together would definitely pull the spotlight off her parents. Sadia glanced around. "I need to talk to you."

Livvy's smile was rueful. "I figured you might, sister. Come on."

Livvy easily navigated her way through Sadia's childhood home, until they were at the back door.

They slipped outside onto the porch, which was blessedly, thankfully empty.

She opened her mouth, but Livvy beat her to it. "I know about Paul, I found out today, I can't believe it either except I totally can, and I'm so so sorry."

Sadia pressed her lips together. "You saw Jackson?"

"Yes." Livvy took hold of Sadia's hands. "I know you probably feel betrayed."

"I do, yes."

"I'm sorry." Livvy grimaced. "I know you don't like getting involved in the Kane family drama."

Sadia laughed, but there was little humor in it. "Well, I suppose it's my family no matter what, so it's my drama."

"I can't tell you how to feel about Paul. I'm pissed at him, and I wasn't married to him. But, like, he wasn't a bad man. He did something dumb." Livvy raised a shoulder.

"So dumb. And the worst part is, I can't even talk to anyone about it."

"You can tell me. And my mom, I guess. And, well, Jackson?"

She studied Livvy for a second. "He told you about us," she guessed. She'd purposefully avoided Livvy lately, fearful her best friend would sense her deepening adoration of Jackson.

"He did. I told him he screwed up, that he sprang a lot on you, and he should talk to you." Livvy's gaze drifted out, across the yard. "He agreed."

Sadia looked, then looked again. Jackson leaned

against one of the pillars of the gazebo that had been in the backyard for ages. They'd played and read and talked in that gazebo as children.

They weren't children any longer.

Someone had turned on the fairy lights that draped the structure, and his perfect, beautiful face and body were covered in a golden glow, caressing his brown skin, his sharp nose, his full lips. He was dressed casually, as usual, but his jeans and sweater looked new. "Do you want to talk to him?" Livvy asked quietly. "If not, I can—"

"No," she responded. "Can you keep an eye on Kareem?"

"Consider it done."

A flash of gratefulness shot through her. She did have the best family.

She lifted her dress and walked out to the gazebo, conscious of Jackson's dark gaze on her. She climbed the steps, quiet and uncertain.

His face softened. "You look beautiful."

She smoothed a hand over her dress. It was sequined and overly elaborate, but that was fine for these parties. "Thank you."

"I was going to crash the party and make a big gesture, like Nicholas did with Livvy, but—" He glanced at the house. "I wouldn't have been good at it. It would have gotten weird, real quick."

She controlled her smile. It would have gotten weird. Jackson did not do his best work in front of crowds of strangers. "That's okay. I don't need or like big gestures either. You can say what you want to say out here."

He scuffed his booted foot against the wood. "Have you checked your email today?"

She cocked her head. "No."

"Can you do it right now?"

Unsure of what this was about, she pulled her phone out of her little sequined handbag and opened her email, refreshing the inbox. A second later, her eyebrows shot up as email after email tumbled into her hand. They were all from Jackson. "What's this?"

"Every email I ever wrote to you."

She scrolled through them, bewildered. "You never wrote to me."

"No. I never sent them. I wrote hundreds of responses to you. That's my entire drafts folder."

She sank to the bench and clicked on one at random while her email continued to load. The message wasn't chatty and long like hers had been, but short and to the point. Like him.

Kareem is beautiful. I'm glad the birth wasn't too difficult. Neither of us is religious, but know that I prayed for you and him.

Another one. **I know you say you miss me and want me to come back, but I can't.**

Another. **Please send more pictures of everyone.**

She blinked and raised her head when he came to sit next to her, and she realized she wasn't sure how much time had passed. "I'm . . . I don't know what to say. I'm not sure why you're giving me these now."

"I laid a lot on you yesterday."

"You did."

"The thing with Paul—" He hunched his shoulders. "I don't want you to feel guilty about it."

"I can't wrap my mind around it. I'm so angry. And I feel . . . betrayed, like I didn't even know him."

Jackson nodded, then reached into his pocket. "Here. Read this."

She took the badly creased note, but didn't open it. "I already did."

"Keep it. Read it again. He felt awful. He signed a confession. And he did it because he loved you and Kareem so much he wanted to be the best man he could be for you."

She lifted the letter. "You should be angrier than me. You've forgiven him?"

"I don't know if I'll ever totally forgive him. But . . . I can't change what he did. I can have some peace in knowing that he was sorry and he loved me." His throat worked and his brows knitted together, the visible effort he was making to communicate his thoughts making her sit up straighter. "You asked me when I first got here why I didn't respond to your emails. I really was scared, terrified you would stop. But I guess, the truth is . . . I was scared of me. I didn't want to take any action that might reveal something terrible about me. I didn't want to hate Paul or Mom or, god forbid, Kareem. I didn't want to be that man. I wanted to be a decent person."

"You are a decent person." One of the most decent men she'd ever known.

"Everything I am now is because of you. You and Paul and everyone else in this family. I shut myself off for years, but deep down, I didn't change." Jackson nodded at the paper. "And I have to believe, that despite one lie, one miscalculation, Paul was always the same decent guy too."

She swallowed past the lump in her throat. "That's a really good rationale." She looked at Jackson, who was so opposite from his brother, but shared so many of the same values. People. Quality. Fairness.

Love.

"I have to go to New York."

Her fingers clenched on the paper. "Tonight?"

"Yes. Don't worry. I'll be back in a couple weeks. Lucy will handle the café."

She bit her lip. "What about us? What do you want from me?"

"I don't want anything from you. My dream is for you to let me love you." He cocked his head. "And maybe, someday, you can love me back. You don't have to love me a lot. A little love is enough."

"You want a relationship."

"I don't care what you call it. I want to fall asleep with you. I want to have a family. I want to travel with you all over the world and then come back to our home."

Her heart somersaulted. "It's not so easy."

"I know. Literally nothing in my adult life has been easy, Sadia. I used to walk away from the hard stuff, but I figured, maybe this one time, I could try fighting for it. And I would fight. But I know it's a lot to ask, for you to trust me."

"It is a lot to ask." But it was more to ask for her to trust herself.

He nodded. "Like I said, take your time. I'll be back."

"Will you?"

"Yes." He leaned down and pressed a kiss on her forehead, and then he started to walk away. He stopped, and turned, a frown creasing his brow. "Listen, so you know . . . I'll be back no matter what. Whether you decide to give me a shot, or whether you want to be friends. Whether you hate me and whether you want me to only have a relationship with Kareem."

She swallowed. "Okay."

He studied her for a long moment, like he was committing her face to memory. And then he walked away.

Chapter 23

THE CROWD would have intimidated Sadia if she wasn't so focused on her task. She wasn't accustomed to New York City, and this place was busy even for Midtown. Her resolve had been firm all the way here, though, and she wasn't about to let something as silly as masses of people chase her away.

She nudged her way past the line, into the restaurant. There was no sign or anything outside, but everyone seemed to know something special was in this building. She assumed social media and word of mouth had lured them to this pop-up. Social media, or the delicious scent of the food.

Food that looked remarkably familiar to Sadia, as she walked past the few tables inside. She spotted mac and cheese. Hot chocolate and cookies and croque monsieurs. Comfort food.

She took a deep breath and walked up to the counter. The cashier and the customer he was helping shot her annoyed looks. She cleared her throat. "I'd like to see the chef, please."

The customer snorted, and the cashier looked amused. "I'm sorry, ma'am. No one sees the chef."

Beneath the long sleeves of her coat, her hands curled. "He'll see me. Can you please tell him Sadia is here?"

"Sadia?"

A woman appeared at her side. She was svelte and well dressed, red hair tied neatly in a braid. She was in her midfifties, maybe, and handsome.

"Yes," Sadia said. She didn't recognize the woman, but her eyes were smiling, if worried.

The woman hesitated, then nodded at the cashier, and took her arm, drawing her away. "My name is Ariel. I'm the manager here. How can I help you?"

"I know this is a bad time, but it's very important I see J—the chef."

"Why?"

"Because I need him."

Ariel studied Sadia for a minute, then relaxed. She tilted her head. "Follow me."

She trailed behind Ariel as the woman led her through two doors that had been hastily rigged with locks—these people weren't kidding about maintaining secrecy over Jackson's identity.

A young sous-chef with a heavily stained apron looked up with a frown that turned into astonishment when he caught sight of Sadia, but she didn't care about him. All her attention was on Jackson, his face damp, hair curling, a fierce frown creasing his brow as he stirred something in a pot.

Ariel cleared her throat, and he looked up, annoyed impatience in his face.

But that disappeared the second his eyes rested on her. "Everyone out," he barked.

The sous-chef and Ariel scurried out so fast, Sadia felt the air whip around her. She couldn't pay attention, though, because Jackson was doing something she'd terribly missed.

Smiling.

It wasn't a big smile, but it reached his eyes, turning them a softer shade of brown. "Sadia?" he asked, so tentatively she wondered if he thought she would be frightened away.

"Hey," she said, and moved around the counter so they were closer. "I don't want to take up too much of your time."

"No, no. It's fine." His hands hovered, as if he wanted to touch her, but then they dropped away. "What brings you here? I told you I would be back."

"I believed you." She glanced around. "This is quite the operation you've got here. You should be proud of what you've accomplished."

He dismissed her praise. "The only reason I've been able to accomplish anything was because I had you in my pocket."

Oh. "I read your emails."

His body tensed. "And?"

"They weren't fancy."

"I'm not fancy."

He definitely wasn't. "I wish you'd sent them to me."

"I didn't know how—"

"No, I totally get that." She reached into her coat pocket and pulled out Paul's letter. It was crumpled and falling apart, but she didn't care. It wouldn't be around for long. "I also reread this. A million times."

"Yeah?"

She contemplated the letter, tracing Paul's signature through the paper. "I'm still disappointed in him, but you're right. I loved Paul, and I will always mourn for him, and as angry as I am at him for what he did, he was a great man. He deserves to be mourned." She took a deep breath. "Kareem can never know."

"I agree."

She swallowed, then reached over to the stove. She flicked on a burner and stuck the letter into the flame, letting it burn.

Jackson said nothing, simply waited while she destroyed the letter and tossed its smoldering remains in the sink, letting a steady stream of water put out the fire. She'd throw away the remnants later.

"I'll make this quick, because you need to get back to your adoring customers. I'm scared, Jackson. I wasn't looking for any kind of relationship when you came back into my life. The timing is all wrong."

"I know."

"You're the wrong man."

He winced. "I know."

She pursed her lips. "And I can't stop needing you."

His head jerked up.

She raked her hand through her hair. "I kept going over everything in my mind. You know I like certainty. What if we couldn't make it work?"

"I'd be really upset," he said frankly. "So would you."

She waited, and then she realized that was it. "Uh, that's not any kind of certainty."

"There's no certainty in the world, Sadia." His smile was tiny. "I know. I've searched everywhere for it. All we can do is care for each other, I think."

She ran her hand over the back of her mouth. "I feel like Paul wouldn't have died if I'd been a better wife."

Jackson took two steps toward her. "No—"

"No, I know. I know that's silly and irrational, trust me. But that's the baggage I'm bringing with me to any relationship I have."

"My shoulders are strong. I'll help you carry your baggage."

Her breath came out in a shuddery sigh. "My god. I do adore you, Jackson."

"You do?"

"Yes. I always have."

"That's . . . good. Great."

She swallowed, feeling like she was teetering on the edge of a precipice. "What if you were to come back to Rockville, once this is done? You can stay in the apartment above the garage, and we can, like . . . date?"

"Date?" He said the word like he'd never heard the concept before.

"Yeah. We could go to movies and restaurants. Fool around in cars."

He frowned. "We already had sex in a car."

She exhaled. "I'm saying I want to take things slow, Jackson. But I'm . . . I'm willing to try." She'd signed up for grief counseling, and she had plans for the café and lessening her work load. It wasn't the ideal time to start a new relationship. But was there ever a perfect time? All she could do was work on herself while she worked on them.

She wanted him. She missed him. She loved him.

If she wasn't in love with him yet, she would be, very soon.

He straightened. "Yes. Fine. Slow would work."

She eyed him suspiciously. He'd agreed far too easily. "I mean it, Jackson. I need time to come to grips with all of this."

"I've waited my whole life for you, Sadia. I can wait for however long it takes you."

Her eyes widened. "Like, literally?"

Jackson's brow furrowed. "What do you—oh!" His alarm was comical. "No, no. Not like that. Uh, though if I'd thought there was a chance in hell of us ever getting together, I might have abstained."

Her smile was shaky, but genuine. "If we do this, you have to let me love you a lot. Because that's what you deserve. All of the love."

He pulled her close, tucking her under his chin. "Then I suppose we just have to work on all of that love."

Epilogue

SADIA FOLLOWED the sound of a child's chattering down the hallway to the kitchen of the café. They were running a little behind schedule, but that couldn't be helped. She and Jackson had spent a good chunk of the afternoon checking over the new stove that had been delivered to the café.

She didn't care at all about kitchen equipment, but he'd been so excited about the new appliance, his enthusiasm had been infectious. Even Kareem had been psyched, and he really didn't care about kitchen equipment, either.

She smiled when she walked in. Over the past six months, she'd been smiling more and more. So had Jackson.

Kareem was hanging off his uncle like a monkey on his back, his arms linked around the man's neck, peering over his shoulder with great interest. Her son had had a growth spurt and was too big for her to carry comfortably now, but not too big for his uncle Jackson.

"Look at that," Jackson said, as proud as a father showing off his baby. "Do you see how well that egg cooks? Have you ever seen—" He cut himself off as he caught sight of Sadia in the entrance. "Uh, hi."

"Please, continue."

His cheeks flushed a charming red. "No, it's fine. Kareem wanted a sunny-side up."

"We're going to dinner," she reminded them both.

Both her men looked less than enthused about that, Jackson visibly gritting his teeth and Kareem grimacing. "Mom, I'm gonna be the only kid there. What if they don't have anything I like?"

Sadia tugged on her ear. "I'm sure there will be something there for you. But now that Uncle Jackson made you eggs, go on and eat them."

Jackson bent his knees and Kareem slid off. Jackson grabbed a plate from above and put the egg and toast on it and handed it to Kareem, who carefully balanced it in his hands and headed to the front to eat. "Make sure you cover your shirt with napkins. I don't have an extra outfit for you," she called after him.

"Okay, Mom."

Jackson shrugged. "Sorry. He said he was hungry."

"He's been to a couple of dinners where there were no kids. This is precautionary hunger. But it's fine. The stove works then?"

His excitement returned and he tapped the new range. "Perfect."

The stove was one of about a million upgrades Jackson had made since he'd bought the place from Sadia a month ago. He'd kept the nostalgic old-fashioned charm everyone adored, but methodically replaced every dated and worn appliance and fixture.

She walked over and slipped her arm around him. It took him a second longer to release the range to hug her back, but he did it easily. He still wasn't a hugger, but he'd gotten really good at embracing her and Kareem.

"You seem to enjoy being a small business owner," she said.

"It's not bad." But he couldn't hide his excitement. He'd begun badgering her to buy the café within a few months of them being together, but she'd held out. Not because he hadn't offered her enough money. He'd offered her too much money. She'd wanted to give the thing to him, but he'd refused that. She'd had to wait him out until he came down to a figure she considered fair.

She might have waited even longer to drive the price down more, but he'd slapped the sale contract down in front of her during one particularly vulnerable moment after a long day of paperwork. She'd signed, and they'd celebrated with champagne. And sex, but they would have had that no matter what.

His hand slipped over her ass, like he'd been thinking along the same lines. "Are you enjoying being *not* a business owner?"

"God, yes." She'd taken on more shifts at O'Killian's while Jackson worked on installing a bar inside of Kane's. She'd thought she might struggle with feelings of failure, but she was mostly relieved to not have the weight of the family legacy on her shoulders. It was back where it belonged, with a Kane.

He pressed a kiss on her forehead, then her nose. "You look nice."

She'd changed quickly in the office, donning her new dress, a simple dark blue jersey fit and flare with dark tights and her sole pair of high heels. "Thank you. Are you going to change?"

He glanced down at his jeans and his button-down shirt and shrugged. "No."

She bit her lip. There was no doubt Jackson was dreading this dinner at Nicholas's house. If he wanted to wear casual clothes to a millionaire's condo, she wouldn't fight him on it. "Well, you look nice no matter what."

Jackson rubbed his cheek against hers and kissed her ear, teasing the sensitive lobe. "Why don't we skip this? We can all go out to a movie."

As much as she adored spending time with Jackson—both with Kareem and alone—she wasn't ready to let him wiggle out of this. He and Nicholas had warmed to each other somewhat, but it was an uneasy truce. They could do with more time together. "Don't tempt me." She leaned back. "Or mess up my makeup. I had to watch four of Jia's tutorials to get my eyeliner like the kids do it nowadays."

He peered at her face. "I honestly cannot tell if you're wearing makeup or not."

"Trust me, I am."

He kissed her, then pursed his lips. "Do I have lipstick on me?"

This teasing, silly side of Jackson was one very few people got to see. Whenever he trotted it out, she thrilled. "You do." She ran her thumb over his lower lip and he nipped at her. "I know you don't want to go out, but if you're very good, I'll reward you later."

His eyes flared and he pulled her tighter. "Is that right?"

"Indeed."

"Mom?"

Sadia considered it a sign of how far they'd come that she didn't immediately leap away from Jackson. When things had gotten serious, she and Jackson had sat down with Kareem and did their best to explain their relationship. Kareem had accepted that news with the aplomb of a child and never seemed particularly troubled to catch them holding hands or hugging.

Sadia squeezed Jackson, then released him. "Yes?"

"I'm done. Do we still have to go?"

"Absolutely," she said firmly, and she couldn't tell if she was being firm with her son or with Jackson.

"Can I ride on Uncle Jackson's bike?"

"Absolutely *not*," Jackson answered. "We're taking the car."

"Ugh." Kareem pouted. "When I get big I'm gonna only ride motorcycles."

"We'll worry about that once we're both older." Jackson put his hand lightly on her back. "Ready?"

"I am. Are you?"

His lips quirked. She knew him well enough to identify the reluctance in his eyes. "Sure."

JACKSON WAS aware Sadia thought he didn't want to see Nicholas, but that wasn't the case at all. The two of them would never be best friends, but he and Nicholas had worked out a tentative truce. They both loved Livvy, and that was enough common ground.

No, he wasn't worried about Nicholas. He was worried about everyone who would be here. Though Livvy had basically moved in with Nicholas, their mother had been a tough nut to crack. This dinner was supposed to be a peace treaty, for both their families.

Save Nicholas's father, of course. He hadn't been invited. Jackson didn't really know what was up with Brendan Chandler and his kids, and he didn't think he wanted to know.

If everything went sour tonight, his sister would be the one to suffer. He was here, though, poised to catch Livvy, and she knew that.

They walked inside Nicholas's condo and Livvy and Sadia squealed and hugged like they hadn't seen each other that very morning. He and Nicholas gave each other guarded, respectful nods. "Thanks for using the door," Nicholas remarked.

Smart-ass. "I always used the door. You changed the alarm code yet?"

"Of course."

"To something that's not your birth year?"

"Yes."

"Or the date of, like, your high-school gradua-
tion?"

Nicholas's eyelid twitched. He didn't respond.

Jackson gave him a thin smile. Predictable people
were fun.

"Grandpa John!" His prior reticence to come to a
grown-up dinner party forgotten, Kareem made a
beeline for the couch and his new favorite relative.
John's face lit up and he opened his arms, hugging
Kareem tight when the boy came close. Since Sadia
was occupied talking to Livvy, Jackson trailed his
nephew.

Kareem snuggled close, clambering into John's
lap with the ease of a child who had never been
denied affection. John readjusted him and grinned
up at Jackson. "How are you doing, son?"

"Well, thank you. Kareem, be careful."

"He's fine." John's grip wasn't so tight as to be
painful, but it was clear he didn't want anyone to
take the child away from him.

Eve rose from the couch and stepped up behind
her grandfather's power chair. She wore an elegant
blue cocktail dress with a bow at the neck.

Jackson gave her a genuine smile of affection.
Oddly enough, he and Eve had become rather
friendly. In many ways, her emotional reserve was
comfortable to him. "Eve."

"Jackson." She ruffled Kareem's hair. "Hi, Kareem."

The boy craned his neck. "Hi."

"Did you have fun on your trip?" she asked Jackson politely.

"Yeah, it was great."

"We saw monkeys," Kareem informed them.

This was one of the many reasons he liked being with this kid. Kareem never ran out of things to say. He was a nice buffer.

"Monkeys!" Eve exclaimed. "Cool."

"And the food was so good." Kareem rested his hand on his belly. "I ate everything."

"Did you eat your plane tickets?" John asked, very seriously.

"No!"

"What about the luggage? Did you eat that?"

Kareem snorted a laugh.

Sadia joined them. Her skin had grown darker in the few weeks they'd been in Karachi. He'd done a pop-up there, mostly so he would have an excuse to get Sadia and Kareem to travel with him somewhere. He'd known how badly Sadia wanted her son to see at least a small portion of the country her family had come from.

Sadia's pride was frequently something he had to work around, but luckily, he liked the challenge.

He'd liked coming home to this place, too. He'd settled into a routine here, and it was a comfortable one. He still tended to avoid people, but it was easier to be out and about when he knew he had allies.

One of his biggest allies now, oddly enough, was Harriett. After discussing it with Sadia, he'd hired the woman back because, as Sadia had put it with an eyeroll, *she wasn't exactly wrong about her cousin being bought off.*

Sadia's pinky brushed against his. Neither of them were given to public displays of affection, which suited him fine. These little touches sustained him through the day. "It was a great trip," Sadia agreed.

"Did Kāne do well?" Eve inquired.

Jackson scratched the back of his neck. He was unused to anyone but his own team knowing his secret identity, but now that circle had stretched to include his family and Nicholas and Eve and John.

He trusted them, but it was weird. "Yeah."

As always, Sadia seemed to sense when he was uncomfortable. "What about you, Eve? What are you up to? Are you working somewhere now?"

Eve shifted. It still startled Jackson how much the girl looked like Maria. There was nothing of her father in her. "I'm taking my time."

Nicholas snorted as he and Livvy joined them. "Your generation takes too much time. You have a job waiting for you at the company."

Eve's expression was tolerantly amused. "I don't want to work at the company. Also, we're the same generation, Nicholas."

"Only technically."

Jackson didn't like talking, but he'd take any opportunity to take the opposite stance as Nicholas, truce be damned. "She's young. She can afford to take some time to figure out what she wants to do." He'd had his business established by the time he was twenty-four, but he'd also had to grow up quickly. There was no reason for Eve not to take her time.

Eve shot her brother a victorious look. "See? I'm fine."

Nicholas directed a narrow-eyed glare at him, and Jackson returned it calmly, though he felt a small spurt of victory.

He couldn't really hate Nicholas anymore, but he could take some enjoyment from these tiny skirmishes.

Kareem rested his head on John's shoulder and gave him a smile sweet enough to melt anyone's heart. "Can we go for a ride in your chair now?"

John laughed and straightened his bow tie. Everyone was dressed up, but Jackson would have had to go buy something if Livvy had wanted him to wear anything other than jeans and a shirt.

"Kareem, be polite," Sadia scolded him.

John waved her away. "Maybe once everyone gets here." His gaze drifted to the front door.

As if he'd willed it, the doorbell rang. John and Livvy tensed, while Nicholas draped his arm around Livvy's shoulders.

Sadia indicated the front door with a subtle nod, and he took the cue, moving to answer it. He nodded at his mother and Maile after he opened it. "Hey." He stepped aside.

Tani was paler than usual, her fingers clenched tight over her purse. She'd overdressed in a pretty black dress, but he remembered that quirk from childhood. His mother had always overcompensated with formality in places where she'd felt uncomfortable. He took Tani's wrap and returned Maile's hug.

Kareem came bouncing up to them. "Hi Grandmas."

Maile gathered her great nephew up in her powerful hands and swung him around until he squealed. "There's my boy."

Tani turned toward the rest of the party. Everyone was dead silent, waiting for what would happen.

As far as Jackson knew, this was the first time their mother and John had been in the same room since the accident. John had been Jackson's surrogate grandfather, but only because he'd been Tani's surrogate father.

Tani didn't appear to register anyone else. She took a few steps toward John.

John visibly swallowed. He wheeled forward, and took Tani's limp hand. "Look at you. You haven't changed a bit."

Tani slowly turned her hand to capture his. "Liar. I grew old."

John's laugh was rusty. He patted his chair. "Yeah, well. So did I."

Her gaze flitted over the power chair. "How is your—you're well?"

"As well as I can be."

"Brendan didn't come?" Her voice shook.

Nicholas cleared his throat. "My father wasn't invited."

"I told you, Mom." Livvy linked her hands with Nicholas.

Her shoulders relaxed. She couldn't tear her

attention away from John. "I know. I was still unsure."

"My son is an ass," John said.

Tani nodded. "He is."

"I got lucky with my daughter, though." John's voice was raspy with emotion.

Tani inhaled sharply. She lifted John's hand to her lips and pressed a kiss to it. "I'm so happy to see you," she whispered.

The room was not unmoved. Sadia came to stand next to him, and he rested his fingers against the small of her back, needing some sort of emotional touchstone. Livvy was dabbing at her eyes with the sleeve of her dress, while Nicholas stood at her side, rubbing her shoulders. Eve had her hands linked in front of her, a smile curving her lips.

Tani and John didn't speak; they simply held hands and communicated in some silent, indefinable way only they could understand.

Kareem punctured the silence with a loud whisper. "Can we eat now?"

Aunt Maile laughed and kissed him. Her dark eyes were wet. "Why don't we do that?"

Livvy jolted. "Yes! Come on. Dinner is served."

Maile patted John on the shoulder as she passed, and they all filed out to the dining room. Everyone except Tani and John.

Jackson glanced over his shoulder in time to see Tani sink to her knees and lay her head against John's chest, but he looked away when her face crumpled and John gathered her close, crooning.

He knew his mother as well as he knew himself. This was something too personal to share.

KAREEM'S WORRIES over the menu were in vain— Nicholas and Livvy had made him a special plate with toast and chicken nuggets, and he happily ate that while the adults enjoyed a fine dinner of roast duck. Jackson didn't speak much, not when there were so many other people to carry the conversational torch. He ate his dinner and contributed a few words here and there and helped Kareem when necessary.

Once upon a time, it might have felt odd to sit there with Kareem between him and Sadia, like they were a family or something, but he didn't feel that way now. They were a family, though an unconventional one. Sadia gave him a gentle smile when she caught him looking at her, and he returned it.

There were absences at the table: Maria, Robert, Paul and Brendan. They were big absences, and every now and then when the conversation ebbed, he wondered if everyone was feeling them too. Then someone would start speaking again, a little louder, as if that could make up for the people who were gone.

Jackson glanced around the table, allowing his feelings to come to the surface. He committed everyone's face to his memory. He committed this moment to his memory. It wouldn't occur again, even if they all gathered at this same table tomorrow.

As they lingered over their dessert, Livvy cleared her throat. "Thank you all for coming. This has gone better than Nico and I could have dreamed. We've wanted to do this for a while, but the timing always seemed off. But since we've managed to come together for dinner, we wanted to take this opportunity to announce something."

Tani dropped her fork with a clatter. "Oh no, you're pregnant."

Livvy's cheeks turned red. "No! Jeez."

Nicholas smiled at Livvy. "We're engaged."

They all stopped eating. Sadia was the only one who looked unfazed, which led Jackson to believe his sister had told her about this announcement. He made a mental note to poke her about secrecy later.

John was the first to recover. "This is wonderful!"

Maile beamed. "Truly wonderful. Oh, Livvy, we'll have to find you the most perfect dress."

Eve raised her glass. She appeared genuinely pleased. "When's the wedding?"

"Next month."

Jackson rested his elbows on the table. He was happy to see the glow in his sister's face, but he'd always be a little wary of the Chandlers. A wedding wouldn't make everything between their families perfect. "Why so fast?"

Tani raised an eyebrow at her daughter. "Because you're pregnant."

Livvy gritted her teeth. "No. I promise, my womb is empty, Mother."

Now Sadia looked nonplussed. "Uh, Livvy, that's not enough time to plan a wedding."

"Sure it is," Livvy said cheerfully. "Between your organizational skills and Eve's party planning background, we can throw something together."

Sadia puffed out her cheeks. She was probably already making lists in her head. "I don't know."

"It'll be tiny," Livvy soothed. "Closest friends and family only. You and Jackson can be my people-maids. Eve and John will be Nico's grooms-people. It'll be great."

How like Livvy, to simply assign him a role. Jackson cleared his throat. "I don't want to be a whatever you called it."

Livvy looked stricken, and Nicholas glared at him. Shit. He'd said the wrong thing.

"He's not saying he doesn't support your marriage," Sadia jumped in, and Jackson gave her a grateful glance.

He hurried to clarify. "I don't want to get up in front of a crowd."

Livvy frowned. "It won't be a big crowd."

It didn't matter. "Let me cook for you," he proposed. It was a spur-of-the-moment offer, but as he said it, he settled into how right it felt. He might not adore Nicholas, but he could pour his love for his sister into his cooking. "That's one less thing for you to worry about. And you know you'll love the food."

Livvy pursed her lips. "I suppose that'll be okay, but our attendants will be imbalanced then.

I wanted family only in the bridal party and I was hoping Mom and Aunt Maile would give me away."

Tani stirred. She picked up her fork and poked her chocolate cake. "Ask your boss to be a brides-whatever."

"Gabe?" Livvy pondered that.

Across from Jackson, Eve choked on her sip of water. "You okay?" he asked.

She waved him off and covered her mouth with her napkin.

"You grew up with him." Tani took a delicate bite.

Livvy brightened. "Yeah, Gabe's basically family. That would work."

Sadia tucked a strand of her hair behind her ear and shoved back her seat. "Okay, we don't have much time. Let me get my journal from the car and we can get started."

The table fell into a discussion of various wedding planning, but Jackson sat back, food dancing in his head.

Chocolate and rich flavors and dramatic surprises. That's what he would give Livvy.

"ARE YOU still thinking about the menu?"

Jackson turned away from the passenger window. He blinked at her, which told her that yes, indeed, he'd been fixated on the wedding menu.

Sadia grinned and returned her gaze to the road. "What's the main entrée going to be?"

"Roast lamb. I'm still working on the vegetarian option." He glanced into the backseat, where

Kareem was fast asleep. "Something less adventurous for the kids, too."

"Sounds like you have it figured out."

"Did you know about the announcement?"

"I had a feeling. Livvy had told me she and Nicholas hadn't wanted to get married until the families could at least break bread together."

"She jumped on it first chance she could get."

"They've waited so long. I don't blame them."

"Me neither."

She removed her hand from the steering wheel to capture his. "You're okay with it, then?"

"Yes. I want Livvy happy."

"Me too."

"It won't solve all of their problems."

"There's no such thing as being problem-free. You can really only hope for someone who's able to share your problems with you."

His fingers tightened around hers.

They pulled into their driveway. Jackson lived inside the main house now, and slept in her bedroom. He'd broached the idea of a fresh start with a new house, but Sadia hadn't wanted to make too many dramatic changes yet in her son's life. She was seeing a therapist regularly now, one she actually liked, to manage grief and her panic attacks, and he'd agreed with that call.

She didn't feel guilty about Jackson moving in, though. The Paul she'd fallen in love with and adored would have been fine with it.

She knew it wasn't totally healthy that she'd separated Paul's actions with the fire from the man she'd married, but it had been the only way she knew how to process what he'd done. Someday she'd be able to be as at peace with her late husband as Jackson was, but it would take her a bit more time. It helped that she could talk about it with Jackson and Livvy.

Not Tani. Her mother-in-law had given her a warning look the one time Sadia had attempted to broach the subject. The woman was older and frailer than Sadia, but it had been enough to intimidate Sadia into silence.

Money aside, no wonder that witness had shut up.

Jackson carried Kareem inside and put him to bed while she went to their bedroom. She shimmied out of her dress and hung it up carefully, and then went to the vanity to remove her earrings.

Jackson entered the room quietly, closed the door, and locked it. He came to stand behind her. His hands slipped around her body and cradled her breasts, slipping the cups of her bra down to get to the flesh. "You said you would reward me if I was good."

She couldn't look away from their reflection. Those long, elegant fingers manipulated her nipples, pressing and pinching until they were long and puffy.

She pressed back against him. "You were very good."

"Tell me what you want," he murmured against her sensitive ear.

"I want to watch you fuck me."

His smile was sharp. He released her to remove

his shirt, and then his jeans as well. She braced her hands on the table, her breath coming faster, though he hadn't touched her yet.

He ran his palms up her side and pulled her back so her body was arched. His cock brushed against her thigh, the wetness of his pre cum dragging a trail across her leg. She'd gone on birth control and they'd both gotten tested months ago. It hadn't taken Jackson much convincing to ditch the condoms.

He pressed inside her, high and deep, and she groaned. God, he felt so good, thick and long. She wanted him to fuck her forever.

The table wobbled as his hips picked up speed and she lifted her head to watch his face in the mirror. His high cheekbones were flushed red, his muscular stomach clenching as he hammered inside her. He switched his attention between his body penetrating hers and her face and jiggling breasts. "Stop." Her voice was a sharp crack in the otherwise silent room.

His nostrils flared, but he stilled immediately, his cock still half inside her.

"Pull out."

He made a tortured sound, but did as she commanded.

Her legs were too wobbly. She managed to turn around and perched on the vanity, hands braced on either side of her. She lifted her leg, feeling no self-consciousness as she placed it on the chair, opening herself up to his gaze.

His eyes were locked on her pussy. Every muscle

in his body was tensed, his cock wet and hard, sticking straight up. It must have been painful, but he didn't touch it. His hands were clenched at his sides.

"You wanted a reward," she purred. A part of her watched aghast. Sometimes she didn't know who she was when she was with Jackson like this, alone. Not a mother, not a widow. Just a woman.

With a man who would do whatever she liked.

"I do," he growled. His tongue touched the corner of his mouth.

"If you give me a very good orgasm, I'll let you come."

He dropped to his knees before she could finish speaking, but she'd let that infraction pass. His tongue slicked up and down her vulva, and found her clit. She bit her lip to keep from crying out when he sucked it hard.

Two fingers found her opening and he finger fucked her while he played. He knew her body now, and it didn't take her long at all to convulse around him.

She was still recovering when he gathered her close, his hard cock rubbing against her wetness. "Now?" His tone was frantic. "Let me fuck you now."

She gave a slight nod, and it was enough. He picked her up like she weighed nothing and tossed her on the bed. She opened her legs and her arms and he was on top of her, his cock driving inside her. Her orgasm taken care of, he was selfish and greedy, pounding into her hard enough to move her up the bed, her pillows cushioning her from the headboard. His mouth covered hers and he groaned. His muscles tightened and released beneath her palms, the wetness between her legs telling her he'd found his pleasure.

He panted into her neck. She stroked his hair as both their bodies cooled. Soon, she'd draw the covers over them both and they'd sleep, but right now, this was nice.

He rolled away and drew her to his side so she could cuddle him as she liked. She traced her fingers over the rose he'd gotten for her, the leaves for Livvy, the geometric tribal design in memory of his father. She shifted over to trace the Japanese phrase he'd gotten because it reminded him of his grandpa Sam.

She'd asked if he was planning on anything else. For Paul or his mother. He'd looked thoughtful and disappeared the next afternoon. When he returned, printed letters had been inked next to the rose.

I am the man I am now because of you.

He released a deep, shuddering sigh. "I want to get married, Sadia," he said.

She snuggled closer. The thought of marriage should make her panic, but there was no fear here. "Not yet. Let's let Livvy and Nicholas have the spotlight for a while."

"Our wedding wouldn't have a spotlight."

He sounded so worried she kissed his arm. "No, but I'd want my family to come. And yours." She wasn't eloping again. "What I meant was, I don't want to pull attention from your sister right now."

He mulled that over. "But soon, right?"

"Yes. Very soon."

"I love you."

She looked up at him. At his dark eyes, his steady strength. She didn't differentiate anymore between love and in love, not when it came to Jackson. She felt both. "I love you, too."

"Always."

There was no guarantee of a future or even a tomorrow, but that was okay. She would take this love for as long as she could have it. She stretched up and sighed into his lips. "Always."